Books by Judith O'Brien

Rhapsody in Time
Ashton's Bride
Once Upon a Rose
Maiden Voyage
To Marry a British Lord
One Perfect Knight

Published by POCKET BOOKS

JUDITH O'BRIEN

ONE PERFECT KNIGHT

POCKET BOOKS

New York London Toronto Sydney Tokyo Singapore

For the best Christmas gift—ever.

Who could have imagined that Santa would arrive
not with reindeer but with a stone-deaf, intestinally
challenged chihuahua named Spike?

This book is a work of fiction. Names, characters, places and inci-
dents are products of the author's imagination or are used ficti-
tiously. Any resemblance to actual events or locales or persons,
living or dead, is entirely coincidental.

An *Original* Publication of POCKET BOOKS

POCKET BOOKS, a division of Simon & Schuster Inc.
1230 Avenue of the Americas, New York, NY 10020

ISBN: 0-671-00040-3

First Pocket Books printing November 1998

10 9 8 7 6 5 4 3 2 1

POCKET and colophon are registered trademarks of
Simon & Schuster Inc.

Front cover and tip-in illustrations by Gregg Gulbronson

Printed in the U.S.A.

1

❦

The New York City subway car—that great metropolitan equalizer—accepted its riders grudgingly. Faces were indistinct, features blurred, but no doubt the crowd included convicted felons, a couple of lawyers, an actor racing to an audition, perhaps a murderer or two, a young mother with a howling toddler, all packed into a graffiti-covered tin car.

And into this cocktail of humanity was tossed Julie Gaffney, all-around nice girl, the sort of person who pays her bills on time and never misses a dental appointment.

She did not blend in with the other passengers.

Julie Gaffney stood out like the proverbial sore thumb, with her fresh-faced good looks, her crisply ironed blouse, and her pleasant expression. It was the pleasant expression above all else that made her so incongruous on a Thursday evening at rush hour, that set her apart from the other commuters on an unseasonably hot spring day, the tail end of an early heat wave.

The other passengers stood as one blank-eyed entity, briefcases carving a path past the lucky ones already grasping a coveted pole, Macy's and Lord & Taylor shopping bags scratching arms and hands and occasionally faces with remorseless pointy paper edges.

Julie Gaffney entered, her own briefcase poised before her like a lance in a commuting joust.

"Brooklyn bound F train," droned a crackly speaker, words pouring forth only as alternate syllables. "Next stop, Forty-second."

The announcement was indecipherable to the unlucky riders who actually needed the information. It sounded like a muzzy horn blast with inflections, the grown-up voices in a Charlie Brown cartoon. Only those with an attuned ear, who already knew what was going to be said, could distinguish the words with any degree of accuracy.

"Does this go to Queens?" a middle-aged woman clutching a map shouted, panic rising in her voice.

"No," Julie said, and immediately the other riders shot her curious stares. There is an unspoken rule on the subway: do not react. Not to the one-armed beggar, not to the man selling yo-yos, or the guy with the paper bag on his head claiming to be an alien. Do not react to anyone. With defiance that could only be described as pleasant, Julie continued speaking to the woman. "You need to go upstairs and switch to the other track—the uptown local. There'll be plenty of signs."

The woman eyed Julie, as if appraising her worth and the potential value of her information. She was enough of a subway rider to know the response was highly unusual. What she saw was a young woman in her late twenties, with blue-green eyes and shoulder-length blond hair streaked by the sun, and a face that combined warmth and beauty in equal measures.

"You sure?" The woman took in Julie's clothes, the pinstripe suit made feminine by a lace blouse and a fanciful gold scroll pin on the lapel.

Julie nodded, and just as the doors began to close, the woman wiggled through the crowd and left the train, adding over her shoulder, "Thanks. You're a very pleasant young lady."

All eyes returned to where they had been, to folded papers or mystery novels or, most common, to the nothingness just above the heads of the other riders.

Julie sighed. During the journey back to her Chelsea apartment, she was free to pause and imagine what life would be like if she weren't in the middle of a crisis at work. Not that every week didn't bring a new set of crises in the advertising business. It was the nature of the industry to operate in a state of high panic.

And it was an industry that Julie had somehow managed to conquer. For in spite of her gentle disposition, she was one of the youngest senior executives in the city, and certainly the only woman in that position. While the rapid promotions had given her pleasure, the large office, and a spacious apartment, there was something missing. That something, whatever it was, seemed to touch every small joy she experienced, whispering, *Yes, your life is good. But there should be more, so much more.*

The subway rattled to a halt at each station, letting more passengers on as a few struggled to squeeze off.

She smiled at the young mother with the howling toddler. The young mother clutched the toddler protectively, pulling the child against her thigh as if Julie's smile had been a ransom note.

And then he slipped in, the old blind man with the accordion, just as the doors closed.

No one paid attention. No one cared on this crowded Thursday evening. Everyone just wanted to get home and to forget all about work and the subway and old blind men with accordions.

He was a regular on the F line, his short, squat body braced for the jolts and turns. Julie smiled and began reaching into her purse for some change. She always gave him change, the old blind man with the accordion and the misbuttoned shirt with a sleeveless T-shirt showing through the transparent fabric. He buffed his palms on his trousers, the accordion hanging loosely about his neck for a moment, and then he began.

There were a few groans as he launched into a song. His selection was not varied, but on the other hand, it was consistent. On most days, he played spirited versions of "Lady of Spain" and "Raindrops Keep Falling on My Head."

Today he played something different.

It took Julie a moment to realize what the lovely song was, slow and deliberate. And when she identified it in her own mind, her vision misted with unexpected tears.

The blind man with the accordion was playing "If Ever I Would Leave You" from the Lerner and Loewe musical *Camelot.*

In her mind, she played the words along with the tune, the beautiful lyrics of love and longing.

Julie was aware that a few people were staring at her with curiosity, but she couldn't help being moved by the music. The song was so captivating that suddenly she wasn't on a crowded subway but in a field of flowers with a dashing knight who was promising, in his roundabout or perhaps direct way, that he would never, ever leave her. She swallowed as the song continued, and she sniffed softly, pressing her lips together to prevent any sound from escaping.

She recalled her dream then. It was the same one she always had, sometimes while she was wide awake, sometimes in the middle of a sound sleep. There was a woman, beautiful and mysterious, emerging from a mist. Her hair was shot with gold, her gown was an emerald green, and her every movement was graceful as a dancer's.

The woman stopped then, her motionlessness all the more obvious because of the continuous swirling of the mist, twirling and hovering about the hem of the gown. She reached down and picked something up. Julie could never see what the object was, for before the haze cleared, a hand, large and strong, took it away. And the woman smiled warmly.

That was always the end of the dream, and the music and the fantasy mingled and curled together so she could not tell where one ended and the other began.

Closing her eyes, she swayed with the music and with the rhythm of the train and with the mist in her mind. And then, all too soon, the music ended. Once again, she was in a subway car filled with strangers, on her way home to an empty apartment.

The blind man walked the length of the car, nodding wordless thanks as coins were tossed into his coffee can. Julie slipped a five-dollar bill into the can, and he nodded, just the way he nodded at everyone else who had given him a dime or a nickel. He left for the car up ahead, and as the train pulled into the next stop, she could hear the vague strains of "Raindrops" through the scuffed metal door.

Yet she couldn't get the song from *Camelot* out of her mind. It put her in a strange, dreamy mood, even as she got out at her station and mechanically stopped at the grocery store for dinner.

Was it possible for anyone to be so in love that they could promise—absolutely and without a doubt—they would never leave? Could romance really last forever?

Standing in the checkout line, she scanned the headlines of the tabloids, about the divorcing stars whose weddings had been reported so breathlessly in the same publications less than a year before, and Julie concluded that perfect love probably was not possible. Her own track record was evidence enough of the transitory nature of modern romance. Nothing lasted anymore. Nothing was permanent.

"Julie?"

It was a man's voice behind her, and she immediately knew who it was. Forcing a smile, she turned to face him.

"Orrin, how have you been?"

"Great, just great!" He twitched his nose, a peculiar habit he had displayed with alarming frequency during their one and only date. "And you? I've left a few messages on your machine, you know. Thought we could get together."

"Oh, yes. Well. I've been so crazed at work, Orrin. I mean, it's really nuts there."

"Yeah, I'll bet. You work at a travel agency, right?"

"No. Advertising. I work at an advertising agency."

"Yeah, whatever." His nose twitched.

"Well, I'd better get going." She clutched her grocery basket and gestured toward the line.

"Yeah. Did I tell you that I've got a big gig coming up next week?"

"How wonderful. Where are you playing?"

"Over at the Cockadoodle Lounge, right after karaoke night Tuesday. I'll be going solo, singing original songs, that sort of thing. More of a concert than a gig, in actuality."

It crossed her mind to ask how he was going to sing and play the French horn at the same time, but she did not really want to know the answer.

"Hope you can make it, Julie." As an afterthought, he added, "It's also nickel beer night. They serve it in plastic cups, and you have to use the same cup over and over again, but it's still a bargain. No cover or anything."

"Great. I'll try to make it, Orrin. Thank you."

"Thanks. And Julie?"

She paused.

"Sorry about the other night."

Julie wasn't sure what he meant. Their one date had been three weeks earlier. In the course of the evening, he had pulled off his shoes and socks to apply foot powder in the middle of a sushi restaurant, requested that she "get really drunk" so she would loosen up, gargled with a gelatin dessert, and engaged in a bit of road-rage banter with a motorcyclist on Hudson Street.

"Oh, no problem," Julie said brightly. "And good luck with the gig."

"It's a concert, in actuality," Orrin corrected.

"Right. 'Bye."

Finally, he waved and left.

Julie took one last glance at the tabloids. No, she had her answer. Real romance, the kind she had always dreamed of, was simply not possible in this world. And as she placed the bananas and frozen dinners and salad bar containers on the conveyer belt, she wondered, with more than a little sadness, had perfect romance *ever* been possible?

The red light was flashing furiously on her answering machine. As she set her groceries on the floor, her desire to hear the messages overcoming a desire to rescue the rapidly melting frozen dinners, she punched the play button.

The first message was from her aunt Tessie in Ohio, reminding her that Aunt Fran in Indiana had a birthday coming up, and a card would be most welcome. Julie nodded at the machine, as if answering, *Yes, yes, I know.* She had already mailed the card that afternoon, as Aunt Tessie most certainly would have guessed. Tessie simply wanted to hear about Julie's social life, the glamorous New York niece living an oh-so-glamorous existence in the city. Not that Julie had ever uttered a single word to reinforce the notion of such a life. That was not necessary—Aunts Tessie and Fran had already filled in the blanks on their own. And they had indeed created a wondrous life for their niece.

Sweet as the women were, it was sometimes difficult for her to bear their well-intentioned ministrations, their constant concern for their orphaned great-niece. Every time Julie felt she was doing well on her own, she would receive a telephone call or a doily-embossed card that did nothing but remind her that she was alone in the city.

The next message was from someone named Dale, a friend-of-a-friend who wanted to ask her about the advertising business. His voice faded in and out, some sort of static on his phone when he called, she assumed. Perhaps he had called on a car phone. In any case, he asked if they could have brunch that weekend, his treat. Oh, and his girlfriend would be there, too.

She was unable to suppress a slight giggle. Why did men always seem to operate under the unshakable conviction that every unmarried woman will fall at their feet in a swoon unless they are fairly warned about a preexisting girlfriend or fiancée or wife?

The third message was from a college friend who gleefully announced her engagement and wanted to know if Julie could be a bridesmaid. Of course she would. And once again, another synthetic gown in some godawful pastel shade and design guaranteed to make the bridesmaids look perfectly ghastly would join the others in the back of her closet. This would make nine such gowns and nine such matching shoes and nine such frilly barrettes and . . .

Another voice drifted out from the machine. It was layered over her friend's message, and through the excited babble, a man was saying something. At first, she wondered if it was her friend's fiancé, perhaps in the background or on another extension of the telephone. But the male voice seemed to be coming from someplace else, someplace distant.

Her friend signed off, and during the slight pause before the answering machine clicked, she could finally hear the words the man was saying.

In an anguished tone, he said simply, "Help me."

2

❧

"Jeeze, Julie. You look like hell today," muttered Audrey the receptionist as she fumbled with pink message slips. Her plunging angora neckline, also pink, revealed the prime reason for her employment, for she could neither type nor take dictation, and her telephone skills were rudimentary at best. But she was more than friendly, and the clients—especially the men—seemed to like her. Really like her.

Audrey rose to her stiletto heels, showcasing a tight miniskirt and a powerful self-confidence. A spy in human resources claimed that according to her file, she was just shy of sixty. She shuffled through the messages.

"You're assistant's out sick today, although I hear she felt well enough last night at happy hour at Donovan's Tavern. Bob what's-his-name—that new guy in creative—says you should call him yesterday. And some guys are waiting for you in the conference room—you know, those big Swedish fellows. My second husband, God rest his soul, was from there. Well, his parents were, anyway, not that I ever met them. Or was it a grandparent? Anyway, he had the same sort of expression."

"Anyone else looking for me?" Julie ran her hand over her hair in a vague attempt at grooming.

"I think that's all, but then I was in the john for a while, so I may have missed a few calls. I had chicken salad for dinner last night, and it never agrees with me. Once when I was in Jersey with my third husband . . ."

"Thanks, Audrey." Julie snatched the messages and hurried down the hall to her office. She was late. Julie Gaffney, queen of the early-morning wake-up calls to other staff members, had slept through her own alarm clock.

"Julie, we need you," called a frantic account assistant from his cubicle. "Debbie called in sick today, and . . ."

"I know, I know. I'll be right in."

Julie stepped into her office and closed the door for a moment, trying to compose herself. It still surprised her every time she walked into the huge space with plush carpeting and prime Manhattan views that this was actually her office. At times she felt as if the real executive who belonged there would walk in and catch her, tossing her back to one of the bullpen cubicles where she began her career more than seven years earlier. But so far it hadn't happened, the career police hadn't booked her yet, and if she managed to pull off the next few accounts and please the clients, she would be promoted once again before the end of the year.

With shaking hands, she retied her silk scarf and reached into her purse for lipstick. She was rattled, and it wasn't just being late for the client meeting that had her so unnerved.

The man's voice on her answering machine, that's what was really bothering her. Last night, after hearing his voice once, she went downstairs to the laundry room. When she returned, there was another message. It was someone from work, but she could barely hear what he was saying.

All she could really decipher was a static sound, and then a clear repeat of the previous plea. "Help me."

That was all she could think about, even as she raced to work. The ad campaign was the last thing on her mind.

With trembling hands, she slicked the lipstick on, hoping she got most of the color on her lips, not bothering to blot. She was about to leave the office when she paused, then reached over to her telephone. All of the lights were blinking like a crazed Christmas tree, and she punched in the number of Ron in the art department, an electronics nut who read *Popular Mechanics* with the same intensity as adolescent boys study *Playboy*.

"Hey, Ron. It's Julie."

"No."

"Excuse me?"

"I said no, I can't do any better with the campaign because the whole idea stinks. Sorry, Julie, but this is a lame one. What made you think you could sell an all-purpose cleanser with a medieval knight? They are extinct, for Christ's sake. And if they ever did clean their armor back then, it was just to wash off the blood from their latest victims. What housewife has those particular cleaning needs? It makes no sense, and Ajax did that same routine years ago. I know you always pull these things off, but this time . . ."

"No, that's not what I want to ask you. Listen, I'm having trouble with my answering machine at home."

Ron paused on the other end. "Excuse me?"

"I keep getting static or something, some sort of interference."

Ron loved this sort of thing. "You mean the messages are hard to hear?"

"Yeah, in a way. But it's because there's a man's voice there."

"A secret admirer?" Ron chuckled. "The plot thickens! Tell me what he says. I never understand what chicks want."

"No, it's nothing like that. He seems to be, well, he seems to be in trouble."

"What kind of trouble?"

"I don't know. He's asking for help."

"Listen, Julie, if every guy who needs help in Manhattan found a way to get on your answering machine, you'd blow a circuit."

She ignored that. "Really, Ron, how could this happen? Can it be someone with a cell phone or something?"

"Nah. You know what you've got? Interference from livery cabs."

"Huh?"

"Livery cabs. There's a city law that their radios can only have so much power, but it's not enforced. Most of those livery cabdrivers have their systems jacked up so they can hear each other in all parts of the city. They can probably call their moms in Benghazi. You know, those cabs with the big bent antennas over their hoods. I'll bet the guy is speaking some foreign language, eh?"

"No. That's just it—he speaks very clearly, in English."

"Weird. What does he say?"

Julie hesitated for a moment before answering. "He says, 'Help me.' "

"That's all? No accent? No pickup request or pizza orders?"

"That's all," she confirmed. "And if there's an accent, it seems almost English."

"Man, that *is* weird. I've gotta go in a second, but don't worry. I'm sure it's a livery cabdriver. And frankly, if this guy is from England and he's driving a livery cab, he *does* need help."

"Thanks, Ron." She smiled.

"No problem. Oh, and Julie?"

"Yeah?"

"The cleanser idea isn't that much of a dog. I'll see what I can do to spiff it up for those Swedes."

"Thank you. 'Bye."

Interference. That made sense. It was simply interference, a technical thing, nothing mysterious.

But his voice. It was so compelling, a voice that seemed to catch her in her chest. It was a voice of warmth and passion, a rich tone to it with just a hint of something else.

She grabbed her briefcase and left for the conference room.

The last message on her machine had been late at night, when she went to retrieve the laundry from the dryer. There had been no other message under his voice. He did not interrupt another call. Instead, this one was clear, as if he had dialed himself. Again, it was the same plea.

"Help me."

By Sunday morning, as Julie opened her eyes following the second sleepless night in a row, one fact was painfully clear. The illustrious advertising agency of Stickley & Brush was close to losing one of its biggest clients, and Julie Gaffney could not for the life of her come up with a single reason for them to stay.

Ron had been right; the Shine-All campaign was

absolutely lame. Usually she could think well on her feet. More than once she had turned certain disaster into triumph, or, as she called it, "pulling a Darrin Stevens." Julie's ability to come up with clever slogans was almost legendary in the business.

It was Julie who had brainstormed and come up with the Burton Tea campaign, the one all the trades went so nutty over. The one that boosted Burton Tea sales by sixty percent. That was last year, a few short yet somehow very long months ago.

But yesterday she had not been able to pull a Darrin Stevens, or even a Tabitha—her name for the small miracles of advertising. Friday had been nothing short of a full-blown Endora.

And now, on Sunday morning, with the brutal rays of sun streaming into her bedroom, there was no denying she would have to think of something spectacular by Monday if she wanted that promotion. She had kept her creative team at work until after midnight Friday, and most of Saturday, the same team that only last year had won a shelf full of awards for persuading the American public to buy a baking soda-based nasal spray and an automobile made in South America.

She was exhausted, but when the telephone rang, she jumped. He had called twice yesterday, or at least left two messages for her. The man who so desperately needed her help.

Sucking in a deep breath, she picked up the phone. "Hello?" Her voice was as tentative as she felt.

There was a slight pause, but she heard someone on the other end. Then came the voice. "Don't kill me," the woman said.

"Peg!" Julie relaxed against her pillow. "How are you? I tried to call the other day, but . . ."

"I need to ask a massive favor of you."

Peg Reilly was one of Julie's first real friends in New York. Even after they stopped being roommates and Peg went on to graduate school and a career as a psychologist, they remained close friends and confidants. Two years older than Julie, Peg had a no-nonsense style that Julie found both amusing and vexing, depending on the circumstance. And Peg's family lived on Long Island, her parents and a married sister with two kids and a minivan, so Julie always had a place to go for the holidays.

"So you have a favor to ask of me," Julie repeated warily. "Just how massive a favor?"

"Very massive," Peg conceded. "You may wish you never met me."

"That doesn't narrow it down much. Does it involve travel to a Third World country?"

"You only wish."

"Does it involve baby-sitting your sister's kids?"

"Ha! Child's play, my dear, compared to what I need."

"Peg, spit it out. You're making me nervous."

"Okay—here goes. Today is Nathan's birthday party." Nathan was Peg's nephew, the older child.

"Go on."

"And Lucy has an earache." Lucy was the four-year-old.

"And?"

"And someone has to stay home with Lucy. So we have a choice, you see."

"We do?"

"Yep. We can either take care of Lucy, who has been in a less-than-cheerful mood with her earache. My sister says she's in a Linda Blair, head-twisting sort of mood, poor thing. That's one option."

"Or?"

"Or we can take cute, healthy Nathan and a hand-ful of his little pals, one or two of whom may have single, eligible, and financially solvent fathers for us to flirt with, and ferry the sweet little guys to a fun-filled afternoon at . . ."

"At? Go on, Peg. Where. Bloomingdale's? That new brunch place on Sixty-fifth and Third?"

"Not exactly. This is the fun part, Julie. We get to drive my sister's minivan! Isn't that cool?"

"Yeah, Peg. Way cool. Especially since you haven't been behind the wheel of a car since the early days of the Reagan administration. What about your fun-loving brother-in-law?"

"Good point! Chuck's in Atlanta on business. Just listen. See, this is where it gets even more fun. You, my dear, lucky pal, get to drive my sister's brand-new minivan! Full sound system, cup holders—this thing is fully loaded."

"And where does the lucky pal get to drive the fully loaded van to?"

"New Jersey."

Julie paused for just a moment. "Why?"

Finally, Peg laughed. "To Knight Times, that theme restaurant. Please, Julie, I'll do anything for you. Nathan's on this knight kick, and since it's almost something historical, they figure they should jump on it. Believe me, it's a vast improvement over the Power Rangers."

"I'll bet it is. He was on the same kick when I saw them a few months ago, but I thought it was beginning to fade. And how much influence did his aunt Peg and her penchant for the odd and bizarre have to do with his conversion?"

"I am proud to say it was almost all my doing. I took him with me a few months ago to some of my village haunts, and he loved those places."

For the first time, the jocular tone left Julie's voice. "Ah, Peg. Was that such a good idea? Those old shops are creepy. Especially that one place with the stuffed dead animals. I swear, the hairs on the back of my neck stand up just thinking about it."

"No big deal. You said the same thing about Bruce."

"Don't mention him. I'm only just speaking to you again after that last setup. Seriously, though. Does

Betsy know you took her only son to a shop that sells magic potions and funky old books bound in human skin?"

"Good old Cauldrons & Skulls. Nope. I did not go into those details. I described it as an old bookstore with first-edition classics."

"Yeah, nice technicality."

"Anyway, how about it, oh great driver? Please? If you can't do this, Nathan will have a miserable tenth birthday and will most likely remain in therapy for the rest of his life. Not to pressure you or anything."

"Well . . . how do I get from the city to Long Island and the fully loaded car?"

"This is the exciting part," Peg enthused. "We get to take the train together in forty-five minutes. Long Island Railroad. Penn Station on an early Sunday morning! Hey, it just doesn't get any better than this."

Julie moaned just once. It might do her good to have a complete change of scenery. Maybe some brilliant idea would come to her, something that would help salvage the account. And Peg was just the person to bounce ideas off. She knew all sorts of subliminal ways to sell products. "Sure, Peg. Count me in. When should we meet?"

"About two minutes. I'm calling from your lobby."

"Pretty confident I'd say yes, eh? Okay. Come on up."

And as Julie waited to let Peg in, she wondered,

should she tell her about the man on the answering machine?

The instant she saw the van, Julie regretted her decision. It was the size of a tank, with only slightly less grace and style, a boxy metallic green monster.

"What *is* this thing?" she whispered to Peg as they walked up the driveway.

"It's the El Caracca. The very car you helped sell to the world last year."

"I had no idea it was so . . . Betsy! How wonderful to see you!"

"Go ahead." Betsy laughed as she emerged, the screen door slamming behind her. "You had no idea the minivan would be so ugly, eh? And aren't you the one who wrote that award-winning copy?"

Julie winced. "If I recall correctly, I emphasized the safety factors. Is this a special paint job?"

"No. It's called Rain Forest Green. Rather special, isn't it?"

"Special. I like that," Peg agreed. Just then, a piercing scream came from inside the house, and both Betsy and Peg ignored it.

"That's just Lucy," Betsy explained.

"I really have to drive this thing?" Julie peered in at the driver's seat, which was covered in a camouflage material.

"The upholstery is Jungle Beige. Goes with everything," Betsy offered.

Just then, Nathan came out of the house.

"Hi, Aunt Peg. Hey, Julie. Today I will answer only to Sir Knight."

"Then good day, Sir Knight." Julie extended her hand.

"Good night, Sir Day," Nathan responded with a flushed smile.

Within a half hour they were on the expressway, van fully loaded with boys, bound for New Jersey. As she drove, Julie managed to duck soda straw wrappers that shot past her head as Peg struggled to maintain order. In the rearview mirror, Nathan waved, his face covered with more freckles than Julie thought possible.

Peg turned to her. "Really, it won't be so bad once we get there."

The restaurant itself was precisely what Julie had imagined—all facade, fakery, and fun. But the boys didn't see the tawdriness. A reverential silence descended over the van as they pulled into the parking lot and accepted a scrolled stub from the ticket dispenser, a plywood creation designed to look like a small turret.

"Wow," breathed Nathan, his eyes widening as he took in the magnificence of the four-story pink castle, complete with triangular flags of no particular meaning and moat with no particular water.

At the door, they were greeted by scads of undergraduate students in costumes of varying degrees of authenticity. Julie overheard one of the girls explain that most of them were from the theater department of the community college in the next town.

"That explains why the wenches are within," Julie whispered to Peg. "Cramming for ye olde political science exam."

Peg pushed the last boy through the door. "I can sure use ye olde ladies' room. Can you get them seated?"

The interior of the restaurant was just the way a Hollywood set designer would imagine a medieval restaurant accepting all major credit cards should look—lots of exposed plastic wood, menacing iron cauldrons, and oversized tools that looked suspiciously like used barbecue utensils.

"That one's to pull out your guts," one boy stated wisely as he pointed to a pair of tongs.

They were ushered into the main room, a darkly lit place that smelled like last night's dinner mingled with something sticky. That something sticky was explained by rows of large plastic soda pitchers. The odor of last night's dinner remained mercifully, for the moment, unexplained.

Once her eyes adjusted, Julie realized the room resembled a large indoor riding arena. The center of the circular space was covered with packed dirt, and off in a distance could be heard the neighing of horses.

The boys filed into a row of chairs at a long plank, with a handwritten sign that read, "Lord Nathan's Party."

"That's me!" Nathan squealed, for which he was alternately punched and shoved by his friends. They sat eagerly, exploring the oversized napkins and plastic wooden bowls and large stainless steel spoons.

"This is so cool," said one kid.

"Awesome," agreed another.

Then their serving wench appeared.

"Good evening, sires, my lady. I am Trudy, your faithful serving wench for this evening," she began. "I have traveled from shores far beyond to serve you the finest foods of the kingdom."

From her accent, Julie placed her as a native of shores no farther than the kingdom of Bayonne, New Jersey. In her hand was a large covered tray, and she pulled the cover back to reveal something made of paper.

Thus, with great solemnity, they were presented with blue and gold crowns and matching bibs.

Peg returned, a smile on her face.

"Thank God. I was afraid I would miss the coronation," she mumbled as she slid into her seat.

"How do I look?" Julie asked. The blue and gold cardboard and paper crown was a subtle accessory to the beautifully accented bib, which read—in faux-calligraphy splendor—"Ye Olde Big Bib."

The bib all but covered her scoop-neck red blouse and very nearly came to the knees on her jeans. She struck several poses for full effect.

Peg laughed. "Perfect! I think you have your new outfit for casual Friday at the office."

"Please. Don't remind me," Julie moaned as she sat back down.

"Trouble in River City?"

"Yep. I'll fill you in later, maybe on the way back. It might ruin the party mood if Lady Julie of Gaffney began bawling like a damsel in distress."

Peg eyed her friend. "Hmm. Later, then. Oh, look. The festivities are about to commence."

A solitary man walked to the center of the arena. Even from a distance, Julie could not help but notice that his legs, in bicolored tights of yellow and orange, were particularly thin, almost painfully so. The puffy pleated shorts, balanced on such scrawny legs, gave the impression of a two-legged pumpkin. Upon his head was a round cap with multicolored spikes for the brim, much like the hat one of the kids in *The Little Rascals* always wore.

The spotlight followed him as he paused and put a long trumpet tied with what seemed to be dozens of ribbons to his lips. It was then that she saw his nose twitch.

"Oh my God," she hissed. "It's Orrin!"

"Who?" Peg asked, but Julie could not answer as Lord Orrin blew his horn. His face reddened with every note, and his left foot tapped, as if he had suddenly become Benny Goodman at Carnegie Hall.

His shoes were pointed.

That's all she could see. It was too much.

Great waves of laughter overtook her, between which she gasped for air before doubling over once again with the weight of the hilarity. Everyone in the party of Lord Nathan stared at Julie as she attempted to quiet herself, bit her lip, fixed her gaze straight ahead, and began the treacherous rise from shoulder-shaking giggle to loud guffaws once more.

Now other lords and ladies of the realm began to stare at her, and even Trudy the faithful serving wench shot her an annoyed look.

"I have to go to the bathroom," announced one of the boys.

"Me, too."

Peg stood up to take them, but Julie waved her hands wordlessly. She attempted to say that she would take them, but she was still unable to speak.

"You'll take them?" Peg asked.

Julie nodded.

"Are you okay?" Peg asked, noting the wary expressions on the bathroom-bound boys' faces. They now numbered four.

Again she nodded, the strains of Lord Orrin's horn echoing in her ears, and took them to the back and downstairs.

"She's weird," one of the boys said to another.

But she was still a grown-up, even if her behavior—not to mention the crown and bib—bespoke otherwise. And like any responsible grown-up, she led them safely to the little lords' room.

"Okay, guys," she began, her voice raspy from laughter. At least she had managed to regain some measure of control. "I'll wait out here in the hallway, and when you're done, we'll all go back together."

They all nodded, except one boy who, from his expression, made it clear that he felt they were far safer on their own than under the guidance of Julie. And as a group they marched into the dungeon-doored men's room.

At last she had a chance to catch her breath. Scrubbing her face with her hands, she relaxed and then took a glance at the corridor.

Downstairs the decor was far more subtle, with plain blue carpet and a row of plastic suits of armor, a printed and laminated version of what seemed to be the Bayeux Tapestry, and a few brightly colored tournament banners. She smiled and strolled over to one of the plastic suits of armor.

It was impressively mounted on a red velvet pedestal, and in the dim light it almost looked real. Almost. The telltale seams gave it away, as did the "Made in Taiwan" stamped on the knight's rear end.

"Poor Sir Knight," she whispered.

Glancing over her shoulder to see if any of the boys had emerged from the men's room yet—and they had not—she walked to the next suit of armor. She assumed that the boys would all exit together.

The next suit was on a fake marble pedestal, and

she was about to go back to the men's room to wait for her charges when she stopped.

This suit looked real.

Blinking, she leaned closer. Although the lighting was just as dim, from a round circle set into acoustical tile in the ceiling above, there was a weight to this one, a sense of permanency the other lacked.

"Impossible."

The suit was magnificent, etched with graceful swirls, richly gilded, and pierced with numerous holes. The ones on each side of the helmet, she guessed, would have been for hearing.

The body of the suit was large, the limbs thick, as if a man with heavy muscles would have worn it into battle. But something disturbed her. Something was wrong.

Then she realized what was amiss. The breast-plate had a massive dent in the center, as if a mighty blow had been struck. The metal had been pounded back carefully, but there was no mistaking the severity of the injury.

Slowly, she drew her hand to her mouth.

He couldn't have survived, was her single thought.

As if in a trance, she stepped closer, and then, mechanically, she joined the figure on the podium. Heat seemed to emanate from the suit.

He was much taller than she was, and languidly, as if it was the most normal, natural gesture in the world, she placed her hand on the visor.

It was hot to the touch.

Suddenly, the world began to spin, and she felt herself falling backward, tumbling helplessly from some great height, her arms flailing . . .

And he grabbed her by the waist.

The force of his embrace knocked the breath from her, and she closed her eyes against the brilliant light.

The sounds of birds chirping from outside filled the room, and a fragrance of leather and cool metal jolted her senses.

She opened her eyes.

From behind the visor, muffled but unmistakable, came two simple words.

"Help me."

3

❧

$\mathcal{J}$ulie stared at the visor, stunned beyond speech.

"Help me," he repeated. The voice was the same, the voice on her answering machine. Yet it was muffled by the metal faceplate, and something else was different.

There was no sense of urgency. His tone was conversational, as if a talking suit of armor happened to be the most absolutely normal thing in the world. Pushing against his shoulders, she wiggled free of his grasp.

"What's going on here?" Stepping back, she realized she was on a stone floor. The pedestal was gone, the carpeting had vanished. Instead of being outside the rest rooms at a theme restaurant, she was in a room filled with what appeared to be medieval armor and weapons.

"Is this some sort of storage closet?"

A snorting sound emerged from the suit of armor, and an arm creaked into position on his hip.

"Please," she continued, her voice rising. This was all wrong, everything was wrong. Even the atmosphere seemed different, brisk and clean and cold rather than the restaurant's recirculated cooking smells. Panic began to mount to her throat, and she wondered if she were losing her mind. "Please, I'm really confused."

"I said"—was it possible for a suit of armor to clench its teeth?—"help me, you dolt," he insisted in a less-than-pleasant tone.

Now, that was a new twist; her thoughts raced crazily. Had he simply said, "Help me, you dolt," on her answering machine, this whole fantasy could have been nipped in the bud.

"Listen." She tried to keep her voice even. "I just need to know . . ."

But before she could complete her question, the suit of armor pulled off his arm and threw it at her; it slammed into her stomach like a ramrod.

"Ugh!" The grunt escaped her lips, and she crumpled forward as the metal arm clanked to the stone floor. Little stars of bursting pain floated about her head as she gasped, clutching her middle. Through a distant haze, she saw that a brown quilted forearm and a large hand had emerged from beneath the airborne armor.

"God's blood, George. A sickly maiden would be heartier than you."

Catching her breath, she was about to speak when she paused. "George?" Straightening, she looked up at the visor. "Why did you just call me George?"

A quaintly unprintable oath exploded from the armor, followed by, "Because, you dolt, I believe it is premature to call you 'sir.'"

"But my name isn't George," she said simply. "It is . . ."

"Do you think I care if you are George or Tom or St. John? You are my replacement squire, and a wretched one at that. I see before me a boy of little wit, other than what is displayed in his attire."

"My . . ." Julie looked down at "ye olde big bib" and reached up where her crepe paper and cardboard crown still rested.

Julie began to remove the crown.

"Leave it be," the armor barked.

"Excuse me?"

"The headdress. Leave it be. You deserve the crown of a dunce. And besides, they are my colors."

"Your colors? Seems to me that metal is neutral. Goes with just about anything."

For a long moment, he stood so still, Julie began to think that she had imagined the entire conversation. She had been simply standing before an inanimate suit of armor and had very quietly but very definitely lost her mind.

That was the most logical conclusion. Her friends had warned her, especially Peg, that if she continued at her current pace, something would have to give. And it certainly had. Unfortunately, that something was her sanity.

Then he pushed back the visor, and Julie's jaw dropped.

The suit of armor possessed the most drop-dead gorgeous face she had ever seen. The sun-darkened skin, glistening with perspiration, was utter masculine perfection, straight black brows, beautifully sculpted nose, just a hint of whiskers on the lean cheeks. And his eyes—they were blue, but a pale blue, the color of her favorite Crayola when she was a child.

"Cornflower blue," she breathed.

The blue eyes narrowed. "You are addled."

"And you are . . ." She was about to say "gorgeous" but stopped herself. "I mean, who are you?"

His armor squeaked and rattled as he began to walk away without answering. It was amazing how even in heavy armor, a man could take strides in obvious anger and ball a fist in fury.

As he moved, she was able to get a better look at her surroundings. It was a vast room with a vaulted ceiling and arched windows. To the left was a smaller section, almost like a church nave, and as he approached that area, she realized the nave was filled with armor, weapons, and ancient battle equipment of every variety and material imaginable. There were upright suits like those in the restaurant, although all of these seemed genuine, and all were proportioned to fit the man with the cornflower eyes. There were golden-hued helmets etched in silver, and silver-hued breastplates etched in gold. There were all styles of head gear, from open burgonets to closed-visor modes.

An oblong table held odd bits of armor, extra gauntlets, arm guards, and elbow pieces. The leg armor and breast and back plates were leaning against a wall next to a stack of doublets with loose waxed-thong ties.

It reminded her of *The Wizard of Oz*, when the Tin Man and the Scarecrow were pulled apart and tacked back together with replacement parts. She could make a small army of men from the pieces on the table alone.

On a shelf of marble were rows of weapons, from maces made of bronze and wood to crossbows, some as wide as a compact car, and arched longbows. Arrows were held in baskets hanging from the walls.

And dangling next to the baskets was a vast assortment of swords and daggers, some with hooked ends, with little in common but glinting edges and frighteningly shaped points.

She could not pull her gaze from the brutal-looking tools.

"Can you identify?" His voice was harsh.

"Sure." She slipped her hands into her jeans pockets, uncomfortable and awkward. Nodding toward the swords and daggers, she smiled. "You're the dentist from hell, right?"

She waited for him to laugh in appreciation of her humor, finally to admit the joke or at least just to explain what was happening. Instead, he waited a few moments, his jaw working as if he were trying to loosen a morsel of cement from between his teeth.

Then, with movements so swift she was unable to prepare herself, he grabbed a small dagger and threw it at her.

"Hey! Watch it! You could have hurt me!" The dagger had come just a few inches from her head.

"That was my intention, George."

"Why do you want to hurt me?" She was unable to keep the disappointment from her voice. Just her luck that the most glorious specimen of a man she had ever encountered would find launching artillery at her a form of entertainment.

In response to her justified question, he threw a sword.

"Hey!" She ducked just in time. "This isn't funny!"

"I know it is not," he said calmly, reaching for another dagger.

"Don't you dare . . ."

But he did dare. The second dagger came even closer to her head than the first.

"That does it." She straightened, mustering all of the dignity her bib and paper crown would allow. "Who's the manager here? I hate to see you let go, but you're completely unfit for this job."

He paused. "I am unfit?"

"Yeah. You're clearly in the middle of some sort of mental crisis. And I think . . . what are you going to do with that arrow?"

As she had been speaking, he calmly pulled an arrow from a basket and reached for a large bow, creaking with every move. For a few moments, he seemed concerned with the arrow's feather end, and she continued talking as he stroked the feather smooth.

"As I was saying, you should really speak to the head of human resources. You're probably not the first employee to go a little around the bend, and . . . hey!"

With great deliberation, he loaded the arrow onto the bow, aimed, and shot the crown from her head.

"Silence," he commanded as she began to speak. "This is not a game."

She glanced behind to see the blue and white crown pinned against a basket with the arrow.

"You will listen," he said, and she was unable to come up with any reason not to listen, especially when he reached for another arrow.

"Good." Again he stroked the feather. "I hope I have your complete attention."

She nodded and was about to reaffirm how very interested she was in what he had to say when he held up a hand to silence her.

"I do not believe you understand how vital the

role of squire is to a knight. Not only in tournaments. They are mere pageants."

He waited for her to respond, and she nodded once to indicate she was listening to every word.

"You must understand that your abilities may very well determine whether the two of us live or die."

Part of her wanted to smile at the melodrama of the moment, but she didn't. This man was utterly sincere in what he was saying. Crazy or not, he truly believed he was a knight who might one day go into battle.

"Although we have been at peace for some time now, that peace has been maintained by our capacity to show force when needed. Do you understand?"

"Yes."

"Very good. I am not an ill-tempered beast, contrary to what you may believe at this moment. But damn it, George, you behave as if you've never been within arm's reach of a weapon."

"Sorry."

"Now, let us begin. I will throw you a weapon, and you must toss it back to me." He put the bow and arrow back on the table. "Keep in mind the shapes, the various weights, and above all the blades, for I have them sharpened to such a degree that you may slice a hair in two. Do you comprehend?"

"Well, sure, but . . ."

And with that, a ferocious-looking ax was lobbed at her. By only the luckiest of chances, she was able to hit the stone floor to avoid the blade.

"Whew!" She grinned, rising to her feet and dusting off her knees. "That was a close one!"

"Do you not understand me?" He was beyond a simple raising of the voice. That had been nothing short of a howl.

Whirling around, he reached behind and threw a pike. Without thinking, she reached up and grabbed it, simply because there was no place else to hide.

"That is an improvement," he barked.

"That was self-preservation," she mumbled.

For the first time, he smiled, and she felt herself weaken.

"Self-preservation is the whole point, George. That, and inflicting a bit of bodily damage. Now, try again, and this time don't catch it so well. Do it differently."

She was still staring at his mouth, when she blinked, realizing he had stopped speaking. "Okay. Wait. What do you mean that I should do it differently."

He cleared his throat, then wiped his mouth with the hand that was free of the gauntlet. "George, you tend to move and catch in a most unique way," he said gruffly. "Has anyone ever commented on your, eh, technique?"

"No. What do you mean?"

"God's blood, George. You catch like a girl."

"Oh." She smiled, looking down. "Sorry."

"Let's get on with this." And with that, he began

a rapid-fire onslaught of weapons and information. She had no time to think or to reason or even to catch her breath. All she could do was attempt to keep up with him and occasionally throw a weapon back at him in anger and self-defense.

But that only seemed to please him.

She had no idea how long the lesson had been going on. Perhaps minutes, perhaps days. All she knew was complete exhaustion. Yet the heavier her own limbs felt, the more her muscles burned and ached, the more energy he seemed to derive from the experience. It was as if he were nourished by her draining energy.

This had to end, she thought, wondering when she would collapse. Enough was enough. She raised her hand to stop the action, to call a time-out.

But he misinterpreted her gesture as a plea for another weapon. Instead of halting, he threw a bronze mace at her head.

She saw it coming, almost as if in slow motion. Yet she did nothing, unable to move fast enough. And the handle hit her directly on her forehead.

He winced at the thunk, then watched her crumple to the floor.

"George?"

There was no answer.

With a sigh, he began to remove his armor, realizing that he could not bend down to the boy impeded by the metal. Poor lad, he thought, shaking his head.

Perhaps they could find him work in the stables. Light work. With gentle horses.

When the last piece of armor was off, he approached the squire.

"George," he repeated. The boy's hair had fallen over his face, and gingerly the knight bent over and pushed it aside. There was a nasty red mark on his forehead but no blood. Indeed, he was rather surprised that such a mild blow had rendered the lad unconscious in the first place.

Perhaps the stables would be too difficult for George. He tried to remember if the queen still maintained her pet rabbits. They might be more to the liking of this vexing lad. Most certainly he would never be a squire, much less a knight. He reached down to loosen the boy's ridiculous neckwear, placing his hand on his chest and . . .

"What!" he shouted, withdrawing his hand.

Could he have been mistaken? Or was the lad malformed?

Swallowing, he again reached for the boy's chest, one side, then the other.

Was it possible?

He scrutinized the boy's face, touching his cheek to see if the skin was as soft as it appeared. It was. And there was not the barest hint of whiskers, although he had reached most of his adult height.

He touched the boy's side, patting down as he reached the . . .

"Hips!" he muttered.

Settling back on his haunches, he stared at the person before him, appraising the features with a different mind from what he had just moments before. This was no weakling boy, no worthless lad.

He tilted his own head to get a better view of the face, noting the delicately arched brows, the long lashes. Was there color on the lips? They were rounded and slightly parted.

"Good Lord," he whispered, astonished at himself. How could he have not noticed before this moment?

His replacement squire, George, was a woman! She was not only a fully grown woman but a comely one at that.

His smile vanished as he remembered another fact. Whoever she was, she was masquerading as a boy. Was it to get close to him? How long would it have taken him to discover the disguise?

Again he touched her face, shaking his head in befuddlement. Tracing her cheekbones, his fingertip rested against her lips. He felt the gentle warmth of her breath.

Then he lifted her into his arms, startled by the lightness of her weight, and carried her to his bedchamber.

"Lancelot," he said to himself, watching as her head rested against his shoulder. "What have you gotten yourself into now?"

*   *   *

It had all been such a strange dream.

Julie sighed, almost awake, anticipating her alarm clock to the right, resting atop the wicker nightstand, and the magazine she had been reading before she fell asleep folded open to an article on the perils of contact lens bacteria.

Still in the realm between sleep and complete awareness, she frowned slightly. Her head ached, and she wondered if she had somehow knocked against something in her sleep.

Then it came back to her, a man dressed as a knight throwing sharpened knives at her head. With a jolt, she opened her eyes.

And she was in a room she'd never seen before, with stone walls and very little furniture. Immediately, she sat upright.

"At last you wake."

She turned, and there he was to her left, the suit of armor. Only now he was a man in a blue tunic, seated in an ornately carved highback chair. On his legs were leather boots that covered his knees, and one ankle was crossed over the thigh of the other leg.

He was as undeniably handsome as she remembered.

"Oh. It's you." Running a hand through her tangled hair, she was unable to take her eyes from him. Charisma, she thought. That's what he had. A moviestar quality that made him impossible to ignore.

Another thought occurred to her. What had happened while she slept? One glance down at her blouse and jeans reassured her that she was still fully clothed. Only the bib was missing.

"Okay," she said, hoping her head would stop aching. "What's going on here?"

"That is precisely what I wish to ask of you, George." He emphasized her name with a slight snarl.

"Hey, don't you dare put this on me. One moment I was in a restaurant in New Jersey, the next I was target practice for someone who thinks he's a charter member of the Round Table. Please tell me, who are you, and where am I?"

"Come now. You know the answer."

"No, I don't! Don't you see, I really have no idea what is happening to me." She was close to tears, and he stared at her for a few moments, as if judging whether she was really upset or simply acting.

"Very well. I am Lancelot. And you, as you must surely know, are in Camelot."

"Oh, please. I'm really not up for this kind of . . ."

"And I must ask a similar question of you." He overlapped her response. "Who are you? And where do you come from?"

He remained absolutely motionless as he awaited her answer.

"All right," she sighed. "My name is Julie Gaffney, and I live in New York City."

"You are from York?" He seemed momentarily confused. "Your accent is most peculiar."

"Well, originally I'm from the Midwest, so I don't have a New York accent." With a grin, as if sharing a joke, she continued, "Your accent is strange, too. I thought you were supposed to be from France. You know, Lancelot du Lac, or whatever."

His blue eyes narrowed. "You *do* know who I am, then. You claimed ignorance, yet you know who I am."

"You're too modest. Everyone knows who Lancelot is, even in New York."

"I am known in York?" That seemed to please him. "But no, I am not from France. Those in Camelot have a singular sense of geography. They assume anyplace that is not Camelot must be in France."

"Rather xenophobic of them, no?"

Again, his eyes narrowed as he watched her. "Well . . . yes. Of course." Then he leaned forward, both feet shifting to the floor. "So why did the citizens of York send a woman to pose as my squire?"

Instinctively, she reached for where her bib had been, and felt her cheeks redden.

"You are too modest." He smiled at her discomfort, and then, in a casual tone, he added, "Why are you here?"

Still mortified, she shook her head, trying to get the image of him discovering her gender from her mind. "I . . . In all honesty, I don't know. Really. I was just . . ." Her voice trailed off as she heard a peculiar noise outside the stone room. "What was that?"

Instead of responding, he remained still, watching her reaction.

"That sound." Swinging her legs over the bed, she stood up, momentarily dizzy, then stepped to the window. There was a large tree obstructing her view, but the noise continued. "Horses. I hear horse hooves and carts."

"It is market day," he said softly. She was not pretending, he realized. She was frightened.

Don't they have market day in York?

"Where am I?" Her back remained toward him, but he could tell by her stiff posture that she was bracing herself for the answer.

"I have already told you. You are in Camelot."

She teetered just slightly on her heels, then braced her palms against the stone frame of the window.

"What year is this?" Her voice was a bare whisper.

"You are ill," he began.

"What year is this!"

"It is the year of our Lord four hundred ninety-eight . . ."

She did not hear what he was saying. There was a buzzing in her head as she took deep breaths, trying to steady herself, attempting to absorb the impossible information.

Absurd facts wove into her mind. Did a place

called Camelot really ever exist? She remembered a history professor in college saying that in all probability, Camelot was simply a myth used as propaganda by the royal houses of England, who all claimed blood ties with King Arthur. If there was a real King Arthur, he was probably an unusually successful Celtic chieftain sometime during the fourth or fifth century.

"The year of our Lord four hundred ninety-eight," she repeated, closing her eyes for a moment. The sounds of a medieval village pierced her ears, and the smells as well, pungent and sweet.

King Arthur. Camelot.

Her professor had said that at that time, success as a chieftain was measured in an ability simply to stay alive and not be axed by a neighbor or member of your immediate family. So the historical King Arthur would have been head of an ancient, marauding tribe of near-savages.

The man behind her, Lancelot, was no savage. Furthermore, how could she understand his language? Why did he seem to speak with only a slight English accent, more mid-Atlantic than most BBC productions?

Suddenly, he was behind her, and his hand, rough and strong and warm, touched her forehead. "You do not have a fever," he concluded.

"No." In a way, she wished she did have a fever. That would explain everything. "How can I understand you? You have barely any accent. I mean, I took a Chaucer course, and even *he* spoke and wrote in Old English. When did Chaucer live?" She felt herself losing control, and she twirled a piece of hair. Lancelot stared at her profile, watching as she wrapped the hair around her finger.

"Good Lord, even Chaucer is eight centuries away," she said, her eyes wide. "None of this makes sense."

"The blow to your head did addle you. I will return with a physician." Lancelot began to leave.

"No, wait. Please, just help me out here."

He paused, so close to her that she could feel the heat of his body.

"I'm losing my mind," she mumbled to herself.

"Well, if that be the case, there are far worse places to go mad."

"I'm serious. I don't know how this happened, why I'm here." Finally, she looked him directly in his eyes. "Doesn't this seem strange to you? Suddenly, some woman dressed in clothing that must be absolutely bizarre to you appears before your eyes?"

"Yes. But in truth, your own confusion is reassuring."

"Why?"

"Because no worthy enemy would ever send such a disjointed assassin."

At last she smiled, and he returned the smile, and a warmth seemed to encompass his features.

"I must go," he said. "You stay here and await my return. We will discuss this matter then."

"Where are you going?"

"It is not a woman's concern."

He turned and began walking to the door.

"You can't just leave me here! I'll leave, I'm going to explore, I'm . . ."

"Remaining where you are," he said matter-of-factly.

"You can't keep me here!"

"Yes, I can," he said simply as he stepped through the door. "Because, fair one, I'm locking you in."

With that, the door closed, and she heard the tumbling of a metal lock.

"Good point," she muttered to herself, wrapping her arms around herself as she gazed out the window.

"Thank you," he replied from the other side of the heavy wood door. Then she heard the distinct sound of his footsteps retreating. And in spite of herself, in utter defiance of her situation, she allowed herself a small smile.

4

$\mathcal{L}$ancelot's long strides carried him down the corridor with his customary authority, heels clicking on the polished marble floor. Sunlight streamed in jewel-like colors through the glistening stained-glass windows, illuminating the smooth stone walls, shimmering and vibrant against the sparkling surfaces. The guards in their brilliant red tunics stepped aside as one to allow him to pass through the massive double door at the end of the hallway, their metal pikes remaining firmly in their grasp.

He was the last one to arrive. The others were already standing by their designated places at the enormous Round Table.

The forty-nine knights acknowledged his entrance with nods, and as always Lancelot felt something deep within him stir to life. It wasn't just the sense of belonging, although that was certainly a vital part of his being. Nor was it the quiet satisfaction of knowing that he, Lancelot, was the king's chosen knight, the one man called on for counsel and advice, the soldier the king selected to ride by his side in battle as well as dine with at banquets.

No, there was something far more basic. It was an overwhelming sense that what they were doing was important, that every citizen of Camelot was living proof of man's ability to dwell in harmony, with as little as possible of the baser elements that had brought down every other great empire.

Camelot alone was different.

They had come from many countries and lands, this magnificent gathering at the table. They had come seeking a place where justice was revered and the good deeds of one individual were celebrated by all. They had come searching for a realm that honored human nature's best and most noble instincts, while quelling the coarser elements that threaten to taint and destroy even the strongest intentions of the most valorous human being. And, to a man, they had vowed to preserve the ideals of Camelot and its king. They almost moved and breathed and thought as one.

Almost.

"How kind of you to grace us with your presence, Sir Lancelot," muttered a voice so softly only Lancelot could hear the words clearly.

He did not have to turn to ascertain the speaker. "Malvern," he said as both an acknowledgment and a continuation of his thoughts. Malvern seemed to possess a character that was unique in Camelot, but unfortunately not in the rest of the world.

He was a most unlikely choice to be invited to this table. The other knights had been forced to prove themselves not only to the king but to the rest of Camelot as well. There had been tournaments to which every citizen had been invited, and careful scrutiny of each potential knight's moral and ethical judgments. The vast majority of those who attempted to join the Round Table were rejected, although most were more than pleased simply to remain in Camelot as ordinary citizens.

But Malvern was different. His father had been a page with Arthur when they were children. When at last Arthur rose to be king, Malvern's father, then on his deathbed, had asked King Arthur to watch after his only boy. Arthur vowed to do so, and gladly. Young Malvern was soon employed as a page, then as a squire, before becoming a knight himself.

Yet he did not fit in with the rest of the men. There was something different about him, a fleeting darkness in his eyes, an occasional display of bad humor, that made the others instinctively pull back. In short, he was not trusted with the absolute certainty the others enjoyed. And Malvern, in turn, did not trust anyone else.

The king had not yet arrived, and the knights stood still, awaiting Arthur, some resting their fingertips upon the rich wood of the immense table, unconsciously feeling the solid might of the piece. It was centuries old already, this mythical table, found preserved in a bog not far from the kingdom. But it was Arthur who had insisted upon its use, upon the fairness of the shape, so that no knight was above or below another. The king himself had polished the wood, exposing the magnificent inlay and the shades of red and brown and yellow that fanned out from the table's center in triangular shapes. As the years passed, the table seemed ennobled, as if an object could absorb the strength of those who rested their hands upon its surface.

And then the king entered.

All of the knights straightened at the sight of Arthur.

The king was easily the tallest man in the room, a stately bearing to him as if he had always worn a crown. On his head was a simple gold circle with a few small stones, rather than a lavish, gem-encrusted piece. His clothing was no more spectacular than anyone else's, his manner straightforward and unvarnished. His face was angular, the nose large but well shaped. A full brown beard circled his chin and jaw; not a jot of gray could be seen. He was a paradox of wisdom without great age, much younger than many who saw him for the first time expected. Still, he seemed to carry himself with a rare majesty. This was not just a man. This was a king.

"Men," he said simply, urging them to take their

seats in the carved chairs. There was the scraping of the legs against the floor, the settling of the knights, the clanking of side arms, and then silence as they awaited Arthur's words.

The king did not sit at the Round Table. Instead, he sat by himself at a separate table, as if emphasizing both the ultimate loneliness of his position and the difference between his knights, no matter how elevated, and the king.

After they were seated, he lowered himself into the enormous cushioned chair.

"Now, do any of you have news of the realm?"

He always began the regular gatherings in that way. A few of the knights nodded yes, and one by one, around the table, they spoke their news.

"Young Carter from just beyond the walls fears he saw an army of giants approaching from the west," stated one knight. "Normally, I would not bother you with this news, Your Majesty. But Carter was my squire for a time, and he is intelligent and not at all inclined to be fanciful."

There was a murmuring of concern, but the king merely smiled. "Young Carter? Is that not the same youth who has become betrothed to the baker's eldest daughter?"

"Why, yes, it is, Your Majesty," said the knight.

"When did he see this army of giants?"

"It was the night before last."

"Just as I thought. That evening, Young Carter

was feted by his future in-laws. I believe he was, well, overserved of the wine. And you may note that to the west is where the common haystacks are piled."

The knight's cheeks turned red. "Forgive me, Your Highness, for wasting your time . . ."

"Nonsense, Sir Eliwlod. I thank you for any information you may have. You are all my ears and eyes when it comes to Camelot." He then smiled at Eliwlod, eliminating the young knight's embarrassment, and nodded to the next man with news.

Lancelot wondered if he should mention the girl, the woman, who had come to him that morning disguised as a squire. Was it important?

The next knight was speaking, and Lancelot rubbed his jaw, thinking about the woman. Surely a stranger in disguise who creeps within the walls of Camelot is worth discussing. Perhaps she was sent by some enemy. Maybe her purpose was to infiltrate the innermost center of Camelot.

But he was reluctant to mention her.

"Lancelot, have you any news?" The king was always astute, and the other knights turned to Lancelot.

"No, Your Majesty." He smiled easily, but that masked a discomfort he felt in the pit of his stomach. Never before had he been less than forthcoming in front of the king and his brother knights. It was more than unpleasant, and a stab of anger at the young woman caused him to clench a hand beneath the table. "Nothing at all."

Another knight continued, but the king's eyes remained for a few moments on Lancelot.

Should he need to mention the stranger, Lancelot reasoned to himself, he would certainly do so. He was simply sparing the king's precious time.

The meeting continued as usual. At the conclusion, King Arthur motioned for Lancelot. It was not an extraordinary request. Often Arthur would seek out Lancelot for his opinion or expertise on certain matters.

"Lancelot," the king began as the others filed from the chamber.

Malvern stalled, making himself the last one out, able to hear what transpired between the king and Lancelot.

"Your Majesty." Lancelot stepped closer. "What may I do to help you?"

"Well, it is not myself I am concerned about." The king placed a hand on Lancelot's shoulder, and as they spoke, the two became oblivious to the presence of Malvern.

Lancelot's brow creased slightly as he listened to Arthur. "I don't know what you mean," he said simply.

"It's you, Lancelot. I'm worried about you."

Before he could respond, the king held up a hand. "Listen to me, please. Hear me out before you answer."

Lancelot nodded, and the king continued. "It is

not that I am displeased with your service as a knight. Nothing could be further from the truth. As always, you are the most skilled of any knight, and my most trusted. It is your personal life that concerns me."

"My personal life?"

"Yes. It seems to me that there is a certain aimlessness at your core. Only I notice it now, but I believe that in time that sense of drifting will encompass you and perhaps lessen your strength both spiritually and bodily."

"I honestly don't understand, Your Majesty."

"This concerns me, Lancelot, mainly because I myself have experienced the same feeling. At one time, I, too, began to feel a futility in my daily life, as if I were performing my duty well enough, but deep down in my soul I did not know why. There seemed to be no purpose to my life. I struggled by day to make the lives of others run smoothly, and I struggled by night wondering why I felt so empty."

"And why was that?"

"It was so simple, I almost laughed. In fact, I did, and still do when I recall my ailment. Lancelot, you need a woman."

Lancelot was about to speak when Arthur again bade him to be silent. "No, I don't mean just any woman. I am aware of how my knights spend their idle hours, and I know that you have not been wanting in quantity. But that is not the same thing, Lancelot. Not at all. And at times I believe a large variety is what exacerbates the feeling of loneliness. What you need is someone special, someone who can both soothe your soul and excite your senses at the same time. Someone who anticipates your needs, and someone in turn for you to need. In short, you require a Guinevere."

Lancelot thought for a moment, pondering what his king had just said. "Your Majesty, nothing would give me more pleasure than to find a woman such as the one you just described. And add to that beauty and intelligence, and I see only one problem with what you have just said."

"Indeed? And what is that one problem?"

"There is only one such woman on this earth, only one woman who could be everything you have just described. And unfortunately, Your Highness, she is not free. For the only woman who matches your description is Queen Guinevere herself."

The king clapped Lancelot on the back and grinned. "I know, I know. I am the most fortunate of men. But I earnestly believe there lives a woman somewhere who will be to you what my dear Guinevere is to me. It is only a matter of finding her."

Now Lancelot smiled in return. "Now, there's the difficulty."

"Who knows? Perhaps, Lancelot, she will find *you*."

Lancelot laughed, and the two men left the chamber together, discussing matters of Camelot, not noticing Malvern, who had been just beyond the door.

He walked away alone in silence, hands clasped behind him, his dark head bowed in thought. And then, all of a sudden, he, too, smiled, a gradual, unpleasant smile.

Lancelot opened the door, and at first he did not see her. For the briefest of instants, he thought she had gone, fled the kingdom, vanished.

And then he saw her.

Still in the comical attire, the strange blue trousers and the blouse, she was curled on his bed, sound asleep. He approached carefully, softening his steps so as not to wake her.

How could he have mistaken her for a lad? In profile, her gender was perfectly obvious. Not only was her gender apparent, so was something else he had somehow neglected to notice fully.

She was beautiful.

Which, of course, could make her more dangerous. That is, supposing she had been sent by an enemy. As he watched her, the notion began to seem utterly ridiculous. What sort of enemy sends a woman alone to vanquish a kingdom? A woman could not possibly brandish such power, especially over men.

Immediately, Helen of Troy came to his mind, but he brushed the thought aside as her eyes began to flutter open.

For a few moments, she frowned in sleepy confusion, then she gasped and sat upright.

"Good afternoon, George," Lancelot said.

She turned toward him, and the alarm left her face. "Oh. Hello. How were things at the Crusades?"

"The what?"

"Never mind. Wait a few more centuries, and I'll explain." Her eyes took in the rest of the room, the late-afternoon slant of the sunlight. She was still in Camelot. It had not been a dream.

And Lancelot was there, standing with a masculine confidence that was both wonderful and irritating. Then she noticed his left arm was holding something from her sight. "What's that behind your back?"

"Aha. You *are* a woman."

"Excuse me?"

"Only a woman can detect the scent of a gift at twenty paces."

"A gift?" She was unable to keep the pleasure from her voice.

Without fanfare, he pulled a bundle from behind his back and handed it to her.

"The king and queen are hosting a banquet tonight, and unless you wish to attend in your squire's costume, this is something for you to wear."

"A banquet? And I can come?"

He nodded.

"You mean I'm invited to a banquet in Camelot?"

"Yes, yes. Of course. Now, open the gift."

She looked up at him with a smile of pure pleasure, and an unfamiliar sensation gripped him. Perhaps it was the color of her eyes, like emeralds. Or the gold of her hair. He pushed the matter from his mind as he watched her untie the present.

The buff brown cloth unfolded to reveal a gown. It had been no hardship for him to find it, for he knew the best seamstress in all of Camelot, and it was really a small matter to . . .

"Oh," she sighed as she held it before her. He hadn't really examined it, but as the rich green velvet caught the light, as the golden belt glittered, he had to admit it was a most lovely gown. Unusual, the seamstress had said. It would take a woman with a rare figure to do it justice.

But the moment he saw it, he knew it would fit her perfectly. He hadn't anticipated the color, however. Now that he saw the gown against her skin, he knew. It was, indeed, perfect.

"And the slippers are there as well," he added. "In the same velvet."

"Oh," she repeated. It wasn't said as a word but as an emotion.

Suddenly, he was embarrassed. "I'll leave so you can get dressed," he said gruffly, realizing that he should leave but wanting very much to stay.

"Thank you," she said, and she reached for his hand. He stepped away, and her hand fell back against her side, and then she clutched the dress again. "Thank you so very much."

"You are welcome." He had begun to walk away, then stopped. "I have forgotten. What's your real name again?"

"It's Julie. Julie Gaffney."

"Very well, then. I must see someone now, but I will return within the hour, Lady Julia, to escort you to the banquet."

She beamed, and he gave her a slight half-bow and left.

"It's really just Julie," she whispered to the closed door. "But Lady Julia will do nicely."

Touching the gown, she smiled. She was just beginning to feel like a Lady Julia.

The queen smiled as her long strawberry-blond hair was brushed. It fell down her back like a great wavy mane, heavy and glorious, reflecting the light that streamed through the windows.

"Mmm," she sighed. "That feels wonderful."

He ran his hand over her hair with tenderness, then lifted a strand to kiss it, his eyes closing.

"Guinevere," he said softly, plainly.

The brush dropped, forgotten, as she turned to face him. Although she was tall for a woman, he towered over her, his strong arms encircling her with strength and passion.

"We should not," she admonished. "Not here, in the middle of the day. We will be caught."

"I don't care."

"My reputation will be ruined," she added coyly.

"But think of how much fun we can have on the road to ruin." His teeth bit lightly on her earlobe, and her knees weakened.

And she was lost. All notion of decorum vanished as if it had never existed.

They didn't hear the knock on the door.

When the knock was not answered, the door flew open.

"Your Majesty," stammered the knight in the doorway.

The king looked up from his wife, her shoulder exposed as she reclined in his arms, her eyes still clouded with desire.

"Damn it, Malvern! Can't you knock? The queen and I are engaged in a private conference!"

The knight blushed, and the queen planted a kiss on Arthur's cheek. "Later, my dear. We will continue our conference later. Perhaps at our magical tree."

The king chuckled. There was an old oak tree just beyond the castle grounds, and it was there they had first shared tender words, first declared their passion. And through the years, that ancient tree still held a special enchantment for them. No matter what had transpired before, simply being at the tree always seemed to restore their love. "I will hold you to that, love. We will pick up exactly where we left off, at our tree."

She smiled and scooped up her silver brush. With a nod toward the knight, she left the room. Both men watched her intently.

"The queen is a beautiful woman, Your Majesty."

"I know it, Malvern. Now, what brings you here at this unnatural hour of the day?"

The knight did not reply at first, and the king, who had wandered over to a desk and begun to survey some documents, looked up. "Well?"

"I do not know how to begin, Your Majesty."

"Just begin."

"This is not a pleasant task. I do not want to say what I have to. Yet I must. I cannot let you be made a fool of. It must end."

The king regarded the knight with mild amusement. He had never been able to warm up to this young man, not at all. There was something dark about him. Arthur could not identify the problem precisely, he simply knew he did not feel comfortable with this one knight. The others he would trust with his life. But Malvern, he was different.

"So I am being made a fool?" The king crossed his arms. "I am king. Many times I am made a fool, Malvern. Now, run along and be a good knight."

The younger man's face reddened.

He was always treated like this, by the king, by the other knights, even by the lowly pages and squires.

Malvern the joke. Malvern the only knight who was undeserving of the rank.

Well, soon Arthur would stop laughing. Soon everyone would stop laughing.

"I have every reason to believe, Your Majesty, that the queen is being unfaithful to you."

There was a silence in the chamber so fraught with tension Malvern thought the walls themselves would begin to tremble. For a moment he was afraid. Had he gone too far? Should he have waited until his plans were further developed?

But that had been the very point of this meeting, to plant the seeds of his scheme, for the king himself to observe every well-laid step.

Malvern swallowed, watching the unreadable expression on the king's face. Suddenly, the king emitted a horrible, lionlike roar.

It had started now. There was no way to take it back. The process had begun.

What had he done?

Fear such as he had never known gripped his stomach. The knight was about to turn on his heels and flee when he realized what the unearthly sound was.

The king was laughing.

It was a hearty, full-throated laugh, his head thrown back, his massive shoulders quaking.

Malvern stared for a moment, uncertain what he should do.

The king's laughter subsided, but he was still smiling. "Thank you, Malvern. That was the best entertainment I have had in many a day. I cannot wait to share it with the queen. Now, off with you. I have some business to attend to."

Malvern did not move. His eyes shifted uneasily, his hands tightened at his side.

"That was not a jest, Your Majesty. It is the truth, although I am loath to say it. The queen has been unfaithful, and she continues to be unfaithful."

The good humor left the king's features. "You speak treason."

"No, no! I only wish to spare Your Majesty further injury!"

The king glared at the knight. He had never liked him, never trusted him. Even listening to the falsehoods dishonored both Arthur and his wife.

Something caused him to press on.

"And with whom is the queen committing this vile crime? Are there many, a few, or just one?"

Malvern hesitated. This was it. Once he said the name, his own life would be in jeopardy. He risked losing everything.

Yet there was no choice. It was intolerable, living like this, being the object of ridicule amongst other knights, amongst everyone. He could no longer exist on the bottom rung. He was born for greater things, and only by bad luck and simple injustice had he been placed in this position.

It was nothing more than simple injustice, and nothing less. If he proceeded with his plan, the injustice would be set right. The wrongs would be corrected. Yes, some people would be forced to suffer. But had not Malvern been suffering, too? Was it not better to rectify an injustice than to let it continue?

"The queen is being wooed by a man much younger than Your Majesty and, if I may unfortunately add, a man much fairer of face. It is a woman's nature, I have noticed, to be swayed by virile youth and callow boasting."

"Give me the name."

"I do not wish to, Your Majesty. I simply wish to warn you, to alert you so that you may see the evidence yourself."

"Give me the name."

"I do this under duress."

The king said nothing, but his expression was far more eloquent than any words. Malvern transferred his weight from one foot to the other, a slow, halting motion.

"Lancelot," Malvern said, unable to keep the venom from his voice.

"Lancelot?" The king was incredulous.

"Yes, Lancelot. I have seen them together. He looks at her the way a hungry man looks at a well-roasted joint of meat, and . . ."

"Enough!" The king held up his large hand. The

knight was silent. "Be gone now, Malvern. I have work."

"But Your Majesty, let me . . ."

"I said be gone," the king said wearily. "Be gone."

Malvern thought of what he could say, something damning that would help to hang Lancelot. But he could think of nothing just then. Before this conversation, he had carefully listed his options, ways in which to respond to any anticipated outcome. But he hadn't counted on this reaction. None of his cobbled responses would work.

This was not what he had expected.

Bobbing a small bow, he left the king, pausing just outside the door, wondering if he could hear anything. But there was nothing but silence. So Malvern, his shoulders rounded in defeat, walked away.

Inside the chamber, the king sank into a chair, the state papers forgotten now, and stared into space.

5

❧

Julie smoothed her hand over the dress, savoring the incomparable texture of rich, slightly irregular velvet. The very fabric of the emerald gown possessed a special quality, an indefinable element missing from anything mass-produced or synthetic. She closed her eyes with pure pleasure, inhaling the scents, so strange and new, that surrounded her.

She was there, in Camelot, awaiting Sir Lancelot himself to escort her to a banquet.

Of course, he was busy at the moment. This knighthood business really took far more time than most people realized.

Her hand slid luxuriously up from her thigh, past her waist and the gold netting, skimming her arm, and then to her mouth, which had spread into a delicious, delighted grin.

She was really there, in Camelot, feeling more alive than she had ever imagined possible.

There was a full-length mirror in the corner of the chamber, and she had stood before it moments earlier in wonder, reaching out to touch the image of the woman there, tracing the carved frame as if daring anyone to deny the vision. It was she, of course, Julie Gaffney. Yet it was a Julie Gaffney such as she had never imagined, never even dreamed possible.

For before her was a pre-Raphaelite beauty, slightly misty in the cloudy, flawed mirror. Her hair seemed to be made of something ethereal, a golden-hued crown that surrounded her, cascading past her shoulders, perhaps a full eight or ten inches longer than she had remembered it being.

The dress hugged her every curve with wanton perfection. Had her figure always been so? Certainly, she had felt less than dazzling at the health club, or in a swimming suit, or even in an evening gown. For the first time, she couldn't find at least a dozen aspects to change or wish for a giant eraser to eliminate some lines and add a few others.

There was nothing she would change, not now.

It was her face that most surprised her. Although her features had always been regular, they had seemed unspectacular, like an uninspired yet competent rendering. As most people had commented, her face was pleasant. But something had changed, the artist had finally been inspired or the brush was of a higher quality, for she was nothing short of radiant.

"Lady Julia." The familiar voice was low, yet her eyes opened.

There he was, Sir Lancelot, standing in the doorway, an unearthly vision of medieval splendor. His blue tunic—another one? she wondered—was a deeper shade, a velvety midnight. The boots seemed more polished, his hair less tousled.

The expression on his clean features reflected the feelings she herself had experienced when she gazed in the mirror. He saw it, too, this change. He, too, was awed by the transformation.

"Lady Julia," he repeated. The tone of his voice sent a shudder up her spine, a thrill. "You are . . ." he began. Then he shook his head and rubbed his eyes with his hand as if suddenly weary. "I need to know something."

"Yes?"

"Who sent you to Camelot?"

That was not what she had been expecting, hoping for him to say. "Who sent me?"

"Yes. I need to know, as will the king."

"I . . . well." She twisted her fingers. "I don't know."

His expression did not betray any emotion. "You do not know?"

"This sounds impossible, but it's true. One moment I was, well . . ." How could she describe a theme restaurant and a children's birthday party? She cleared her throat, grasping for words. "I just seemed to appear."

His eyes narrowed. "In my weapons room?"

"Well, yes. As a matter of fact, yes."

"And from what kingdom do you hail?"

"I'm from New York, in the United States." There was no recognition on his face. "Of America."

"And where be this kingdom?"

"It's across the ocean. Way, way far away from here. In fact, it hasn't been discovered yet. At least, I'm pretty sure it hasn't been discovered. A Viking or two may have rowed over, but . . ."

"If this kingdom has yet to be discovered"——he nodded wryly on the last word—"then how can you know of its existence, much less claim it as your native land?"

"In all honesty, this is the strangest part of all." Suddenly, she felt like an errant child explaining a broken window. Even to her own ears she sounded unconvincing. "You see, Sir Lancelot, well. You see, this is going to blow your mind. Really. As incredible as it seems . . ."

"Yes?"

"I am from the future, from about, whoa——let's think about this." She gazed into space, counting off the centuries with her fingertips.

Lancelot simply watched her as she spoke, then slowly, with great deliberation, crossed his arms.

"Wow," she said at last with a sheepish smile.

"I'm from about fifteen hundred years from now. Give or take a half century."

He did not respond. He did not even blink. Had she not seen him move earlier, she would have sworn he was inanimate. Finally, he closed his eyes. "The blow to your head has addled your mind."

"No! I'm absolutely serious!"

"Come," he looked at her quizzically, as if she were a specimen under glass. "We will not speak of this until later. Perhaps then your senses will return."

"You don't believe me."

"Lady Julia," he said plainly. "You appeared in my weapons room dressed as a boy. You were knocked on the head, and I discovered you are not a boy but a woman fully grown. Then you claim to be from a thousand years in the future. Would you believe such a tale, under such circumstances?"

She was about to say yes, absolutely, of course she would believe. But he stopped her.

"Let me phrase this in a different manner," he explained in an avuncular tone. "Imagine if I appeared in your own chamber, wherever that may be."

In her mind, she saw her bedroom in Manhattan, the dresser and the carpet and the drapes open to the city skyline.

"Now," he continued, "what would you think if a man in strange clothing suddenly appeared and claimed to be from, let us say, fifteen hundred years in the past? What would you do, Lady Julia?"

She could see it now, standing in her room and seeing a man dressed as a medieval knight step from nowhere.

"I suppose I would have called 911," she admitted. "I would probably call for help."

"Would you assume the person was perhaps ill?"

"Yes," she said softly.

"Or that perhaps that person might wish to do you harm?"

"Well . . . I see your point, Sir Lancelot. But please, I'm not crazy or out to hurt you. I'm as confused as you are over this whole thing."

"I doubt it," he mumbled. "Well, I do not believe we will be able to resolve anything at the present time. Perhaps you'll be able to recall your past after a hearty meal."

"But I do remember where I'm from. It's just that you refuse to believe me."

He ignored her statement. "Come. Let us go to the banquet, Lady Julia. I shall be pleased to attend with you, for you are . . ." He seemed to be grasping for the right words. "Tonight you must be . . ."

What would he say? That she was beautiful? Elegant? Perfection itself?

"You are my third cousin once removed," he said in triumph.

"Excuse me?"

"Well, how else can I explain your appearance?"

"What do you mean, my appearance?" She touched her hair, the softness. Was he blind?

"Your being here," he said gruffly. "I have to say *something*. Well"——he grinned, crooking his arm—— "shall we?"

"I . . . well." She hesitated. "Sir Lancelot, don't you notice anything different about me? Not just the clothes."

With a frown, he surveyed her from the top of her head, slowly down her entire length. Then, with equal languor, he traveled from her slippers to her head once again.

"I was right. Absolutely right." He nodded.

"Yes?"

"The other gown would have been too small for you." He brushed his hands together. "Shall we?"

"Oh, damn." She shook her head with a small smile. "Might as well. I don't suppose you brought me a corsage."

"A what?"

"Never mind." She took his arm, and they descended a narrow, winding staircase.

"You are exquisite," he whispered from just behind her ear.

She had been busy gathering the folds of the gown. "Pardon me?" She looked into his eyes, and he smiled.

"I just said watch the step." He nodded forward.

"Oh. Thanks."

And he touched the small of her back as they made their way to the ground floor.

There was a large room with Persian carpets and a heavy cupboard with glittering gold plate on display, but before she had a chance really to survey the furniture, they had stepped outside.

At once she was enveloped by sights and sounds and fragrances of such extraordinary magnificence she felt certain she had fallen into some wondrous dream. Lancelot smiled at her reaction, the response of all newcomers to the place.

She spun to gape at the rosebushes that framed the doorway they had just passed through.

"They're blue! Blue roses!"

"I know they are," he replied, walking over a beautifully arched footbridge. Below was a sparkling creek with strange flora and rainbow fauna nodding with the current. A green and yellow fish with red fins jumped over a rock.

"That fish! Did you see it? It looked like something from the Disney studios!"

Casually, he glanced at the stream, just in time to see another fish, this one turquoise and purple, leap after the first fish.

"Yes, Lady Julia. Those are indeed fish."

Her mouth remained open, and with the tip of a finger he touched her chin gently to close it. Yet her eyes maintained the expression of such pure astonishment that at last he chuckled.

"I see myself in your eyes," he said, guiding her past a marble fountain that was running with wine and surrounded by blossoms of impossible freshness and beauty. Another fountain offered fruit nectars, and there was even one for cool water.

"I never imagined such a place could exist," she breathed.

It was true. Camelot made the rest of the world seem hopelessly dowdy.

They walked through the streets of a great walled city, the late-afternoon sun glowing with yellow warmth in a cloudless blue sky. Birds flew about, dotting the horizon with fabulous colors and songs unlike any she had ever heard, exotic yet familiar, as if fantasy had become reality. Vast buildings were set apart, constructed from the same pink stone as the walls, all twinkling as if made from diamond chips. The pavement was of the same stone, and it, too, glimmered underfoot.

There was no dirt, other than the patches of rich soil from which spectacular flowers rose as tall as small trees, with blooms of such astonishing colors—reds blindingly brilliant, oranges so vibrant they glowed, and, again, the blues, royal and peacock and deep blues—she felt her eyes squint at the unaccustomed beauty of the sight. It was as if the color intensity had been turned up by some unseen twist of a knob. Everything was bigger and brighter and just better than anyplace else.

The people themselves were no less magnificent. The clothing was simply cut, really no more than well-tailored tunics, the women's dresses buffed the glimmering pavement, the men wore the same thigh-high boots and shorter tunics that Lancelot wore, in equally dazzling shades. The fabrics themselves were exquisite, shimmering with every movement.

The attire almost overshadowed the people, but not quite. For in the faces of the people she saw such hope and joy and contentment, pure happiness that made every feature on every person shine.

Horses trotted by, pulling carts made of fine wood or carrying a lady or a gentleman or a laughing child. Yet there was no manure, not a single bit in sight.

"There's no horse manure," she stated, turning to Lancelot, who had just accepted a perfect red apple from a smiling vendor. There were vendors everywhere, with a staggering array of foods, steaming hot bread and elaborately decorated cakes, every sort of roasted meat imaginable, fruits and vegetables, from tropical mangos to roasted corn dipped in butter.

But no one paid. The vendors were simply handing out the marvelous food, their fee apparently nothing more than a smile and a nod.

"Of course, there is no manure. The horses go only outside the gates, beyond where today's tournament was held." He bit into the apple, a trickle of the juice running down his chin.

"You mean the horses are toilet-trained?"

He laughed. "Not exactly, Lady Julia. They prefer to do that sort of thing away from the city."

"I don't understand. Isn't it natural for them just to go as they walk?"

"Not in Camelot. They instinctively know." He shrugged. "The king has a saying, one I think can be understood only after a visit to Camelot."

"Let me guess," she began. "The streets are so clean, you can eat off them?"

"No." He held his face toward the sun, and Julie just stared at him, at the way the light played off his shoulder-length black hair, the way his very skin seemed to glow with vitality. Then he looked down at her with utter seriousness. "The king says we in Camelot have rendered the rest of the world obsolete."

Julie was about to speak out about the sheer folly of such a statement, when she glanced around her, at the people, at the gardens that seemed to thrive on every corner. She realized it was not a statement of arrogance or caprice. It was simply a statement of truth.

"Oh," was the snappiest reply she could manage.

Lancelot seemed to understand, and he laughed.

Julie looked up at the expanse of the castle, holding onto his arm and the strength it offered.

"How can the castle defend itself?" She knew enough of medieval life to notice the distinctive lack of any fortification. Then, even as she spoke, she realized she was not in the Middle Ages, nor was she in the Renaissance or any other time identifiable from her own paltry store of knowledge.

This was Camelot, a place as timeless as it was strange, as foreign as it was familiar. Simply Camelot.

"The castle does not need to defend itself," Lancelot explained. "That is why I am here, and the other sworn knights." He paused, staring up at the castle. "Should an enemy ever get this far, it would be too late. We would have already failed."

A question suddenly occurred to Julie. "You've asked me this already, so now it's my turn. Why are *you* here, Sir Lancelot?"

"Because there is to be a banquet tonight."

"No, I mean here, in Camelot. What made you decide to leave your home and risk everything to be here?"

Lancelot glanced at her, his head tilted slightly as if viewing from a different angle might help clarify the question and the thoughts that led to it. He paused, then sat down on the edge of a wine fountain. Patting the space next to him, he urged Julie to settle as well.

The reflection of the deeper blue of his tunic made his eyes darker as well, from cornflower to sapphire. His leggings and high boots were black, the same midnight shade as his hair and eyebrows.

"Unlike you, I know the answer." His voice was

probing, firm. "But first, Lady Julia, why do you imagine *you* are here? Perhaps we both came to Camelot for the same reasons."

Julie paused, not certain how to answer. Why *was* she there? Then it came to her, the most logical and crazy response of all: the truth. "I really don't know exactly. But maybe it's because I've believed in Camelot all my life. I just failed to realize it. In the back of my mind, it has always been here, always existed, although the reality is far better than I could have imagined. I went about my life feeling half empty, only half satisfied—like wearing only one glove on a cold day. Something was missing. And then, suddenly, here I am. I really don't know much more than that, Sir Lancelot. Just here I am."

Lancelot was staring at her with his Crayola-colored eyes. And she met his gaze with her own, watching as an almost silver beam of recognition seemed to light his stare from behind.

"It was precisely like that with me," he began. "I do not recall much of life before I arrived here as a young man. I do remember dirt and mud and sickness and hunger. I remember a woman, not my mother but a woman with whom I must have been in love. Yet if that had been the case, I would have recalled her more fully—she wouldn't be just an image in the mist, impossible to reach. She must have been a dream."

He stared straight ahead for a moment. Then, as if startled back to the present, he continued, his voice again solid and certain. "Those things I do remember. But they fade with every day I remain in Camelot. And I think we are both here for the very same reason, Lady Julia. The same reason children dream of Camelot, the same reason men great and small know the story of this place."

"What reason is that?" She could barely speak.

"Because we believe in Camelot."

He took a deep breath and continued. "We believed in its existence when others told us it was myth. In our hearts, we knew it to be a true and just place, which is what everyone knows. But we also believed, emphatically and even against all evidence to the contrary, that Camelot is a real place. And thus, we are here. We are here because we believe."

Julie nodded, understanding that his words were absolutely true. Inexplicable, perhaps, but true.

"Does that mean you've come to the conclusion that I'm probably not a threat to you or to Camelot?"

Instead of answering, he simply shrugged. His face was again unreadable, and she realized he was still not sure of her intentions. And his mistrust hurt her. For some reason, she wanted his trust, longed to have him look at her without the unmistakable alertness that never seemed to leave his expression.

Lancelot rose to his feet and gestured with a nod toward the castle. "Come. I'm hungry."

A light breeze blew a fragrance of sweet wine

from the fountain and fresh flowers. The air itself was delicious.

With one glance over her shoulder at the splendor of Camelot, Julie and her knight entered the castle. As she stepped through the wide, arched doorway, her automatic reaction was to tighten her grasp on Lancelot.

"Wow," she murmured.

She glanced up at the ceiling, so very high she could barely see the paintings on the top. The interior of the castle was even more sumptuous than the exterior, but by then her senses had all but gone numb. There was only so much splendor she could take in at one time.

And then they were in the Great Hall.

It was like a massive Technicolor dream, in a spectacular, larger-than-life setting. The long tables were laden with every food imaginable, and a few beyond even the powers of fantasy. Large joints of roasted meats, steaming platters heaped with glistening vegetables, ornately embellished pastries and cakes, all resting upon lush tapestries and gold-embroidered cloths.

And the people, the citizens of Camelot. They, too, were more vivid than ordinary folks. They seemed to glow with health and joy, all of them, no matter what their age or gender or position in the kingdom.

Lancelot guided her to a chair, and she settled with relief. They were up front, with a view of the entire hall.

"I will return shortly," he said softly. "Remember, should anyone inquire, you are a distant relative of mine." Then he left.

She needed the time to herself. As if in a daze, she simply watched the swirl of activity around her.

She was really there, in Camelot, she told herself once again. It had become almost a chant, a mantra to grasp and hold, like a prayer.

Camelot. She wracked her mind trying to recall any details she could regarding the place.

In junior high school, she had read and savored all the mystical novels by science-fiction writers and the Victorian epic poems. Yet the specifics that had so entranced her at thirteen eluded her as an adult. All she could recall was the tale of young Arthur, of his meeting with Merlin, being tutored and schooled and trained by his mentor, and his eventual triumph as the mighty and wise king. From there, the myth branched out into many versions. Every land seemed to have its own interpretation, variations to suit each country and each regional taste. The French Arthur was more romantic and passionate, the German more disciplined. Lancelot was either a victim of Guinevere's treachery or a faithless playboy. But the gist was always the same: Arthur wooed and won the beautiful Guinevere. They married and became paragons of virtue. Then a knight arrived, a man as mysterious and virtuous as he was handsome and dashing.

And the young Guinevere, alas nothing but a

weak female after all, fell in love with Sir Lancelot. And something was rotten in the state of Camelot.

From that moment on, the magic of Camelot turned into mud. Again, the legend was open to all sorts of renditions, but one thing was constant. The affair, whether it was pure or lustful, destroyed the kingdom and its people.

Julie took a deep breath, wondering what point in the scenario they were up to at the present time.

How much time was left for this enchanted land? How many more days until the fragile enchantment was broken forever?

Hundreds of people were dining at the banquet. Colorful cloths covered the tables, banners hung overhead with magnificent tapestries over the fireplaces. It should have been unbearably warm in the Great Hall, but it was perfect, just perfect.

So she took a deep breath and continued to survey the hall, the wonders that were in every corner to savor and enjoy, just there for the asking.

Thus far, the king and queen had not yet appeared. Lancelot had explained that they would arrive later. They did not want to interfere with their subjects' comfort in any way, and so they delayed their own entry into the hall until the thirst and hunger of the masses had been slaked.

Then there was a trumpet blast. It did not sound like a normal trumpet—its tones were deeper and richer, more velvet and mellow. As one, everyone in the hall stood up, Julie a mere beat behind the rest.

And into the hall, to thunderous applause, walked King Arthur and Queen Guinevere.

Julie had seen, on television, the impact of a president on his people. She had heard the strains of "Hail to the Chief" and watched as the press corps or administrative assistants dutifully sprang to their feet and applauded. This was different.

Unlike the reception offered to a head of state, even royalty, this was more like the unrestrained acclaim after a once-in-a-lifetime theatrical performance, the opening night of Olivier as Hamlet, or the first startling performance of *Oklahoma!* or Brando and Tandy in *A Streetcar Named Desire*. This was the way it must have been the night a young Leonard Bernstein took the baton from an aging maestro. This was the Beatles on Ed Sullivan.

This was nothing short of unfettered adoration.

She could see them clearly now. By his side was a tall woman, slender and graceful as a dancer. When she turned, Julie could see a face not of great beauty but of tremendous character. She, too, was younger than expected. Upon watching her smile and touch hands, speak quietly with a woman with a child and then caress the child's bare head, Julie revised her original opinion.

Guinevere was beautiful.

Hers was not a cookie-cutter beauty or a trendy

look that goes in and out of style with the change in hemlines. Queen Guinevere possessed a loveliness that dwarfed mere prettiness. There was a glow about her, an aura. And then her face lit up with recognition. A warm smile turned her fine lips. She extended her hand.

And Lancelot, Julie's Lancelot, received that hand with reverence and pressed his lips to the back of her hand. Slowly, he turned her hand and pressed his lips to her wrist.

Julie glanced around her to see if others were as stunned as she was, but no one else seemed to notice. Perhaps that was a typical greeting in Camelot. Perhaps, as someone new, she was simply unaware of the custom. But from the queen's furious blush of pleasure to the intensity in Lancelot's eyes, Julie doubted it very much.

The fatal flirtation between Guinevere and Lancelot had already begun.

Her eyes studied the scene, wondering if the king had caught sight of the brief spark between his wife and his trusted knight.

He had. To Julie the expression on his face was as unmistakable as it was fleeting. There was a brief darkness there, a burst of anger that erupted and vanished swiftly.

Beside the king, within an arm's length, another man stood alone.

Her gaze rested on him instinctively. Although

he wore the same festive clothes, the same brilliant colors as everyone else, there was a darkness about him that all but screamed wicked. His skin did not have the pearlescent quality of the others. And his eyes. They flashed in Lancelot's direction, then in hers. The eyes were pure malevolence.

"Oh, no," she whispered. "Lancelot, you have an enemy."

"Indeed," came a man's voice, seemingly from nowhere.

She jumped, eyes wide.

Then she saw the speaker. He was an older gentleman, with a head so large and bony, the only relief from the angles was provided by his sparse, snowy tufts of hair. His nose was bulbous, his eyes deeply circled and a watery, red-rimmed blue. Then he smiled with imperfect yellowed teeth, a smile that reached his tired eyes and made them glow, and she felt as if she had known him forever.

"My dear," he said. "I've been expecting you."

Unlike the others in Camelot, his clothing seemed to be those of a pauper. He wore a flowing brown robe patched together with large, uneven stitches. There were spots and stains splashed over the rough fabric, and a large hood formed a cowl in front and was hanging limply down his back.

"You've been expecting me?" She gasped. "You know who I am?"

"Of course I do," he replied with an indignant

nod. "You are Miss Julie Gaffney. I trust your journey here was not too uncomfortable?"

"You know about my journey?"

"I should hope I do, Miss Gaffney. Or is it Lady Julia now? I prefer Lady Julia myself. Much less common, in my own opinion. One should make the most of names. They reveal so very much about one's character and aspirations. Take Lancelot, for example. Would he be considered nearly as heroic if his name had been, say, Igor or Buster? I think not! Granted, Shakespeare claims that a rose would smell as sweet and all of that, but still I beg to differ."

"Shakespeare?" She felt herself reeling and gripped the table. "Shakespeare! How can you know of Shakespeare when he won't be born for another thousand years? And me! How can you know who I am?"

Again he smiled. "I should hope I know of both you and William. After all . . . well. Now, my dear, what was that you were saying before? You know. About Lancelot having an enemy."

She was so shocked she simply answered the old man. "I was just thinking aloud."

"About Lancelot and Malvern?"

"Is that the knight's name? Malvern?"

"My very point about names," he concluded, as if that had been the sole focus of their conversation. "Malvern. It's not the most pleasant of names. Yet it is a name that can go either way, so to speak. As Lester

Spurnick once wrote, 'Names are the hats of our souls.' "

"Lester Spurnick?"

"Indeed, my dear. One of the great writers of the twenty-first century. Oh, forgive me! He's a little after your time."

Julie blinked in confusion. Then, not quite knowing what else to say, she extended her hand. "Excuse me, I'm afraid I don't know your name, while you seem to know mine—and a great deal more."

"Ah! Forgive my lapse of manners. That is what comes from living alone, my dear. Keep that in mind. I am Merlin."

"Merlin?" Now she sank into the chair. "Of course," she mumbled. "First Lancelot, then Arthur. Why not Merlin?"

"You are not losing your mind, Lady Julia." He laughed. "This is all real. You are here, in Camelot."

She reached for a goblet and took a sip. It was wine, incredibly sweet and flavorful and impossibly delicious wine. She had never tasted anything quite like it.

"Naturally you haven't. It's the Tuesday house wine, and this is the first time you've been in this particular house on a Tuesday night," Merlin replied to her unspoken thoughts.

"How do you do that?"

"I'm Merlin."

"Of course." She took a second sip, much larger than the first. "You're Merlin."

The rest of the people in the hall began to sit down or mingle or call for more sweets or seconds of the main courses. She hadn't eaten yet. How could she, with all that was happening around her?

"Well, you simply must," he answered, reaching for a gold plate and selecting samples of food, his blue-veined hands trembling slightly as he moved. There were small dumplings, little ears of corn, several fruit tarts, and some skewers of meats. "We can't have you starving in Camelot, now, can we?"

Satisfied, he placed the food in front of her. Much to her surprise, she realized she was ravenous, and with decidedly unladylike enthusiasm, she devoured the entire plateful.

"Now, that's better." Merlin smiled as if the meal had appeased both of their appetites.

"Mr. Merlin?" she began. And he discharged a brittle, delighted laugh.

"Merlin. Just Merlin." He coughed, running a finger under an eye to catch a tear. "Just Merlin."

"Thank you," she said, "Merlin. But can you please do me a favor and explain all of this to me? And then explain it all to Lancelot?"

"Now, why would I do that?"

"Because I would sincerely like to know how on earth I got here."

"And spoil all the fun?"

"The fun?"

"Why, of course! No, my dear. You will find out soon enough. And if I tell you, it will all be ruined. All of it. Sometimes the old saying is indeed true."

"I'm almost afraid to ask." She sighed. "What old saying would that be?"

"You know very well. 'No pain, no gain.' "

"But that's about exercise, isn't it?"

"Not originally. That's what happens with all the really good sayings. They get mangled over the years. Did you know that 'Feel the burn' was first coined by an exhausted blacksmith named Miller who spilled molten iron on his foot? Needless to say, it was not meant as a particularly happy expression. For centuries, 'Feel the burn' was synonymous with 'Woe is me.' How that Fonda woman got ahold of it and twisted it all around, I'll never know. Oh, here comes Sir Lancelot, the man himself."

"So you will tell him that I'm not out to sabotage Camelot, won't you?"

"Of course not!"

Lancelot wove his way to her side, stopping to smile or shake hands with all those he passed. She swallowed as he approached.

"Merlin." Lancelot grinned, extending his hand to the sorcerer.

"Sir Lancelot," Merlin responded. "I've just been conversing with your third cousin once removed. Delightful creature, your Lady Julia. Absolutely delightful!"

Lancelot seemed pleased as Julie smiled in discomfort. Why wouldn't he just clear everything up with a few words? It would take but a moment, just a brief moment, and Lancelot would no longer view her with suspicion.

"Perhaps," Merlin answered. "But then you could never be sure, could you? No matter where you end up, no matter with whom, you could never be completely sure. Not of yourself, not of him. For that is true magic—genuine love—and one of the few things beyond my power. Think about it, my dear." Then he turned to Lancelot. "Forgive me, Lancelot! I was just finishing up our previous conversation about how to train a spaniel. Oh, the king is beckoning me. Good evening, Lady Julia, Sir Lancelot."

He walked away with uncertain strides, bobbing greetings at everyone, especially young women with trim figures.

"How to train a spaniel?" Lancelot inquired.

"Well, sort of. Have you eaten yet?" She was eager to change the subject.

"Yes. I thank you, and I apologize for abandoning you."

"You were busy with the queen."

"Well, she asked me several questions, and my answers took longer than we had anticipated. Shall we sit down?"

She nodded and allowed him to hold the carved back of her chair as she sat. She had to speak to him and wasn't sure when she would get another chance.

If she would get another chance.

Every corner held a surprise for her in Camelot. She could not risk waiting for a more opportune time.

"I need to speak with you," she blurted out.

"What plagues your mind?"

"All right, here goes." She took a deep breath and squared her shoulders. "Sir Lancelot," she said in a low voice. "I do not think you should be so flirtatious with the queen."

The smile immediately left his face. He was very large and seemed on the verge of becoming very angry. But the realization of what this dalliance would lead to made her press forward.

"If you continue this, Sir Lancelot, you will destroy not only yourself but King Arthur and the queen and Camelot. You will destroy everything you believe in, and once gone, it can never be brought back. It will vanish forever."

"Stop it."

"I'm serious . . ."

He grabbed her upper arm, and she felt an explosion of pain, but she did not wince. "You do not understand."

"It is you who does not understand," he rasped. "Do you realize by just uttering the words, by just hinting of something of a base nature between the queen and me, you speak treason?"

She nodded.

He stared at her for a long time; she barely breathed. Finally, he dropped her arm in exasperation. Yet the anger remained in his voice. "Lady Julia, you misunderstand. I am a favorite of both the king and the queen. Nothing more. I would rather tear out my own heart than do anything to disrupt their happiness." Lancelot stood, knocking over his chair. Some of the people around them quieted, watching the two, the tension obvious to all who witnessed the scene.

Slowly, with great deliberation, he set the chair back on its four legs.

The witnesses included the king and his knight Malvern, who whispered into his sovereign's ear.

Lancelot saw none of his king's reaction. His fury was directed at the addle-brained woman in the green gown.

"Let us leave now," he said between clenched teeth. To him, the discussion was over.

"Others have noticed," Julie said as softly as possible. With a clenched fist, he hit the back of his chair, oblivious to the stares, and turned to leave.

Julie rose swiftly, gathering the velvet skirt and following after him, running to match the distance he traveled with his long strides.

"Others have noticed," she repeated as they walked through the hall.

He paused. "What do you mean?"

"That evil-looking knight."

"There are no evil-looking knights in Camelot, although I'm beginning to think there is an evil-looking lady or two."

"He's dark, has mean eyes. He was there tonight, behind the king. Wearing a yellow and black tunic. He was watching you and Guinevere. They both saw you kiss her hand."

"That is nothing . . ."

"They saw you kiss her wrist."

He was about to speak, then just shook his head. "You have misunderstood whatever you saw."

"I believe I understood exactly what I saw."

For a few moments, he glared at her, then he grabbed her arm and began walking in taut, explosive silence. And as he walked, he increased his speed, the free arm pumping in anger, the other dragging Julie at his side. She stumbled, and he did not notice. She tried to slow the pace, and he only walked faster, ever faster.

Her head was spinning, and she tried to catch her breath, but he seemed to have forgotten her very existence for the moment.

"Please, can we slow down?"

There was no reaction.

"Please," she repeated, her voice rising.

At last, he stopped and looked at her as if she were an unwelcome intruder. Without speaking, he began walking again at a slower pace, his hand still gripping her arm like a vise.

In silence, they reached his home. He kicked the door open, then bowed and gestured for her to enter first. Hesitantly, she did, and he followed.

"Where should I . . ." she began.

"I don't care," was all he said before slamming into his own room.

Julie stood alone in the vast hallway, her arms folded over her chest, and wondered how her well-intentioned warning had gone so terribly wrong.

Upstairs, Lancelot clenched his fists. An unfamiliar feeling ran through him, an uncomfortable sensation that seemed to weigh him down, a gnawing burden that he could not yet identify. Something was not right. Something was amiss.

Until the arrival of Lady Julia, everything had been in order, in harmony.

Ever since he had been a citizen of Camelot, his life had been straightforward and pure. Each trial that was presented to him, from battle with the king to the long hours discussing honor and justice with his brother knights, every single test was met with triumph. It was as if each day were preordained, and he liked that feeling.

And it helped him forget those dreams he had still, dreams of the woman in the fog, calling his name, holding his hand. He had to forget what went before, because that was over. Whatever it had been, whatever significance she had once held was gone, and gone forever. He was confident that his place in Camelot was everything he needed, everything any man with sense enough to treasure it would need.

She was not the queen, the woman who had haunted him and haunted him still. But the queen was beautiful and kind, and he recalled Arthur's words, praising Guinevere in every way. When he had kissed her hand, he had remembered those words and inhaled the fragrance of the queen's perfume. That was it. Nothing more.

Yet she had blushed. Lancelot had observed her face reddening, and that reaction had stirred something deep within him. He enjoyed it. He was gratified and pleased that his simple kiss had so pleased the queen.

Now, all he could envision was the indignant, self-righteous face of Lady Julia. She had just been jealous. That was it. Lady Julia was simply jealous.

No. That was not it, and he knew the fact well.

What bothered him was her absolute certainty and her fearlessness in telling him exactly what she was thinking. Most men would not have dared to fire his anger. But this stranger, this Lady Julia, had no such qualms.

What if she were right? About the king, about Malvern. What if she were right?

"Damn her," he swore aloud in the solitude of his chamber. "Damn her for finding me."

6

❧

All alone, Julie stood in the cold, vast hallway. The green gown seemed less charming now, as if the beauty of the garment had more to do with pure enchantment than with the quality of the fabric or the design. Whatever had made it so wonderful was gone. Whatever had made Julie herself feel so wonderful had vanished as well.

The stone walls were dark and empty. She was lost and so very alone. The urge simply to succumb to her emotions and cry was overwhelming. But she refused. That would be too easy, too cliché.

It was rather ironic. There she was, a typical damsel in distress, being tormented by the classic noble knight himself, Sir Lancelot.

There was no sound from upstairs, where he had just stormed in anger. Somehow she had never imagined Lancelot in anger. Perhaps that was part of the problem. To her, these characters had always been mythical figures. As real as they may have seemed, they were not in fact real. They were the fanciful renderings of writers. They were the glorified illustrations of Gustave Doré, the gentle, idealized images of William Morris or Edward Burne-Jones.

But this Camelot was different, a place of human beings with all their frailties and desires. Here Lancelot was not just a valorous knight on a horse, riding in the heat of battle to right a wrong or to defend the defenseless. He was much more than that.

This Lancelot was a man.

From above, she heard a thud and could only assume that he had assaulted another chair.

In spite of her unaccustomed anxiety, she smiled in the darkness. Somehow she could not envision Edward Burne-Jones painting a lavish canvas of Sir Lancelot kicking a chair in hot-tempered fury.

She glanced around her, wondering where she should spend the night. Although she could go up the narrow, winding back staircase to the room she had been confined to earlier in the day, she was not eager to fumble about in the night.

Turning around, she saw a wooden bench against the wall. That would do as well as anyplace. She shrugged. And so she settled on a too-short bench, in a too-cold hallway, by herself.

Somehow she fell asleep from pure exhaustion. It was a dreamless slumber, and even in her sleep she was aware of the hardness of the wood and the chill of the night air on her ankles.

Then the chill seemed to go away, and she felt warmth. Half asleep, she tried to turn on the bench and bumped into something solid. With a start, she was fully awake.

Sitting at her feet on the floor, with his back against the bench, was Lancelot.

"I do not understand your accusations," he stated flatly, as if they had been engaged in an active conversation and he was responding to a comment.

"Sir Lancelot?" With a sigh, she sat up, pulling her feet against her body, the full skirt making a tent over her legs.

He did not look at her. His gaze remained straight ahead, fixed on the black nothingness.

"I do not understand your accusations," he repeated.

"Oh. About you and the queen?"

He nodded.

"Lancelot, I am not trying to hurt you in any way, and I'm sorry if what I said offended you. I'm just trying to protect you."

"Protect me? You are but a woman!"

"That may be so, but I know a heck of a lot more about you than you realize."

"Tell me, then." There was challenge in his voice.

"Well, for one thing, you're in love with the queen."

"Ha! There you are wrong!"

"Then you *will* be in love with her soon, and she will return the affection."

He just shook his head.

"It's true. You love her because you see her as a paragon of virtue, as the perfect woman. She's your ideal, isn't she? Don't you envy Arthur, just a little, because he's lucky enough to be married to Guinevere?"

Finally, he turned to face her. "I . . . of course not. This is absurd." Although his words were of protest, he spoke them without his usual fervor. "Go on. Tell me what happens next."

"Do you really want to know?"

He returned his focus to the darkness. "Of course."

"There are different versions. Some things remain the same, however. In all of the renditions, Arthur is devastated by your betrayal. He will never be the same, and his powers will ebb as his faith in man dissolves. You and the queen will run away. At least, that happens in most interpretations of the Camelot myth."

"Myth?"

"Yes, myth. Don't forget, to me this was always an ancient tale." She tried to sound as casual as possible, fully understanding that if he believed her, what she was telling him was nothing short of shattering. "Anyway, you and the queen run away, but both suffer for your betrayal. She loves both you and Arthur, but you she loves as a woman loves a man. Arthur she loves much the way you see her now—as a bastion of virtue and good. The sad thing is you both love the same thing, really. And that very love is just twisted and misdirected."

"Misdirected?"

"You both long for a romantic love as well as a pure, almost holy love. By definition, the two are opposite."

"No. You are wrong there, Lady Julia. The two can coexist. But it must happen between the right people for the right reasons."

"Perhaps. The bottom line with you and the queen is that there are elements in your characters that bring out the best and worst of human nature. You are both noble and selfish, generous and greedy."

He was about to interrupt. Instead, his head dropped forward. "Then what happens?"

"You are banished from Camelot, which really won't matter much because Camelot as you know it will no longer exist. You become either a monk or a hermit and die a miserable old man."

"Well, that's something to look forward to," he said with bitterness. "And the queen?"

"Poor Guinevere joins a convent and dies a miserable old woman."

He straightened a leg and remained silent.

"You're not arguing or yelling. You're not even laughing at me."

"I should do all three. But somehow, well, there is something about what you say that disturbs me."

"It's because it's true, and some part of you knows it."

He didn't disagree. "I do not understand how you could know such things. I have told no one of my feelings for Guinevere." Then he seemed to be lost in his own thoughts. "It is not Guinevere, perhaps, that I love. It is the idea of a woman such as the queen that I love. The ideal."

"That's not reality. Believe me, I'm an expert on romantic reality."

"You are?" He turned toward her, his forearm resting on the bench, touching her ankle. "How can you be an expert?"

"Sir Lancelot, any woman who has reached her late twenties in my time is an expert on romantic reality. There are books and magazines, radio and television shows entirely devoted to the topic."

"So you get your knowledge from books?"

"Ha! I wish." She smiled and took a deep breath. "I've gone on more first dates and blind dates than I can count."

He began to ask a question, and before he could deliver the first syllable, she anticipated his confusion. "A 'date' is a particularly heinous form of late-twentieth-century torture. Before the nineteen-hundreds, the term was 'to court,' which sounds much more pleasant, doesn't it?"

"How terrible is a date?" Now he, too, had a small smile.

"How terrible? I'd go into details, but you're only a medieval knight, accustomed to violent death, mayhem, and occasional dismemberment. Don't want to churn your stomach."

"Please explain."

"Well, most of my dates are called 'blind dates.'"

"In the literal sense?"

"No. I think the term came about because in most cases, it would be better if the dates couldn't see each other."

"Ah. I believe I understand."

"Yep. Unfortunately, some human experiences are universal."

"So you, too, have been disillusioned."

"I don't know if I'd go that far," she began. Then she stopped. How could she describe the past several years of her life? She'd had lots of first dates, several seconds, very few thirds. There had been some kind men, some not so kind, others were rough-edged guys, even a couple who seemed as lost and lonely as she was. But no sparks, no thrill when their hands brushed, no looking into their eyes without being able to pull away.

In short, she had never before met a Lancelot.

"I guess I was disillusioned," she admitted. "I just never realized it."

"How could you *not* realize it? Good Lord, I'm

aware of the deficit every moment of every day. Yes, I serve Arthur, but at times it seems such a hollow mission. As a man, I want so much more. I want . . ." He reached up and grasped her wrist but didn't seem fully cognizant of the gesture. "I want something to hold onto. There has to be more to devote my life to than just myself, Arthur, Camelot. There has to be more."

"I'm sure there must be," she said softly.

"You claim to be from the future."

Taken aback by the sudden change in topic, she paused for a moment. "Well, yes."

"Do you mean to tell me that in the next thousand years, mankind will still be facing the same basic problems as now?"

"A thousand and a half, actually."

His voice rose. "In the next fifteen hundred years, we'll still be lonely and miserable?"

"Not everyone, I suppose."

"No. Not everyone. Just people like us."

"You don't believe me," she concluded.

"Lady Julia"——he patted her hand then withdrew his own——"I just think that man will most certainly find a way to remedy his most basic dilemmas by then. War, hunger, disease, and above all loneliness will surely be considered ancient ills by then. Well before then, in truth."

"I hate to burst your bubble, but if anything, those issues will be far worse. By my time, wars will no longer be man-to-man battles but push-button annihilations. Millions will still starve every year, and the rest will watch it on television. Humans will live longer in general, but they will die of horrible diseases that don't even exist yet. And yes, as crowded as the world will be, as packed as the cities in my time are, and as hard as it is to find some peace and space, there will still be loneliness and despair."

As she spoke, tears began to sting her eyes. "It will be far, far worse than anything you can imagine here in Camelot. You have no idea, Lancelot. And I'm glad. I really am. There are so many awful things. Just so many awful things."

He moved beside her on the bench, slowly taking her into his arms. "Hush, Julia." He smoothed her hair, brushing it from her forehead, from her temples. "It's all a dream. Simply a bad dream."

"But it's not! Don't you understand? Everything that happens then has its roots here, in Camelot! All of the pain and corruption and disaster begin with you and Guinevere."

"Poor Julia," he murmured tolerantly, rocking her gently as he would a child. His large, callused hands were astonishingly gentle. "What a burden you bear."

"You don't believe a word of what I'm saying, do you? Fine. Then let me ask you this." She leaned back to look at his face. It the partial darkness, with her eyes still clouded with tears, his expression was hard to determine. "Doesn't it strike you as peculiar that I know so much about you? Not only about what you've done but about your thoughts and desires?"

"Not really. It's probably only women's intuition. I've learned never to underestimate the powers of a woman."

"This is not just women's intuition. I'm trying to warn you. This is a chance not only to save you but maybe to save the future for me as well. Maybe that's why I'm here."

"So you feel that of all the millions of people in your own time . . ."

"Billions," she corrected. "There are billions of people."

"I stand corrected. So then, of all the billions of people in your time, of all the scientists and physicians and theologians and kings, you alone were somehow selected as the best possible choice to save the world?"

"Well"—she relaxed against him—"I guess when you put it that way, it sounds a bit far-fetched." It was comforting being there, feeling the warmth and strength of his body. "Then I wonder why I'm here at all."

"Perhaps it's to help me."

She pulled back and gave him a speculative glance. "So, of all the billions of people who have ever lived, or will ever live, somehow you alone were selected to be helped by someone from the future?"

He smiled. "When you phrase it that way, Lady

Julia, I believe I should just say that question may take time to answer."

Closing her eyes, she allowed herself to savor the pure luxury of being held, of being taken care of—even if only for a brief moment. And in spite of being in a strange land, in an uncertain time, simply being with Lancelot seemed almost perfect.

"We're very alike, you and I," he said as he stroked her shoulder. "It seems neither of us has found precisely what we're looking for."

"And what are we looking for?"

With a low chuckle, he shook his head. "That is part of the problem. We don't know, Julia. We don't know exactly what we're seeking. All we can do is hope that when it comes along, we'll be astute enough to recognize it."

He was right. The instant he said those words, she knew that she, too, had been on a quest. And she, too, had no idea how or when that quest would end.

As she mused, drowsy and content, his hand continued to stroke rhythmically, first on her shoulder, then to her neck, gently against the line of her jaw. Then with his thumb he traced across her collarbone, and suddenly she wasn't drowsy anymore.

Instead, every nerve in her body was jolted as his thumb glided up her throat, then tilted her chin toward him. She held her breath as his lips found hers, softly at first, tender as the unfolding wings of a butterfly. She reached up and touched the side of his face, the roughness of vague whiskers, the lush softness of his hair. He moaned and pulled her closer, still gentle yet with an awakening undercurrent of something unfamiliar, perhaps even dangerous.

His arm braced her back, hand splayed between her shoulder blades, as her arms encircled his shoulders, feeling the hardness of his muscles. The kiss deepened into something much more intimate, far more compelling, as he gently pried her lips apart.

Then, without warning, he pulled away, breath ragged. His eyes were hazy, unfocused.

"Julia," he rasped. "Forgive me."

She was too stunned and muddled to speak. "I . . . please."

He dropped his head for a moment, then looked back, his gaze now clear. "I'm sorry, Lady Julia. I have no wish to take advantage of you."

Her lips still warm with the heat of his kiss, she tried to smile. "Maybe I would like to take advantage of you," she admitted before realizing what she was saying.

He took a deep breath and grinned. "Ah, Lady Julia. If only," he began. Then he stopped. "Come." He rose to his feet, lifting her with him, and after the briefest of pauses, he set her softly on the stone floor that no longer seemed as cold or as hard as it had before. "I'll take you to your chamber."

After taking a few steps, he stopped and turned back to her. Then he smiled, and she felt something deep within her stir, something warm and unfamiliar. Wordlessly, he reached out his hand, and she took it. In his grasp, her hand felt small and fragile, and his thumb lightly caressed her palm. Together, they climbed the stairs, and he took her to the room she had been in earlier in the day.

Much to her disappointment, and somewhat to her relief, he left her alone in the chamber to chase the slumber she knew would most surely elude her.

The morning sun fell across the kingdom, illuminating the sparkle of the stone walls, touching the vivid blooms, embracing everything with its clean warmth. The citizens were just beginning to stir, the women sweeping the already pristine sidewalks, the tradesmen rolling out their carts, the children stretching sleepy arms over tousled heads to face the new day.

The king stared out the palace's arched window at the splendor of his Camelot. For it was his, as much as any land could be shaped and formed and nurtured by a single man. Below, and as far as he could see, were the fruits of his toil. Every tree and flower, each building and pathway and road, above all the people—all had been coaxed and encouraged by Arthur himself.

He rubbed the bridge of his nose. He had not slept much the night before. His mind was troubled, and his wife, sensing his unease, had urged him to tell her what he was feeling.

And for the very first time in their marriage, he did not. He purposely kept his worry to himself. For how could he confess to Guinevere that he no longer felt sure of her, that he was feeling the first uncomfortable tug of something so unseemly and abhorrent that he was loath even to articulate the thoughts in his mind?

At times like this, when he was troubled, she had always been a source of comfort and wisdom. But not now. Not with this dilemma.

"Your Majesty." The voice was behind him.

The king did not need to turn. He recognized the speaker. "Malvern. I did not hear you."

"I knocked several times, Your Highness, but you did not answer."

The king remained at the window. There was a bird in the tree below, chirping and hopping from branch to branch.

"I need to speak to you on a matter most serious." Malvern watched his sovereign's back, the ramrod-straight carriage, the noble grace of his hands, clasped behind him as he stood.

Malvern hesitated for just a moment. Once he spoke the words he had labored over so carefully, there would be no taking them back. Even more than the day before, when he had been but testing the waters with a cautious toe. This would be it. This was the golden chance he had been waiting for, and fate had smiled upon him, upon Malvern, to give him this opportunity.

He cleared his throat. His practiced words deserved an elegant delivery. "Your Majesty," he began. His voice had just the right tone. The reedy, unpleasant pitch that sometimes annoyed him was gone. He spoke again with more confidence. "Your Majesty, I have a weighty matter to discuss with you."

"Go on, Malvern. I'm listening."

Malvern willed himself to stay calm and ignore Arthur's dismissive manner. He could not afford to let his temper get the best of him, especially at this moment. He took a deep breath.

"Your Majesty, I believe you noticed your queen's reaction to Lancelot at last evening's banquet."

Slowly, the king stepped toward the window, resting a palm on the uneven glass. Malvern did not see Arthur's jaw tighten or his eyes narrow.

"Are you listening, Your Majesty? This is vital to the well-being of Camelot."

"I am listening. Continue."

Malvern swallowed. Was the king really paying attention? It was impossible to tell. He pressed on. "The entire court is commenting on the queen's blush when Sir Lancelot touched her. Just a touch. Of course, it was a touch of a most intimate kind. As you witnessed, Lancelot rubbed his lips against the soft flesh of her wrist. Some say they saw his tongue touch her wrist, but I for one did not see that. I was at the wrong angle, but still . . . well. No matter. And her reaction was that of a besotted schoolgirl! The court is abuzz. There is talk of nothing else."

Of course, that was not true. But Malvern knew that the king would never ask, and even if he did, any impassioned and sincere denial would be taken as the opposite. No, Malvern was quite safe in this bit of embroidered tale-telling.

The king said nothing.

Malvern waited for an explosion of anger, for some flash of passion or fury. But there was no reaction from the king.

Now he was worried. What if the king did not care? What if the royal romance had been extinguished long ago, and Malvern, as always, had been the last to know?

How typical, he thought. How absolutely typical! This is precisely why he had to take matters into his own hands. Why, if he did not rectify the situation, who would?

The king still showed no indication of any emotion. Malvern had to think, and he had to think fast. Now. There was no time to dawdle. The king would not allow Malvern much more time. Already he had impinged upon the royal chamber. There may not be another chance.

"Are you finished, Malvern?"

"No! No, Your Majesty!"

The king remained silent, waiting, back still to

the room, and Malvern said the first thing that came into his head. "Lancelot intends to overthrow your throne!"

The words burst forth as if they had a life of their own.

Very slowly, the king turned to Malvern. "What did you say?"

This was it. One wrong word, one errant syllable, and Malvern would ruin his life. A falsehood discovered would earn his disgrace, banishment, perhaps even death.

With every bit of strength in his possession, he began. "There have been whisperings. Lancelot is attempting to raise an army to take over Camelot. His aim is to gain both the queen and the crown in one swoop."

"Whom has he contacted in this quest?" The king's voice was so neutral and even, he could have been asking for a cup of water.

"He has contacted many of the knights, Your Majesty." Malvern held his voice steady, even as he realized the king would want more information.

"Has he contacted you?"

"Yes. Yes, he has, three times." Three times?

"Do you know the names of the other knights?"

Now, this was tricky. He had to say no but somehow make it seem as if he knew more than he was telling. He had to make himself invaluable to the king.

That was it! He alone could render this service for his king!

"The other knights?" Malvern frowned as if in deep thought. "Lancelot told me, but forgive me, Your Majesty, I was so appalled and shocked, I do not recall the names."

"I thank you, Malvern, for this information. Should I have more need of you, I will have you contacted. Good morning."

That was it?

The king again turned to the window.

"Your Majesty, I must urge you to . . ."

"I said good morning!" the king snapped.

Never before had Malvern heard King Arthur snap. Malvern began to leave the chamber, wondering if Arthur was angry at the information he had just been given.

Or was he angry at Malvern? Did he see through him?

Malvern left the chamber as silently as possible. Uncertain. Frightened.

It was early still. The castle was sleepy, the guards were changing posts. A young maiden—was she new?—rushed by with a silver pitcher, her face intent.

Think, Malvern said to himself as he paced the corridor. *Think*.

As he walked, he passed the king's closet. The young maiden with the pitcher must have just come from there. It was where the king usually slept, but this morning it looked untouched.

Just one peek, Malvern promised himself. Such luxury. Although the room was sparsely furnished, it was elegant, beautiful. The room of a man.

No. Better than that. The room of a king.

He was about to leave when something caught his eye.

It was the sword Excalibur.

Why was it in the king's closet? Usually, the magic sword was locked away. He had never even been alone with it, such was its power. For that sword, the mystical weapon, was the very key to Camelot.

Arthur's own weapon. Just one closer look . . .

There was a cloth resting on the hilt. Ah. That was it. The king did not sleep. Instead, he cleaned his beloved sword with that soft cloth. The jewels twinkled at Malvern, almost winking.

What was the worth of this object? Impossible to calculate. It was precious enough for its materials. Add the sorcery, the history, Arthur's love of it . . . well. Only Guinevere herself was worth more to the king.

What would he do without it? Where would the king be without Excalibur?

Malvern did not think. He simply took the sword, wrapping it in the cloth that had been used to polish it. There was no one in the hall, and Malvern picked up his pace. Quickly. He had to get away from the castle quickly.

Running now, he was at last outside, panting, his heart pounding with fear. He leaned against the trunk of an old tree.

"What have I done?" His lower lip began to tremble. *Think*, he told himself. There must be something he could do, anything. He had to get rid of the sword. He had to . . .

Then it came to him. Of course! A strange sense of calm flowed through his body and coursed through his limbs as his plan unfolded in his mind.

It was nothing short of perfection. It was nothing short of brilliant.

This was the key to his future. He wrapped the sword more securely, tempted to unwrap it and kiss the blessed sword.

Not now. Soon. Very soon.

He straightened and began to walk with a slow, deliberate pace. He knew exactly where he was going. He knew exactly what had to be done.

7

⁎

The morning was glorious.

Julie loosened the silk ribbon at the throat of the nightgown Lancelot had handed her when he led her to the room. Slipping from the bed, she spread her arms wide as if to embrace the world.

That was exactly how she felt. The sun was full in the azure sky, there was a fragrance of spring everywhere, and never had she felt more alive.

In the corner of the room, folded neatly on the chair, was yet another gown. How had it arrived?

The same way Lancelot had produced both the nightgown and the green dress. The same way she herself had come to Camelot.

The same miraculous way she had been in Lancelot's arms. Everything was a wonderful, enchanting marvel. It was all she could do to stop herself from twirling about the room in childish celebration.

She skipped to the chair with the new dress. This

one was a shade of blue that matched the sky precisely. The low, square neckline was softened by sleeves that puffed slightly before falling into graceful folds of an unexpectedly lovely yellow.

"It's just like the sun and the sky." She sighed at the colors. Bordering the wide bell sleeves and the neckline were bands of embroidered silk. If possible, this gown was even more lovely than the green one.

And when she tried it on, the fit was just as perfect, and the reflection in the mirror confirmed what she knew.

But there was something else. Her complexion was glowing, first thing in the morning, with no makeup and very little sleep. And her eyes were brighter, more vivid. Had her lips always been shaped that way, with just a tint of rose? She touched her skin, then her hair, which was shiny and soft.

It didn't matter if the changes were real or simply the product of sudden and unexpected happiness.

She left the chamber and went down the staircase, really looking around at this place that was Lancelot's home. It was clean and simple and almost completely void of personality. There was nothing she could see that offered any hint about the character of the man who lived there.

The house was empty, and in the main room was a trestle table laden with breads round and square. She picked up one as she glanced around the room.

As beautiful as the day was, she was unable to

forget completely the conversation with Lancelot. He did not believe her, not completely. He was not convinced she was from the future. And worse, he was only beginning to understand the danger his flirtation with Guinevere held.

"I have to stop this," she said, tearing off a piece of the roll and eating it, only remotely aware of its delicious flavor.

But how? How could a mere woman, the medieval equivalent of an unpaid intern, make an impact on someone like Lancelot? She had tried in earnest to speak to him, and it was a resounding failure. If only she knew someone. If only there was someone she could trust.

Then it came to her, absurdly and clearly: Merlin.

Although they had only spoken once, she knew that if she could express herself fully, he would understand the importance of backing up her story to Lancelot. Then all would be well. It had to be.

She wondered how to find him. He must be around someplace. Perhaps there was a retirement home for elderly wizards. Maybe she could chant something, and he would appear in a puff of multicolored smoke. Or she could close her eyes and click her heels together.

"I've lost my mind," she said aloud. And then she laughed, realizing that her wild thoughts were no more insane than the notion of an account executive from the Madison Avenue firm of Stickley & Brush taking a sudden, unannounced sabbatical in the kingdom of Camelot. She began to laugh harder, imagining the interoffice memo, something along the lines of "This year, Camelot. Next year, Brigadoon."

Yep. She had definitely lost it.

She picked up another roll and strolled outside, inhaling the sweet air and the fragrance of the strange blue roses climbing Lancelot's wall. Although there was no formal garden, no area delineated or marked as such, the whole outside seemed to be a vast, wonderfully planned landscape.

"Hello, Lady Julia."

It was the voice of a very young man, and she turned to see a boy of about fifteen who looked slightly familiar.

"Oh, hello," she began. "I'm sorry. I don't seem to remember your name."

"I know. It's confusing here. I'm Nathan."

He had dark hair and freckles. The more she looked at him, the more familiar he seemed. Perhaps she had seen him at the banquet or walking about.

"How are you enjoying Camelot?" Nathan asked, chomping on a handful of raspberries.

"Very much, thank you. I have a question for you." She tried to sound as casual as possible. "Do you happen to know where Merlin lives?"

He nodded. "Follow the footpath behind the castle. It will take you right to his home."

"Thank you, Nathan."

"You're welcome, Lady Julia." Then, with a bantering grin, he added, "Good day, Sir Knight."

Automatically, she responded, "Good night, Sir Day."

Nathan vanished into the bushes before she could say anything else. "Hey, wait a minute!"

But he was gone.

Was it possible? The young man seemed to be Nathan, Peg Reilly's nephew from Long Island. Only instead of being ten years old, he was at least fifteen or sixteen.

This was absurd. More than absurd. This was insane. And the oddest thing of all was that the utterly absurd insanity, the non sequiturs and oxymorons—taken together as a whole—made perfect sense.

Rubbing her temples, she put it out of her mind. It was all so unbelievable, so complicated. Instead of dwelling on the lunacy of the situation, she decided to do something sensible.

She went in search of Merlin the Magician.

So involved was she with what she would say to Merlin and how she would act and the importance of the visit that she never saw the man who was waiting for her to leave. Hidden in the bushes, his eyes followed her every move.

Just waiting.

As Nathan had said, the home of Merlin was impossible to miss. In fact, Julie guessed that it was the only bona fide fixer-upper in the entire kingdom.

She followed the footpath around the castle, noticing a peach orchard as she passed.

She turned down a small slope, and there it was, Merlin's house. She knew it immediately, the slanted angle of the roof that seemed about to tumble over at any moment, the large chunks of missing plaster that exposed the framework of the structure. The place was a mess.

And it was also identifiable as Merlin's by the simple sign that read "Merlin's House."

Tripping over a loose flagstone, she approached the door, which seemed to be in danger of slipping off its hinges. Before she could reach the house, the door swung open.

"I've been expecting you," said Merlin. "Come in, Miss Gaffney. Or do you prefer 'Lady Julia'? We never did establish your choice last evening."

"I . . . either. I mean, thank you."

He was wearing the same brown robe he had worn at the banquet, unless, of course, he had several identical ones with similar stains and tears. It was disturbingly possible.

"My, what a lovely gown you have on," he commented as she entered his home. She smiled, trying to think of how best to approach the topic of Lancelot. Should she be direct? Or perhaps begin another subject before switching?

Then he returned her smile, with his imperfect

yellowed teeth, and she felt as if she had known him forever.

She did not have a chance to speak first.

"I know why you are here to see me," he explained, brushing off papers for her to sit on a red-upholstered stool. The room was low-ceilinged and dark, with dust swirling in the corners and a faded parrot cackling in the corner as it threw seeds across the room. "That's Charo," he nodded toward the bird.

"Charo?" She repeated stupidly.

"Yes. Now, let's get to the point." His accent was definitely English, straight from the Royal Shakespeare Academy. He was more British than anyone she had ever heard outside a Noël Coward play. He continued. "You are worried about your knight. And indeed, you are quite right in being worried about him. Quite right."

Somehow, she wasn't surprised that he knew exactly why she had come. "Yes, I am worried. I'm afraid he's going to get into trouble, big trouble."

"Precisely."

They stood for a few moments, looking at each other. Charo tossed some more seeds. Then Merlin brushed his palms together.

"Well, that's that. If you'll forgive me, I have some things to do. I believe you can find your way out."

With that pronouncement, he stepped over to an enormous desk covered with papers and oddly shaped glass beakers, some with lavalike substances bubbling over small blue flames, others filled with clear or pastel solutions. There was a large basket of feathers, and he dropped two into a blue liquid, and a small mushroom-shaped cloud puffed overhead.

"Excuse me?" Julie asked.

Merlin jumped. "Oh, yes?"

"Can we talk a little more?"

"No need, no need. You'll figure it out, my dear. It will all come to you."

"How can you be sure?"

He did not respond, stooped over his desk. He slipped a pair of strange-looking glasses over his rounded nose, the sort of glasses she had seen in practical joke shops, with spirals for lenses. Yet he was working intently, as if the glasses really helped.

"Why am I here, Merlin?"

He did not look up, and she was about to ask the question again when he answered. "You're here because you want information from me. Quite simple."

"No, I mean why am I here, in Camelot?"

Slowly, he raised his head, then removed the glasses, blinking a few times before he spoke. "The answer is within you, my dear. It's always been there. You just can't understand it yet."

She thought of the night before, of the time with Lancelot. What was happening to her? What was happening between them?

And what if she found herself forced from Camelot just as mysteriously and swiftly as she had arrived?

"Please, Merlin. You alone can help me persuade Lancelot to proceed with caution. He doesn't believe he's in such serious danger. Not with the queen, not with anyone."

"I'm afraid he'll find out rather soon, then."

"But if you come with me, and explain where and when I'm from and that the warnings I am giving are not the product of an addled mind, we have a chance of saving him, of saving Camelot!"

"The product of an addled mind, you said? Interesting concept, my dear. I don't believe I've ever thought of myself as addled, although perhaps you are not alone in your assessment of my situation. Thus, I thank you."

Julie was again perplexed by his words but decided to press on. "So will you help me?"

Again he blinked. "Help you with what?"

"Help me explain to Lancelot why I am here!"

"And why is that?"

"Excuse me?"

"Why are you here?"

"To ask you about Lancelot!"

"No, no. I mean, why are you in Camelot?"

It was all she could do to keep herself from throwing her arms up in exasperation. "That's what I'd love to know!"

"Indeed? Well, then that's certainly something to ponder."

"Do you know why I'm here, in Camelot? Is it for me or for Lancelot? Or is there another reason?"

His thin lips curved slightly into the ghost of a smile. Gone was the scatterbrained magician, and Julie very nearly stepped back from the sense of power he suddenly seemed to exude.

"I know the answers to all of your questions, Lady Julia. Now you must find the answers for yourself. That is the only way."

Fragmented images swirled in her mind like photographs strewn on a floor. She saw her hand resting on Lancelot's arm, the expression on his face when it was so close to hers she could feel him. The images dissolved into feelings, the way his skin felt against hers, his breath against her ear, then the tumultuous emotions, and she swallowed hard and looked back at Merlin.

"You know the answers, my dear. You just need to discover the questions."

Then he returned to his desk, slipped the glasses back over his eyes, and began working once more. She had been dismissed, with more questions than she had entered with.

"Thank you," she said weakly. "Um, I'll just let myself out."

Charo screeched and threw part of her perch as Julie backed away. A bleeping sound began, like a telephone ringing, but she barely noticed. Outside the day was still magnificent, although she was oblivious.

For as wonderful as Camelot was, she was beginning to realize that maybe, just maybe, Lancelot was the most remarkable thing there. He was not a man who did anything in half measures. Nothing but a full-tile effort would ever be good enough, would ever satisfy Sir Lancelot.

And it was possible that no matter what she said or did, he would continue to charge headlong into disaster.

The instant she set foot in Lancelot's home, she knew he was there. The emptiness she had felt that morning was gone, replaced by a presence that seemed to fill every corner and permeate each square inch.

"Julia?"

His voice washed over her like a cool breeze, invigorating, intoxicating. Then he came down the steps, and she reached behind to steady herself.

Had there ever been such a man?

"Hello." Her voice was as unsteady as she felt.

"Are you unwell?"

"No. No, I'm fine."

He was clad in yet another blue tunic. But this one was slightly more tailored, accentuating his form to perfection. There was something else about him, a larger-than-life quality that made him absolutely magnificent. It was a unique blend of personality and physical appearance, strength of character mingled with strength of body.

"Your gown is lovely." He reached out and touched her sleeve.

"Oh, thank you," she replied lamely.

And then he laughed, and she did as well, at the absurd tension that had somehow made them feel awkward, made her feel awkward. With that gentle sound, all of the uncertainty simply melted away.

"There is to be another banquet tonight." His hand remained on her sleeve. "Would you wish another gown for the evening?"

"No, no. This one is just fine. Perfect, really."

"It is not the gown," Lancelot said softly. "It is you. You who are perfect."

His hand slid up her arm and rested for a moment on her shoulder, then against the bare skin of her neck. It was a vulnerable spot. A man of his size and power could easily cause harm, and as his thumb stroked the column of her throat, she marveled at the feeling. For instead of fear or concern, all she felt was joy and security. No matter what, he would protect her.

Then he frowned slightly. "The lace in the back is coming unfastened."

"The hazards of trying to dress myself," she said lightly, then realized how it sounded. "I mean . . . well. You know what I mean."

He nodded, and without hesitating, he undid the

velvet lace, pulled both ends tighter, then tied it into a bow. "There." He gave a satisfied pat. "I fear I make a far better ladies' maid than you make a squire."

"Well, that's something to consider if the Knights of the Round Table ever go out of business." The instant she said the words, she wanted to take them back, but it was too late. "Lancelot, you know I was just joking."

"Were you?" A darkness came over his expression, as if he were suddenly in a faraway place. Then he offered a flash of a smile that did not reach his eyes. "Shall we away to the banquet?"

"I . . . yes. Of course." She accepted his arm, and together they walked to the castle, small talk masking any matters of substance they carefully avoided.

The evening's festivities were similar to the previous night's, and still Julie felt the excitement of the place. It wasn't simply being at a banquet in a castle. Nor was it merely the thrill of being with Lancelot, although that, too, was felt in force.

There was something greater, grander perhaps, in simply being there, in Camelot. It was as if legend had collided with reality, elevating both to a new plain. It was the best of the two, the lofty ideals and the mere humans who were able to live and breathe the dream.

It was nothing short of invigorating in a way she had never before imagined possible, as if every child-hood expectation, from Christmas mornings to birthdays to sleepovers and summer vacations, had finally been met and exceeded.

Other citizens of Camelot were beginning to recognize her, and the nods and smiles and "Good evening, Sir Lancelot, Lady Julia," filled the air. The sumptuous fragrance of the many foods mingled with the other scents she was beginning to identify simply as Camelot.

It was like being the most popular person in the lunchroom, the homecoming queen. Yet there were no lonely faces sitting by themselves over limp cartons of milk or stale sandwiches. There were no outcasts, no social pariahs.

In Camelot, everyone was the homecoming queen or star quarterback.

Lancelot led her to a dais by the king and queen's table and helped her settle onto a bench. Another knight was speaking to them, but she heard little of what he was saying. She just watched Lancelot's face, the animation of his features and the intelligence of his eyes, those beautiful cornflower eyes.

Now she wasn't hungry at all.

She stared at him, his face almost in profile, his gestures somehow graceful and masculine at the same time. Suddenly, a young squire tapped him on the shoulder. He nodded and turned to Julie.

"The king wishes to speak to me on some matter. I will return in but a moment."

So Julie sat and watched and listened by herself,

glancing down at her gown, stroking the fabric and swirling designs with her finger in the nap. The noises from the banquet would rise occasionally, then be replaced by the rise of laughter, or the sporadic silences that seemed to descend momentarily, only to be replaced by more laughter.

She sat and waited for her knight to return to her side.

"Your Majesty." Lancelot entered the small chamber just beyond the Great Hall. "Kirwin said you wish to speak to me?"

"There are rumors." The king's voice was heavy, weary.

"Rumors?" Lancelot stepped forward, watching Arthur's face. It was placid, as usual, yet there was something else there. And Lancelot identified the difference.

Arthur seemed reluctant to look him in the eye.

"What sort of rumors, Your Majesty?"

"Rumors that you have decided to conquer my wife."

Lancelot waited for the king to announce that his statement was a jest, or to laugh outright at the atrocious nature of what he had just said. But he did not. Instead Arthur traced his finger along the edge of a thick candle and waited for Lancelot's reply.

"Your Majesty . . ."

"Is it not true that you have long admired the

queen?" The voice didn't even sound like Arthur. There was a sharpness, a bitter quality Lancelot had never heard.

"Of course, I admire the queen," Lancelot replied. "She is my queen, my good king's wife."

"Do not play with me! You know very well my meaning. Do you love her as a man loves a woman?"

"No! Your Majesty, I do not know who has . . ."

"Do you deny kissing her palm? Lingering as a lover and watching the color rise to her face? Do you deny that?"

Lancelot took a deep breath. This was exactly what she had said, Lady Julia. This was precisely what she had warned him of—well before now, before this.

"I do recall kissing her hand in the courtly fashion, Your Majesty. Nothing more."

Arthur finally glanced at Lancelot. He looked back at the candle, at the yellow wax he had pressed with his thumb, then his gaze returned to Lancelot.

"Is there anything else you wish to confess? I will go easy on you, Lancelot, if you should confess any plans you have now."

Lancelot shook his head. What was he speaking of? Perhaps he knew of Lady Julia, that she was a stranger, that he did not know where she was from, only her strange tales of another land and another time.

He was bound by honor to his king. Yet he could not offer Lady Julia. Not now, perhaps not ever.

"I have no plans, Your Majesty." He would leave it at that. He would not elaborate, for he would not lie to his king.

Arthur stared at his knight, watching as he paused and formed his answers so carefully.

"Enough," Arthur said at last, his voice weary. "Get back to the banquet."

"Your Majesty . . ."

"I said enough!"

Lancelot reached out his hand, but the king had turned away. "Yes, Your Majesty." He backed out of the chamber.

Almost immediately, Malvern stepped from behind a black curtain. "Was I not right, Your Highness? Did you not see the way he faltered when he spoke? He has plans, that one!"

"Malvern, please leave me alone." The king closed his eyes.

Malvern smiled and did as he was told. All in all, it had been a most satisfactory meeting. Most satisfactory indeed.

"Lancelot." Julie smiled up at him as he returned to the banquet. Then her smile faded as he sat beside her. "Is there anything wrong?"

He nodded to an older gentlemen before answering. "Where did you get the information about me and the queen?" he whispered, and she was forced to lean forward to hear his words over the din.

"What did the king say?"

"Just answer me," he gritted between clenched teeth.

"My God, what happened?"

He glared, and she realized he was in no mood to speak until he heard from her. She spoke quickly and softly. "The stuff I told you about you and Guinevere is part of the Camelot story. Everyone from my time knows it. Everyone a year from now will know it."

"There is something else. I don't know what, but there is something else. The king stopped before telling me. What else is there, Julia?"

"I don't know." She thought of all the possible versions but could come up with no other story line that didn't begin with Lancelot and Guinevere. "I honestly don't know."

Confusion and discomfort seemed to radiate from Lancelot, although outwardly he was the same strong knight. She alone could feel his emotions, and they seemed to twist her own insides.

"I feel sick," she mumbled.

"Don't show it. Whatever we do, we must smile and act as merry as possible."

"I can't eat."

"Then don't. But we must stay, at least until the king and queen make their progress."

In a short while, the king and queen did indeed appear, just as they had the night before.

Lancelot stepped toward his queen and kissed her hand. Only this time, Julie saw a disconcerted expression cross King Arthur's face, as if he suddenly felt unwell. He stared at Lancelot, and Malvern whispered something into the king's ear.

Arthur's shoulders slumped slightly, and then he seemed to recover his regal posture. Yet he was not the same man she had seen before. He was pretending that he was in high spirits, but his eyes had lost their brightness, replaced by a wan, unhealthy dullness.

And Lancelot and Julie stayed, and smiled, and somehow made it through the evening. At last, she felt his hand on the small of her back.

"You look rather exhausted," he said. And gracefully, with others, they were at last able to leave.

They walked in silence, both lost in their own thoughts yet very much aware of each other. Then she stepped in something and stopped for a moment.

"What is it?" Lancelot asked.

She looked down at her slipper. Horse manure. She had stepped in horse manure. Their eyes met, and the same thought ran through both their minds.

Things were beginning to fall apart in Camelot.

8

*I*t was a relief to return to Lancelot's home, as if the solid stone walls could keep the changes at bay. Of course, that was but a comfortable illusion, for even he was on the cusp of realizing how drastically his world was beginning to shift.

Without preamble, he took her into the main room, building a fire in the massive marble hearth as he spoke.

"The king has altered. You noticed it, I saw it in your expression this very evening."

"Yes," she replied simply. At this point, there was no use or time for flowery words or nuance.

"He confronted me about Guinevere again. How can he accuse me of something that was nothing more than a fleeting, misdirected thought?" He stared at the fire, a clenched fist raised at his side in frustration. "And how can I deny those errant thoughts and remain honest?"

There was an anguish in his voice now, and Julie

sank to her knees on the bare, cold floor, feeling nothing but the chill of his words.

"There is nothing you can do about thoughts. You cannot control them." She watched his features in the orange flicker of the new fire.

"But that's just it—I used to be able to control the ideas in my mind. It's as if that ability, that strength, has vanished."

"And do you believe it's my fault, this weakness?"

"No." There was not much conviction. "It's just that you may have come upon me when I am doubting myself for the first time."

She wasn't sure if she should speak. Perhaps he needed to sort through his own feelings, at his own pace. But there wasn't time for that. Things were moving too rapidly.

"Lancelot, I need to say something."

He turned to her, eyebrows raised in silent encouragement.

"I think Malvern is up to something."

"Malvern? Please, Julia. He's the last person I'm interested in at the moment."

"He shouldn't be." She wanted to phrase the words carefully. "I believe he has said something to Arthur. I'm not sure exactly what, but I think he is setting you up to be framed for something."

"Framed?"

"Yeah, you know. He'll do some evil, traitorous deed and be darned sure you're blamed."

"Lady Julia, Malvern is a Knight of the Round Table. As such, he has sworn an oath of allegiance to King Arthur as well as to his brother knights. Perhaps I do not always see eye-to-eye with Sir Malvern, but he would never do anything deceitful or treacherous to me or any other knight."

"I think you're wrong," she insisted quietly.

"Where you come from, wherever that may be." Their eyes met, and he looked away before continuing. "Where you come from, is Malvern part of the tale?"

"No. To tell you the truth, I'd never heard of him before coming here."

"Then how can you cast aspersions on his name?"

"Because before, in the versions that have come down to me, there was no need of a Malvern. You and Guinevere were enough to destroy Camelot."

"How can you . . ."

"How can you not see!" She shouted, raising her voice to counter his. "Are you blind? Honor and trust is one thing. But Lancelot, dear God, you're taking your faith beyond the realm of sense. This is just plain stu—" She stopped.

"Say it."

"No. No, that's not what I meant to say."

"Yes, it was." In two strides, he was towering over her. "You were going to call me stupid. Well, Lady Julia, I would rather be stupid in your eyes than dishonorable to the rest of the world."

"Please. Forgive me." She reached her hand up toward his, a pleading gesture. He ignored her hand.

"Forgive you!" From his full height, he seemed a giant. "Forgive you," he thundered again. "Now I see the depth of your destruction. You're a one-woman catastrophe. No wonder the place from which you come is such an inventory of disasters. It's because of you, isn't it? Now you've come here, to this formerly peaceful kingdom, to wreak your own special havoc."

His boot touched one of her slippers. "Tell me, do you have hooves under the satin?"

While part of her wanted to laugh at the ridiculous ferocity of his accusations, another part—the larger part by far—understood his confusion and fear. He was absolutely serious. This was a man raised in an age of superstition and sorcery, in a place where Merlin was an acknowledged wizard and blue roses were more common than weeds.

There was so much she wanted to say. Instead, she just shook her head. "No."

Her hand was still raised, and suddenly he pulled her to her feet. With a gasp, she teetered before him, and he encircled her waist to keep her steady.

"Look at me," he whispered. "Into my eyes. Swear that you do not mean to do me harm."

Her head fell forward. How could he even think such a thing? He didn't believe her. She was the enemy.

She didn't realize something could hurt so very

much, cause her pain so sharp a physical wound would be welcome in its stead.

"Look at me!" He demanded, squeezing hard.

"I . . ." she began.

And she looked at him, at the man before her. If only she could dismiss him, an archaic man who was not part of her real life.

But she could never dismiss him.

Wearily, with anguished eyes, she looked up at Lancelot. She was too tired, too emotionally wrecked to continue. Her gaze was raw, unguarded.

He stared at her, surveying her expression, wondering if she could possibly be pretending. Perhaps she was really an enemy, or an enchantress bent on his destruction.

But that was impossible. No one could feign such an expression, such utter sadness.

Then, in a clarion flash, it became obvious to him. No matter what else had happened, no matter what would transpire in the future, at this moment there was no pretense between them, no guards. Everything now was real and pure.

A low moan escaped his lips. His grasp tightened, and he pulled her to him. "Julia," he rasped. He held her against him with such force that her feet were no longer touching the floor, and her entire body seemed to twine around his.

She closed her eyes, savoring the closeness as much as hoping that the volatile emotions between them would not turn to venom. He raked his hands through her hair, her face tilted toward his and illuminated by the dim light. Slowly, she opened her eyes.

He gazed at her with such an expression of undiluted hunger that she held her breath, her own features mirroring his wanton desire. Then his mouth descended upon hers, and she felt the solid strength of his arms and shoulders, and nothing else was important.

Exquisitely aware of every sensation, it was as if the closeness heightened every nerve, sharpened every feeling. An odd hum seemed to vibrate between them, created by their energy and fueled by their passion.

Her hands skimmed over every part of him she could touch, gliding over the finely honed muscles, and he pulled her closer, ever closer.

Together, they sank slowly to the floor, bodies still entwined, and they both felt the cold smooth stone but only as it contrasted with the heat of their flesh. Gently, very gently, he eased her into the crook of his arm, and for a moment she just stared at his face. In the firelight, she could see his features and was surprised by how very accustomed to him she had become—the way his eyelashes fell upon his cheek when he lowered his gaze, the distance between his nose and his mouth, the heavy feel of his forehead as she cupped it in her hands.

There was a familiar warmth to him, a realness she had never before experienced. He held her gaze for what seemed an eternity, then his hand rose to her collarbone, pushing aside the fabric of her blouse. She swallowed and let her eyes close. His other hand moved under her hair, along her back to cup her neck. Her trembling was stopped by his mouth on hers, tenderly at first and then hard and demanding. He pulled her into the circle of his arms, hands running over her back in a heated caress, his tongue parting her lips, coaxing a deeper response. She let the sensations overwhelm her, curling her arms around his neck and into his hair. She could feel his desire as he began trailing kisses down her throat to the swell of her breasts. She reached out her hands to touch him. The muscles of his shoulders and chest, so hot and smooth, moved at her touch.

And then the world spun into a haze of sensations, of contrasts, as their clothing seemed to melt away, and then there was skin against fabric and stone and, above all, each other. Nothing else existed for them, not time or place. Just each other.

For long moments, they simply lay in the dancing strobe of the fire. He eased her against his body, shielding her from the cold, covering her with the clothing they had shed. And soon she fell into a deep, blissfully untroubled slumber.

Lancelot remained awake, and he shifted slightly, careful not to disturb her. She sighed in her sleep, and her hand rose up to her cheek. With a soft smile, she again fell still.

He stared at the ceiling, dim in the glowing ember light, amazed and awed by what had just happened. Idly, he twisted her gold hair around his index finger, wondering how such a thing could have happened to him, how such a woman could have entered his life and in an instant change it forever. For there was not a doubt in his mind now, that was precisely what had happened.

Where had she come from? The answer, whatever it was, had become almost immaterial. For the strange things she said now seemed to be coming true.

If she was, indeed, from the future, her predictions suggested not only his downfall but his ruin as a knight. Everything he now stood for, everything he had battled for and believed in and struggled against would be for nothing. He would be Lancelot, the fallen knight. The scoundrel. The betrayer.

The thought was intolerable.

There was only one other thought that was more devastating. And as he inhaled the scent of her, the thought became almost a physical threat to him.

What if she vanished as swiftly and inexplicably as she had arrived? What would he do if he awoke alone on the stone floor, in front of a dead fire?

"No," he whispered harshly, closing his eyes against her temple.

She began to stir, and he held his breath, not wanting to wake her, not wishing her to witness the dread he would be unable to hide at this vulnerable, raw moment.

"Go back to sleep, my own love," he urged. With another sigh, she did, and eventually Lancelot, too, found slumber.

*　　　*　　　*

She awoke to the sound of birds.

For a long moment, she lay very still, afraid to move for fear that everything would be revealed as a dream. His heavy forearm was wrapped protectively around her waist, and his face was buried against her shoulder.

This was real.

The rest of Camelot could very well prove to be a hallucination, a pleasant side trip of her own hopes and desires. But everything that had passed between them had been honest and genuine. Picture-book images of a fairy-tale town were one thing. The emotions and caring and, yes, love they shared hours earlier had nothing to do with fantastical castles or whimsical flowers.

No matter where they had been—Camelot or Jersey City—it would have been every bit as enchanted. Because the sorcery came not from anything on the outside. It came from them, from their very souls joining. They alone possessed the magic.

She closed her eyes, bathed in an inner warmth and certainty that filled her with astonishment. It was a sense of yes, of course, this is what it should have been all along. This was meant to be. And this is what it will be forever.

No matter what happened that day or the next day or the rest of her life, she had something to treasure, something rare and magical to cherish.

For Julie Gaffney had finally experienced the one perfect night.

9

Julie sat up, realizing something was wrong, rubbing her sore elbows and wondering how she had managed to sleep on a stone floor all night. Immediately, she knew the uneasy feeling she had was because she was alone, not because she was on the floor.

"Lancelot?" She spoke softly, then repeated his name, a little louder. "Lancelot?"

He appeared at last, dressed for the day, hair damp and looking impossibly fresh, clean, and wonderful.

"Good morning," he nodded as he laced his tunic.

Suddenly, she felt shy and pulled the gown up around her chin. "Good morning. Where are you going?"

"I need to train, Lady Julia. Breakfast is on the table, and I'll be back as soon as possible." There was something distracted about his manner, a brittleness that was so in contrast with the generous warmth of the night before.

"Oh," was all she could think of to say. Grasping the fabric of the gown, she added, "Um, I hope it goes well."

He looked at her for a moment with a strange expression. "Thank you," he replied curtly. He started to leave but paused. "I . . ." he began. Then he stopped, as if thinking better of whatever he was about to say, and he left.

"That was odd," Julie said to herself. Strange as his departure was, she felt no morning-after weirdness, that awkward sense of "What *was* I thinking?" when seeing him in the unforgiving sunlight. Instead, she had been just happy to see him at all, no matter how briefly, no matter that she was sitting on the floor naked and holding a rumpled gown.

Slipping the gown over her head, she stood and went to the table, where an assortment of breads and fruits were spread, looking very much like a still life too lovely to disturb.

But hunger won out over art, and she took a roll made out of some sort of marvelous grain. What was it about the food in Camelot? Everything tasted better there, more intense, as if even the simplest of items had been infused with extra flavor.

The simple roll. Although it looked like any other bakery roll, the texture was different, a crispness over a glossy sheen. The fragrance was fresher, potent and grainy, and then the feel when she bit into it, her teeth sinking past the crust and into the softness that managed to be airy and chewy at the same time. There was a pot of churned butter, and she spread it on the roll wantonly. The butter, too, was different, filled with a creamy flavor she had never imagined.

She reached for a strawberry the size of a fist, bit into it, and the sweet juices ran down her chin, sticky and sublime. The perfume of the fruit was an explosion of sensations, tart and sugary and luscious, smelling slightly of the earth and slightly of nectar.

Camelot had raised the Continental breakfast to an art form.

She finished her meal, enjoying every last glistening grape, each bite of honeyed melon.

For a while, she remained where she was, seated at the table with the remains of breakfast, looking at the room, at the stone walls and the large pieces of furniture. It was really quite magnificent, in a testosterone-charged medieval knight sort of way, like an *Architectural Digest* spread of a film director's rustic Lake Tahoe getaway. But it needed something, and she bit her thumbnail trying to figure out what was missing.

Then it came to her: a woman's touch. Lancelot's home was all rough edges and hard surfaces. And she grinned. That's what she would do while he was gone! She could look around for all of those little things that could soften a room, make it inviting and pleasant and just plain wonderful to enjoy.

Funny, she thought as she stood up and cleared the table. She had never had an urge to be domestic before. The furniture in her Manhattan apartment had been bought from a showroom floor, accessories and accent pieces, carpet and ashtrays. She had just pointed to a room display, handed over her credit card, and forgotten all about decorating.

But now she wanted to make Lancelot's house a real home. He'd be so surprised, so pleased. Or maybe he wouldn't notice a thing, being a man.

Hands on her hips, she surveyed the room. Flowers. That's what she needed. Big vases of fresh flowers. But first, some fabric. That's what all the magazines and catalogs seem to do, drape yards and yards of fabric.

The table. She nodded. Of course, the big table needed some fabric. But where would she get some?

On a hunch, she went upstairs into the bedroom she knew was his. There was a massive double-door wardrobe, and she hesitated for just a moment.

Was this the right thing to do? She wasn't snooping. She just wanted to see if there was any cloth, that's all. She threw open the door and found at least a dozen of his blue tunics. With a grin, she looked at them, the various hues, the slight differences in the material and cut.

"Oh, Lancelot," she sighed. "You need to hit Brooks Brothers."

She was about to close the door when she saw

some cloth sticking out, preventing the hinge from working. Before shoving it back into place, she paused. Was this a bundle of cloth?

With a yank, the whole bundle fell to the floor. "What the . . ." she began, and stopped.

Wrapped inside the cloth was a sword. Not only was it a sword, it was the most magnificent sword she had ever seen in her life, could ever even imagine. It seemed to radiate light and was studded with diamonds and sapphires and emeralds.

And it was incredibly heavy. Yet holding it was an amazing experience, awe-inspiring and confidence-building at the same time.

"Oh, no," she said aloud. "Lancelot, you've forgotten your sword." Then she smiled. He, too, must have been befuddled this morning when he left in a daze.

Feeling like a wife chasing her husband to the train station with his forgotten lunch, she went in search of Lancelot.

After all, how could he train properly without his sword?

Guinevere braided her long hair slowly, gazing off into the empty space.

What was wrong with Arthur?

Perhaps he was ill. No, no. He would tell her of an illness. Just a fortnight ago, she had helped ease his tired muscles after a long day in the saddle.

Maybe there was trouble at one of the borders. There was always the threat of some insurrection or other. But that did not make any sense, either. There was always a great deal of excitement when the knights heard of an uprising. And in truth, her Arthur had done such a wonderful job as king, those little skirmishes were as far between as they were insignificant.

With a sigh, she selected a ribbon, a purple silk one. Arthur loved to see ribbons in her hair.

There was a knock on the door.

"Come in," she said absently.

"Good morning, Your Highness." It was one of the new maids, a girl from up north with fresh-scrubbed cheeks and freckles.

"Good morning." The queen smiled. "How do you like Camelot thus far? I do hope you do not suffer from homesickness."

"Oh, Your Majesty! I've never been so happy in all of my life! It is just wonderful, everything is just wonderful." The girl blushed, then bobbed a curtsy. "Forgive me, Your Highness. I almost forgot why I came to your chamber." Stepping closer, she handed the queen a folded parchment. "I found this outside your door. I don't know who left it, but I thought it might be important."

"Thank you," the queen replied, taking the paper. Then she touched the young woman's hand. "And I'm so glad you like it here in Camelot."

The woman smiled. The queen had just won over

another subject, and the young woman vowed there was no better queen anyplace on the face of the earth. "Thank you, Your Majesty," she said as she backed out of the room.

Guinevere opened the parchment: *Meet me by our oak midmorning.*

She smiled. Arthur. It was at that tree that he had wooed and won her, and it had always seemed enchanted to them. The tree would work its magic, as would their love. She had not a doubt. Her sweet Arthur. And so she began to hum.

The moment she saw Arthur at their special tree, all would be right. She just knew it.

Lancelot could not get an image out of his mind. And as he settled with his back against the old tree, he realized that he had no desire to rid his mind of that image.

It was, of course, a vision of Lady Julia, the way she looked that morning with the sun shining behind her, streaming through the heavy glass, bending and arching as it touched her, drenching her skin and hair in a golden glow.

Golden. That was the word for Lady Julia. She was a golden creature.

Yet for all of her ethereal qualities, she was still a woman, a real woman, as he had suspected all along. And as the previous evening had confirmed.

Lady Julia. Julia. He closed his eyes, smiling at the memory.

He didn't care that Malvern was late for their training. Malvern had suggested that tree as their meeting place, asking Lancelot to help him with some new weaponry of his secret design. And so there he was, in partial armor, lounging under an old tree. He hoped Malvern would join him soon, for the breastplates were fiercely hot and uncomfortable.

Poor Malvern. Lancelot felt obliged to help him, the misfit knight, the one with no friends. Perhaps Malvern had truly managed to design some wonderful piece of armor. Maybe. Just maybe.

The smile faded as the unwelcome visage of Malvern entered his mind. Lancelot was beginning to believe that Lady Julia was right about Malvern.

And secretly, he was just beginning to acknowledge the possibility that she was, indeed, from the future. How, he didn't know. Why, he didn't know, either. But he had seen sorcery with his own eyes, had witnessed some of Merlin's spells.

So why was Lady Julia's tale so difficult to believe?

And then he knew the reason.

It was because Lancelot did not want to believe she was from the future. He would rather she was just a slightly addled young woman. For if that was the case, she wouldn't vanish back into her own time.

That was it. That was the fear that had been

haunting him. And strangely, once he articulated the fear in his mind, it seemed to lose some of its power.

He had seen the expression on her face last night, that morning. She would not leave him willingly. Of that he was sure.

Lancelot crossed his arms, eyes still closed, and waited for Malvern's arrival.

Malvern cleared his throat softly, waiting for just the right moment. He walked cautiously, hoping to gain the king's attention without undue clatter. That was one thing he would have to work on. He would learn to move gracefully, regally, as would befit his new status as the king's most trusted knight.

The king did not take note of his arrival.

Again, he cleared his throat, a little louder this time. It was vital that all went smoothly this morning. He glanced over his shoulder just to assure himself that he was, indeed, alone with his sovereign. No one else could hear what he was about to say. There could be no witnesses to give testimony later, to swear against Malvern.

Finally, Arthur turned to him, and Malvern very nearly gasped. Never had he seen a man so altered! There were dark circles under his eyes, lines bracketing his mouth. But it was his posture that was so striking. Instead of his usual patrician-straight stance, he seemed bent just slightly, shoulders a bit rounded.

A dangerous new thrill uncoiled in Malvern.

What if the king became unable to rule? What if he became so incapacitated the other knights were forced to turn to the most trusted of them all?

Malvern's own posture stiffened. It was more important than ever that he be established not only with Arthur but with the others. And soon. Because from the looks of Arthur, it was uncertain how much longer he could be a viable king.

"I fear I have some bad news, Your Highness."

The way the king looked up, eyes dull, listless, made Malvern fight to keep himself calm. This hadn't been in his plan, not originally. All he had wanted was to see Lancelot destroyed.

But fortune, it seemed, had grander plans for Malvern. And who was he to turn his back on fortune?

"Yes?" The king had been watching him. "You have news?"

Malvern nodded. "I have reason to believe that even as we speak, the queen is meeting her lover, Lancelot, at the old oak tree."

"The tree by the peach orchard?"

"Yes."

"But that is *our* tree. It is *ours*." The king seemed to be speaking only to himself, disbelieving, stunned.

"Now it is *their* tree, Your Majesty."

The King shook his head, as if to alter the news, as if to take back the words.

"Perhaps we should go there." Malvern kept his voice silky. "Perhaps we should watch."

"No." He wiped his mouth with the back of his hand, distracted. "No, never. I cannot see that. I will not see."

Malvern remained calm. He could not panic, not now, when he was so close to everything he deserved.

"Come with me . . ."

"No!"

This was not what he had expected. The king was losing his sensibilities too quickly, before Malvern had a chance to establish himself.

"I may be wrong, Your Highness. If that be the case, there is no need for you to worry about Guinevere or Lancelot. No need at all. Perhaps we will be most happily proven wrong."

"I refuse to spy on my wife."

"Your Majesty, such a base word for finding out a truth! Maybe my sources were wrong, and . . ."

"What sources? Who told you all of this, Malvern?"

"It matters not." Malvern offered a vague, conciliatory smile.

"Tell me!"

He managed to keep the smile on his face. "It is someone new in your service. It really matters little."

Arthur seemed distracted, as if unable to add dissimilar thoughts to his already burdened mind. "Let us go. Let us see what transpires under our oak tree."

"After you, Sire." Malvern held his hand before him, offering the way.

But Arthur paid little heed.

Lancelot was half-asleep, the sun pleasant and clean on his face, his mind conjuring visions of Julia.

"Sir Lancelot?"

At once he was on his feet. "My queen." He bent over her hand, his armor clanking. "Forgive me. I was not expecting you."

She laughed. "Oh, Lancelot! This is most humorous! You see, I received a note from Arthur to meet him here, by our tree."

Lancelot joined in her laughter. "I'm afraid it may become rather crowded. I'm meeting Malvern here to train."

"Malvern? Why, Sir Lancelot, I'm rather surprised. I did not know you were special friends with the Prince of Darkness."

"Is that what you call him?" Lancelot grinned.

"Among other things. I'm sorry, but I simply do not trust that man."

He looked down at his queen, so lovely in the breeze, her hair tied with purple ribbons.

And all he could think of was Julia.

"It is most interesting you feel that way, Your Majesty. You are the second woman within the span of a day to offer the same opinion."

"And would that other woman happen to be Lady Julia?"

Lancelot felt his face flush, and the queen placed her hand on his forearm. "How wonderful, Lancelot! Please, tell me more! I am in a mood for a tale of romance."

"I . . . I don't know where to begin," he started, then laughed. "I don't know where to begin, because I have yet to figure out how it happened. One moment, my life seemed empty, and the next, well. I feel full to the point of bursting. I just don't know what the nature of the fullness is."

"Lancelot." She stepped forward. "I'm so happy for you, so very happy indeed. You deserve joy, and the two of you seem so very right together. She is a beauty, my knight. But there is something more. I see it in her eyes, in her carriage. She's a rare one, and I am looking forward with great pleasure to knowing Lady Julia."

Lancelot felt a tightening in his throat. This was what he had been searching for—not an ideal of a woman but Lady Julia. Now his life felt whole. Now he could be the knight he had always dreamed of being, the most honorable, of the very best service to his king and queen and countrymen. And all because he was no longer alone but with his Julia, his partner, his life mate. He would ask her to marry him the moment he saw her again.

Hang Malvern! Training could wait! New weapons could rust!

Now he was complete.

A feeling of such perfect happiness, such pure exultation in the world, washed over him that he leaned over and kissed his queen's hand.

"Thank you, my dear queen," he whispered. "I can only but . . ."

Then there was a terrible, animal-like roar. "No!"

Lancelot's first thought was that a wild man was about to attack the queen. In a blaze of movement, he positioned himself before her, shielding her from danger.

He had no sword, just the breastplates, and he looked about frantically to find a weapon.

"Arthur?" the queen asked. "Arthur!"

And Lancelot stopped, realizing the mad thing was his own king.

"Your Highness!" He sank to his knee, head bowed.

"You! How could you! Our tree!" the king sputtered, almost incoherent.

"What can you possibly mean, my own love? I came here to meet you, at your request!" The queen reached out and touched Arthur.

"Then why were you two in an embrace?"

"We were not, my lord! Sir Lancelot confessed his love for Lady Julia, that was all. And you sent me this note." She patted the small string purse at her waist, but it was empty. "Funny, I thought I put it into my bag. But nevertheless, it was you I was hoping to meet here."

Arthur took a deep breath and looked to Lancelot.

"My king." He raised his head. "The queen speaks the truth. And, Your Highness, why would I arrange a tryst in partial armor?"

Arthur closed his eyes. "I know not what madness has overtaken me. My two most trusted . . ."

"I'll defend you!" Malvern shouted.

The king, queen, and Lancelot all turned toward the voice. Malvern, his eyes wide with panic, pulled his sword and pointed it at Lancelot.

"Malvern, stop this nonsense," Lancelot sighed.

Malvern glanced at the other two and saw it, that same look of mistrust and loathing. He would not allow it to happen again! Never! It must not continue!

"He's lying, my lord! He's raised an army and will attack you, and then the queen will become his mistress!"

Lancelot then did the worst thing imaginable, the only action that would drive Malvern over the edge.

He laughed.

It was a deep, rich laugh, and the queen, too, smiled just slightly. Arthur looked at his wife and shook his head in dismay; then he also began to smile.

Just then, Julie came through the clearing, and at first all she saw were the faces of the queen and

Lancelot, and she, too, began to smile. Then she looked at Arthur, a bit uncertain; still, he seemed to be relaxing.

Lancelot saw Julie and began to wave. Then he saw the sword she was dragging.

"Excalibur?" he mumbled.

From Malvern's throat erupted a growl, and he charged Lancelot. That was all he saw, all he cared about. To kill Lancelot. To wipe that sneer from his too-handsome, smug face.

Julie saw the lunge, and instinctively she thrust the sword between Lancelot and Malvern.

There was a mighty explosion of light, a thunderous howl of the air itself. Julie grasped for Lancelot, blinded, deafened by the blast.

A hand grasped hers fiercely, fingertips brushing, and the last thing she shouted was Lancelot's name.

10

"Julie?"

There was a bad taste in her mouth, metallic and warm.

"Julie? Aunt Peg's coming in a second, so you'll be okay."

"Nathan?"

She opened her eyes to see Nathan, wearing a paper crown and bib, peering down at her. Something was wrong.

"You're so young!" she exclaimed.

"I am not young. I'm ten years old."

Gingerly, she rose to her elbow. There was blue carpet below her, and suits of armor on podiums, and a lot of little boys in crowns and bibs. The red-lighted exit sign glowed at the end of the hallway.

"Julie! Thank God. One of the kids said you were hurt," said Peg, running down the corridor. The other boys were with her, in various states of gaping at her and pushing each other. Then Peg paused. "What are you wearing?"

Wearily, Julie looked down at the blue gown. Poking the tip of her foot up, she saw the embroidered slippers.

"I . . . I . . ." She could not speak.

"You sweet thing." Peg's eyes were soft. "You dressed up just for Nathan and his party. Really, Julie. You're absolutely wonderful. Here, let me help you up."

Every muscle in her body ached as Peg pulled her to her feet. "How long was I gone?" She felt mechanical, as if all of her emotions had been left behind someplace.

"Oh, about five minutes, I suppose. You haven't missed much—they just brought out the chicken, and the joust will start at any moment. That dress is lovely, by the way. What kind of material is it? It's so strange, but it goes with the sword."

"Excalibur," she whispered, lifting the sword by the hilt.

"Wow! Cool! Look at this!" Nathan reached for the sword, but Julie pulled it away.

"Careful. It's, um, it's really sharp."

This was all a nightmare. But unlike any other nightmare, she had managed to bring her clothing and props along when she awoke.

"Damn, Julie," Peg breathed. "This sword looks real. I mean the stones and whatever it's made out of. It's glowing."

All she could do was nod. It was just as heavy as

it had seemed in Camelot, as she was dragging it over to the tree.

Taking a deep breath, she tried to comprehend what had happened. The dress and sword had come with her to the present time. That would mean that someplace, maybe, Lancelot was still alive. Perhaps he was searching for her. Or perhaps he had no memory of Lady Julia, of their time together.

"Julia?"

His voice. It was his voice, Lancelot's.

"Lancelot?"

She spun around, trying to locate the direction of the voice. It was coming from a suit of armor on a pedestal.

Handing Excalibur to Peg, she followed the voice.

The boys clapped with glee, and some other people who had wandered downstairs to use the rest rooms clustered around them.

"Hey, Ethel," said one man. "Get the kids— there's another show down here!"

The arm moved in the suit of armor she had been examining before, when she had first gone to Camelot so very long ago.

Five minutes before.

Without hesitation, she stepped past the boys and calmly climbed alongside the suit of armor.

"Julia?" The voice was muffled behind the visor.

"It's me," she said, delight welling up in her. He was right there, with her!

"Help me!"

She lifted up the visor to see his face, his glorious face. His eyes shifted, his head held by the helmet.

"Where are we?"

"We're in New Jersey, Sir Lancelot," she soothed.

At that, everyone broke into applause.

Just then, Julie saw something from the corner of her eye. A movement, someone furtive, ducking toward the exit sign.

"Lancelot, look!"

Still stunned, he glanced in the direction she had pointed. It was only a brief glimpse of a dark man in a black tunic, but they both knew who it was.

"Malvern," he seethed. He tried to move, to go after him, but was hindered by the armor, fixed to the pedestal.

"I'll go," Julie began.

"No. No, he's dangerous," he began.

Suddenly, an official-looking man in yellow tights and a red name tag that read "Manager," clutching a clipboard to his side, pushed through.

"What the hell is going on?" he demanded. Then, seeing the confusion on the bystanders' faces, he smiled and spoke through clenched teeth. "I mean, may I please inquire what is your pleasure, lady fair? Thou doth playeth with a suit of armor worth a king's ransom."

"It was a few coins. Hardly a king's ransom," said Lancelot from his metal confinement.

"And who are you, good Sir Knight?" The manager was doing everything in his power to stay calm. "Have you come to take part in the tournament?"

"I am Lancelot."

"Crap," the manager muttered. Then, with a brighter expression, he gestured to Julie. "Come down, lady fair, and helpeth us beyond yonder exit sign."

"Why does he speak like that?" Lancelot asked Julie.

She did not answer but looked over at Lancelot. A thought crossed her mind. "Are you wearing anything in there?"

"Oh, crap," moaned the manager.

Lancelot tried to glance down. "I'm not sure. But I would imagine I am."

A few women who had joined the group craned their necks in anticipation. One or two fumbled for their cameras.

Julie surveyed the armor. "Here, let me help you." Carefully, ignoring the manager, she loosened the straps and unhinged the armor. It had been glued in places, and a few fragments were fastened with twist ties.

The helmet came off first, and there was an audible sigh from the women, including Peg.

"He's gorgeous!" one woman shrieked. "Marvin, hand me a folded dollar bill."

"This ain't Chippendale's, Ethel. I'm keeping the money," Marvin snapped.

By now, the crowd had doubled. Groups were positioning themselves on the steps. A large pack of women who had arrived on a tour bus elbowed their way to the front.

Julie continued working, removing the leg and arm pieces, and at last the breast and back plates.

Lancelot, wearing his blue tunic and thigh-high boots, was free. The figure he struck was magnificent, with the blue-black of his shoulder-length hair and the powerful muscles evident even through his clothing. There was wild applause and a few whistles as he helped Julie step off the fake marble podium.

He took the sword from Peg, who had been standing with her mouth open, watching the scene unfold. "Thank you." He smiled. All Peg could do was preen.

Lancelot walked over to the manager, doing a brief double take at the boys wearing paper crowns and bibs. The boys stared, suddenly shy and stepping aside with deference. He reached the manager.

"May I speak to your king?" Lancelot inquired with a crisp bow.

The manager glared. "Yes. Follow me hither into yon office, and we will call him on ye olde phone."

The manager stalked ahead, and Lancelot again turned to Julie. "Why *does* he speak like that?"

Peg grabbed Julie's arm. "Hey, listen. It was great what you guys did. The kids loved it, it's made Nathan's birthday. But I have a terrible feeling the manager's 'king' is going to come in a white car with a siren. Maybe we should head out the back way?"

"Are all the kids here?" Julie asked.

"All present and accounted for," Peg confirmed.

"But they haven't eaten, and the show has just begun."

"Julie, they've had more of a show than they dreamed of. We'll stop off at McDonald's for Happy Meals. Believe me, the kids are in heaven."

Julie looked as the boys circled around Lancelot, who was giving her a perplexed look even as he hefted the sword.

Peg shook the car keys. "Hey, guys. We're going to the kingdom of the Golden Arches. Last one in the van has to share his fries."

At that, the kids, pulling Lancelot, ran to the parking lot. Julie and Peg were close behind.

"Julie, why didn't you tell me about this guy?" Peg whispered. "He's fabulous! I mean, to meet us here and dress up as Lancelot. How can I ever thank you?"

Julie smiled and ran ahead to Lancelot. Slipping her arm through his, removing a clinging nine-year-old, she leaned close. "Are you okay?"

"Where are we?" They stepped into the parking lot, and he gazed at the seemingly endless rows of cars and vans. "What are those?"

"You'll be fine. Those are cars, the way we get around from place to place."

He looked at her, his expression one of utter confusion. "Cars?" Then he paused. "Malvern. We have to find him."

"I know. But Lancelot, we're on the turnpike. He'll never find us. He'll get lost here, and I bet he'll try another one of his stunts and get arrested."

"Arrested? You mean stopped?"

"Yep. I think we can forget all about him."

"No. No, we can't. That would be a mistake, Lady Julia. He'll be as dangerous and devious here as he was back in . . ." He simply stared at the sights, the highway, the cars. "Where are we?"

"We're in New Jersey. Remember? You came back with me into my time. We were at the tree, all of us. Remember?"

All he could do was nod. There was so much to tell him, so much he needed to know. "This is where I'm from, Lancelot. You wanted me to tell you, so I decided to go one better and show you."

In the distance, an eighteen-wheel truck was blowing its diesel horn, cars were zipping by, the garish billboards advertising whiskey and airline packages to Las Vegas. A jet flew overhead, and he ducked, large hand over her for protection. Embarrassed, he turned to her, his arm still slightly raised against the threat of the airplane, the other holding onto Excalibur.

"A discussion would have been just fine," he muttered.

"Hmm?"

"You could have *told* me about this place. I may not have believed you, but a discussion would have been quite sufficient." Again, he stopped. "We have to return Excalibur. Arthur cannot rule without it. We must return the sword."

"First, we have to get our bearings, okay? Let's just get through the next few minutes, and we'll go from there." She continued pulling him toward the van when he paused.

"What's that smell in the air?"

She sniffed. "That's just the air. It's like this all the time."

He just nodded, his eyes taking in every sight.

Finally, they reached the van, and the kids piled in first.

"Peg," Julie began. "I hate to ask you, but would you mind driving? I'm a little shaky."

"Damn. If you're a little shaky, you'll be a lot shaky after riding with me."

"Really, Peg. I just can't."

Peg looked at the van. "I don't know. Maybe. If you keep the kids quiet."

"I will. Promise."

Reluctantly, Peg slipped into the driver's seat and began adjusting the mirror and steering wheel.

Lancelot just stood, until Julie fastened him with the shoulder harness into the front seat and climbed into the back with the kids. They pulled out of the parking lot just as a police car with flashing lights pulled in.

"You'll get used to it," she whispered.

Peg, who assumed Julie was talking to her, smiled. "I hope so."

Slowly, he touched the harness, trying to pull it away from his neck.

They were on the turnpike, passing other cars, changing lanes. The children were throwing their crowns and singing. Peg put a rock station on the radio. A Bruce Springsteen song blasted from the stereo speakers by Lancelot's side, and he was jolted. One hand was gripping the seat, the other clutched the seat belt, and his face was ashen.

"Really, you will get used to all this," she shouted, reaching forward to stroke his arm.

"The question is . . ." His voice was hollow. He swallowed, then continued. "The question is, do I want to get used to this?"

He turned back to look at her, his expression bleak. It was then she noticed small lines around his mouth and a few lines under his eyes. He looked tired and defeated.

Julie tried to smile, but it was a forced cheerfulness. From his reaction, she knew he was in for a terribly rough adjustment. And she realized something else, something more important and startling.

Outside Camelot, Lancelot was no longer perfect.

11

Dinner at McDonald's with Sir Lancelot, lately of Camelot, was not a roaring success.

Perhaps had the boys been less intrigued with the knight and left him to gather his thoughts for more than a few seconds at a time, the transition from Knight of the Round Table to Guy Carrying Happy Meals Back to the Kids' Table would have been more graceful. Maybe if he hadn't been so concerned about the sword Excalibur, resting in a van in a McDonald's parking lot, he could have regained his equilibrium.

As it was, Lancelot wore an expression of mounting confusion as the boys bombarded him with questions. They seemed to accept as a matter of course that Sir Lancelot was, indeed, eating a Quarter Pounder with them near an off ramp on the New Jersey Turnpike.

"There is something wrong with this food," he whispered to Julie. There was a tentative quality to his voice and manner, as if it had taken a great deal of thought to work up the nerve to question any aspect of his new surroundings.

"There's nothing wrong with the meal, Sir Lancelot. This is the way it is supposed to taste."

"And for this"——he held up the orange wrapper, lines of congealed cheese hardened on the paper——"for this, one exchanges coins of the realm?"

Peg had been watching the exchange with amusement. "Yeah. Go figure. Nathan, get the straw out of your nose. Thank you."

Lancelot shook his head and put the rest of the hamburger down, giving it one last wary look, as if the sandwich would stand up and dispute his opinion.

"So tell me," Peg began, sipping her coffee. "What's your real name?"

Julie glanced at Lancelot, who seemed relieved to be on comfortable ground.

"My full name," he stated boldly, "is Lancelot du Lac."

Peg paused, then grinned. "Right. I'll play along. Lancelot du Lac, eh? Any relation to the Long Island du Lacs?"

He considered the question for a moment. "No. I do not believe so."

"Peg." Julie gathered up the papers and napkins from their table. "We really have to be going . . ."

Peg ignored her. "So, Lance, you don't mind if I call you Lance, do you?"

"Not at all," he replied gallantly.

"So, Lance, what do you do in Camelot?"

"Do?"

"Yes, do, as in to earn a living." Peg punctuated the question by eating a French fry.

"Well, I help the king keep peace and harmony throughout the kingdom."

"Of course. And when you say king, I assume you're referring to King Arthur?"

"Yes."

"Aha. Between you and me, Lance, what made you go bad?"

Julie stopped filling a tray with half-empty soda cups, and Lancelot simply tilted his head, as if he hadn't heard correctly.

"What do you mean by 'go bad'?" Julie asked, keeping her voice as level as possible.

"You know, all that stuff that happened," Peg replied blithely, handing out packets of towelettes to the kids.

Lancelot shifted in the plastic chair, and Julie placed her hand on his forearm. "What stuff that happened?"

Peg laughed. "You guys are good! Really, you ought to take this show on the road. Nathan? Sir Lancelot wants to know about the bad stuff he did in Camelot. It seems we have managed to snag the bold knight before he betrayed King Arthur."

"What did you say?" Lancelot's voice boomed,

silencing the garishly lit restaurant as other patrons stopped, trays in hand, and looked with genuine concern at the large man in the blue tunic who had suddenly become unpleasantly animated.

"Shush," Julie started. "It's not a good idea to shout in places like this."

Nathan was not in the least bit deterred by his glowering knight.

"Sir Lancelot du Lac was the fallen knight of Camelot," he began, as if reading a school report. "At first, he was King Arthur's favorite. But eventually, he proved himself to be a . . . well, he was just a bad guy."

"No," Julie interrupted. "That's not true. The whole thing with Guinevere never happened. There was no romance between them, absolutely none, so there was no betrayal."

"What thing with Guinevere? What on earth are you talking about?" Peg asked.

"You know, the fatal triangle."

Peg shrugged in bewilderment, and Julie continued more emphatically, as if stating the facts in a more certain tone would clarify the situation. "The lovers' triangle of Arthur, Guinevere, and Lancelot. That's what destroyed Camelot, but I changed that . . ."

Lancelot had been staring at her, his blue gaze penetrating with intensity.

Julie continued. "You see, one version of the legend had Lancelot and Guinevere falling in love, and the whole kingdom falls apart while poor Guinevere joins a convent and Lancelot becomes a monk."

"A monk!" Lancelot shouted. "Can you imagine, me a monk?"

Again, the restaurant hushed.

"What's going on here?" Peg asked, no longer entertained by their act. "You're beginning to frighten the kids. For that matter, you're beginning to frighten me."

"Please, Lancelot. We'll go into this later. Nathan." She turned to Peg's nephew. "Could you please tell me more about Sir Lancelot?"

"Sure." The boy eyed Lancelot before beginning. "Lancelot stole Excalibur from Arthur."

"I did not!" Lancelot's face was mottled with outrage. With a palpable effort at self-control, he took a deep breath and spoke to Nathan in a calm, smooth tone. "What else happened?"

"Well, first, he got a wicked crush on Guinevere, but she never really liked him back. Not that way. That's where the crone came in. He was so totally bummed out about Guinevere that the crone saw her chance."

"The crone?" Julie asked, perplexed. "Who on earth is the crone?

"Go to the other stuff," urged one of the boys. "The cool stuff."

"Well." Nathan began to tick off the offenses on his moist, salty fingers. "Lancelot stole the sword

Excalibur. He ran off with it; some say he sold it to Arthur's enemies to make his way back to France. Others say he was trying to raise an army to conquer Arthur and to rule Camelot for himself. He had this evil woman with him, a witch they called the Crone of Camelot. She was really ugly, like over a thousand years old and all wrinkled with hairs on the tip of her nose. But she cast a spell on everyone, especially Lancelot, who thought she was beautiful. So did everyone else, but at night she'd get all ugly again. When she was pretty she called herself Lady Julia, which I'm sure you know, Julie, since you dressed up like her."

"I think she should have dressed up as the crone," suggested another boy. "That would have been much more fun."

"Nah," said Nathan. "You know girls. They usually want to be the pretty princess. Anyway, Arthur could never recover from the betrayal. And without Excalibur, well, we all know what happened then."

Julie was frozen with shock. They had assumed he stole the sword. What else could they have concluded? That before things could be put right, before he could explain what had happened, Lancelot decided to go to New Jersey?

And she was a crone?

"Was Lancelot ever found?" Julie's voice was a bare rasp.

"Nah. But he also killed the gallant Malvern. Well, not only Lancelot. He didn't act alone. The real mastermind of the whole thing was the Crone of Camelot. It's like she possessed him or something."

"Yeah," added a kid with ketchup on his cheek. "Just like *Fatal Attraction* or something."

"Your mom let you see that movie?" asked another.

"Well, not really. But I saw an ad for it once. Go on, Nathan. Tell us the rest."

Nathan was just beginning to savor the topic, speaking with scholarly animation, when he was interrupted.

"I . . ." Lancelot began. "I did not . . . never . . ." He began again, and suddenly he stopped and stared at Julie. His expression was one of pure incomprehension, his eyes wide but unfocused, his mouth just slightly opened, as if he would speak to refute it all, yet no words alone could possibly begin to resolve what he had just heard.

Then he looked at Nathan and the little boys, all watching him, apprehension shadowing their freckled, unguarded faces.

Again, he turned to Julie.

"I . . ." His voice was a hoarse rasp. "My God, my God," he said quietly, almost as a prayer. And then his heavy shoulders slumped forward, and he shook his head slightly, as if negating the world.

"Lancelot, I'll take you home," she whispered.

At once, an expression of hope sparked momentarily on his face.

"No, no," she rushed to say gently. "Not to your home. To mine, in the city."

"The city?" He mouthed the words mechanically.

She was about to speak; instead, she just nodded.

Peg stood up. "Well, kids, shall we go back to Nathan's for some cake and the goodie bags?"

At that, all the boys cheered. The confusion of the moments before left the children but not the adults. Peg turned to Lancelot and Julie. "So, should I drop you guys off? If I were you, I'd grab the chance. I haven't driven a car on the Long Island Expressway since high school."

"Do you mind? Sorry about not driving the van back," Julie apologized. "It's just, well, I want to get, eh, Lance back home as soon as possible."

Peg nodded, and Julie took his arm. He did not respond, and she walked him back to the van.

The ride to New York was very quiet for the adults.

Lancelot's eyes did not widen in wonder at the sights of nighttime Manhattan. He did not "ooh" or "ah" at the bombardment of lights or at the throngs of people marching or strolling or simply standing on the streets and sidewalks. The bustle of Broadway on a Saturday night, with the flashing marquees and the glorious theatrical tawdriness, did not even cause him to turn his head. Instead, he stared straight ahead, focused, it seemed, on someplace just down the street that must be better or more familiar.

When they reached Julie's apartment, he remained in the van as the women stepped out.

"He's fabulous, Julie. Really." Peg gave a concerned glance at the front passenger seat, where Lancelot remained immobile. "I'm sure you guys can work out whatever problem you have."

The tone of her voice implied an absolute lack of conviction.

"I don't know, Peg. This one is much worse than someone with an adored ex or a domineering mother."

Peg nodded. "He's not from around here, is he?"

"Nope."

"Does he have a job?"

"Nope. He did until recently, but I guess you would say there was a restructuring at the office."

"Poor guy. Being laid off really messes with men's psyches. It's a whole identity thing. They don't know who they are anymore without their job to tell them."

Julie looked at her friend and smiled. "You know, Peg, you're absolutely right. Especially in this case."

"Can he find similar work here in New York?"

"I'm not sure. His talents are rather specialized."

"Well, if the job exists, it's right here." Peg studied Julie's features. "Hey, if you need to talk, give me a call."

That's what Peg had always said, and, as always, Julie knew she meant it.

"I might take you up on that."

The kids in the van were quiet; some had even fallen asleep. Nathan was flipping through a Camelot comic book, occasionally glancing over at Lancelot, comparing the cartoon image in his book with the genuine article in the front seat of the van.

There was an uncanny resemblance, even down to the blue tunic and black hair. Only the Lancelot in the comic book had evil eyebrows, thick and pointed, while the Lancelot in the car seemed nice, with kind eyes that sparkled in the beginning but now seemed sad. And he paged on, looking at the other people in the comic book. Then he looked at Julie.

"No doubt about it," Nathan said to himself, hoping someone else would be curious and ask what he was talking about, but no one did.

Peg looked at her watch.

"Well, I should get the kids back to their respective cells. Thank you again, Julie. It was . . . well, fascinating. I'm sure this is a birthday Nathan will never forget."

"Neither will I," Julie confessed.

She opened the door to the van, and Lancelot did not move.

"We're here." Slowly, she unbuckled his seat belt and shoulder harness, and automatically he slid out of the car like a mindless toy. He stood on the curb, face expressionless.

Suddenly, he turned to Peg.

"Thank you, Peg. I hope young Nathan had a good day."

Peg and Julie were both taken aback by his sudden declaration.

"Um, you're welcome," Peg replied. "Thank you for going out of your way for a kid's party, Lance."

Lancelot smiled, a sight far more unexpected than his restored powers of speech. His face was dazzling, even in the shadowy glow of a streetlight. Yet his expression was not one of genuine joy, although Julie alone was aware of the difference. She had seen him really smile, with his eyes incandescent and his face full of warmth. This was imitation delight, a poor substitution for the real thing.

"Going out of my way?" he repeated. Then he looked at Julie, again the completely charming, completely artificial handsome man. "Out of my way." He seemed satisfied with the words. "Yes, Lady Peg. I am out of my way, vastly so, but I will find my way soon, I hope."

Peg hesitated, as if wondering if she should leave Julie with this strange man. One of the kids shouted that he had to be home by eight because his grandmother was coming in from Queens.

"The queen?" Lancelot blinked.

"No. I'll explain later." Julie began to push him toward her door. "Thanks again, Peg!" she shouted over her shoulder.

Peg watched the two as Julie's doorman opened the front door.

"Whatever," she whispered, climbing into the van. Nathan had jumped to the front seat.

"Aunt Peg, look at this comic book. Doesn't this guy look sort of like Lancelot? I mean, the one we had today?"

Peg gave a quick glance, began to put the keys into the ignition, then stopped. "Wait a minute, let me look at that."

She pulled the oversized book into her lap and stared at the image. It was a book she had gotten for her nephew at one of her odd lower Manhattan bookstores, the one Julie always thought of as "creepy."

Nathan was right. The image in the book *did* look exactly like Julie's friend, the guy who never did give his real name.

A shiver went through her for just an instant, a small shock, like touching a frayed electrical wire. Then, just as quickly, the feeling passed. She had an urge to laugh and almost ran after Julie and her friend to say what had happened.

"Nathan," she said in her best wise-aunt tone. "I'm sure Julie's friend simply dressed up to look like the Lancelot in the book. Remember last year, when Jeff was Freddy Krueger for Halloween? Same thing. It may be impressive, but it's still just dressing up and pretending."

"Oh, yeah?" Nathan offered. "Then who is this?"

Still smiling, Peg looked at the small figure to the left of the evil-incarnate Lancelot.

It was a surprised-looking squire in a blue crown and a bib that read, in blurry, cartoon-distant letters, "Ye Olde Bib." But in spite of the indistinct smudge that was part of the background scene, she could see the squire's face clearly. And the features were as unmistakable as they were familiar.

The squire was Julie.

An oath exploded from Peg's mouth.

"Aunt Peg! Mom says you're never supposed to say that word in front of me!"

"I know, Nathan," she said as evenly as possible, trying to concentrate on merging with the traffic while keeping the trembling of her limbs to a minimum. "But sometimes that word is the only word that works."

"Yeah. Well, look at this picture. It's the Crone of Camelot when she was dressed up as Lady Julia. See? She's wearing the exact same dress. And check out her face."

The same word came out of Aunt Peggy's mouth when she saw the illustration.

That seemed to satisfy Nathan and the few still-awake, grinning boys in the van.

And in her mind, Peg repeated the word all the way to Long Island.

The doorman gave Julie and Lancelot a most peculiar look, eyeing the flashing Excalibur, glancing again at the very large Sir Lancelot. Then, in the manner of most New York doormen, his expression went carefully blank, and he bounded over to the open elevator and punched her floor.

"Good evening, Miss Gaffney." He touched the bill of his cap. "Sir," he added warily to Lancelot.

"Hi," she replied, hoping nothing difficult would occur for the next few minutes. She stepped into the elevator and waited for Lancelot to join her.

"What is this small chamber?" he bellowed, poking the sword into the space beside Julie.

"It's an elevator," she explained between clenched teeth. The doorman's face remained impassive.

"Any trouble, Miss Gaffney?"

"No, not at all. It's just, well, my friend is from out of town."

Lancelot was touching the sides of the elevator, sword at his side, knees bent in case he needed to spring into action.

"Ha!" he shouted when the lights blinked. "I saw that!"

Julie patted Lancelot's shoulder. "He's from way, way out of town."

"I see," said the doorman, who really did not but was used to the eccentricities of tenants.

"I'll be fine." She smiled, and the doorman hit the close button.

The double metal doors began to slide shut, and

Lancelot whirled, sword extended, and threw his entire body between the doors.

"Devilish contraption! Be calm, Lady Julia. Right will prevail!"

"No, no . . ." she began as the doors sprang back.

Before she could continue, he grabbed her by the waist and lifted her off the ground. In a moment, they were back in the lobby.

"Listen, Lancelot. It's really all right. This machine brings us up to my apartment, and since I'm on the seventeenth floor, this is the best way."

Another resident entered, a dapperly dressed gentleman with a small, crunch-faced dog under his arm. He calmly picked up his mail and proceeded to the elevator bank. The doorman, who had been watching Julie and Lancelot now with undisguised fascination, belatedly sprang into action. He greeted the newcomer, then dashed ahead to the elevator.

"Stop, sir!" Lancelot shouted to the man with the dog, sword raised in the right hand, Julie tucked under his left arm. "That is a fiendish chamber! I beg you, do not enter!"

The tenant looked them both up and down, then turned to the doorman.

"When is the next co-op board meeting?" he asked the doorman from over his half-moon reading glasses. The dog growled from its underbite.

"Week after next, sir."

"Good." And he stepped defiantly into the elevator.

"I warned you, good fellow." Lancelot shook his head.

In response, the man slammed the close button with force, glaring at all of them as the doors slid together.

"Could you please let me down?" Lancelot unceremoniously allowed her to slip from his grasp, but she managed to land upright. "Listen to me. The elevator is safe. I promise you."

"Stairs." It was more a demand than a question.

"Really, just let me show you . . ."

"Sir?" The doorman smiled. "The staircase is just beyond the laundry room."

"I'll take the stairs," Lancelot concluded.

"It's seventeen floors!" Julie wailed.

He simply glowered at her, then took long strides to the stairwell.

"Wait . . . please! You don't know which floor to . . ."

The stairwell door slammed behind him.

Julie stood for a moment.

"No offense, Miss Gaffney," said the doorman. "But the other residents may not enjoy seeing such a big guy charging up the steps with a knife."

He was right.

With a sigh, she followed Lancelot, pausing for

just a moment. "It's not a knife," she corrected. "It's a sword."

"Yes, Miss Gaffney."

She saw Lancelot above her on the staircase. Was he taking them two at a time? She raced to catch up to him, panting his name, her sides aching, legs shaking.

After what seemed like hours, the torture finally ended on the seventeenth floor, with an infuriatingly calm-looking Lancelot, Excalibur propped by his side, leaning against the wall.

Unable to speak, she gestured weakly down the hall. He made an "after you" gesture with his hand, and she tried to smile and staggered ahead.

Then she realized she had a problem. "Keys," she gasped. "I left my keys in Camelot. In my jeans. I have to go down to the doorman."

Gallantly, he stepped ahead and opened the stairwell door. She shook her head and went over to the elevator.

"Please, just stay there," she said, and pressed the button. She stepped in and returned within two minutes with the spare keys.

By now, she had almost caught her breath and was able to open the door without shaking.

"Well, this is it," she announced.

She looked at her place with fresh eyes, the way Lancelot would be seeing it. As impressive as it was, as filled with pricey furniture and expensive paintings and rare carpets, she felt about as much emotional attachment to the apartment as she would to any Holiday Inn room.

He said nothing as he entered, but she could tell that his eyes were taking in everything, from the oversized leather sofa to the antique coffee table. There was a massive entertainment center, complete with a thirty-two-inch television and a professional-quality sound system. He barely glanced at it, and his gaze moved on to the dining room. A large mahogany table with four chairs, and six more matching against the wall, gave the appearance that she had dinner parties every night of the week. In truth, she usually ate her take-out Chinese food, salad, or frozen dinner in front of the television, by herself.

"Is there a place we can keep this safe?" He held the sword, and it glimmered, sparkled in her sleek living room.

"Oh, sure." She looked around, wondering where to put something as priceless as Excalibur. "Maybe under my bed?"

"Under your bed?"

"Well, I'll wrap it up in something soft. It's just that in this town, anything of value should be hidden—or taken out of this town."

He remained silent, merely raising an eyebrow as he handed her the legendary sword. She wrapped it in her one extra quilt and shoved it alongside mismatched shoe boxes and her old Barbie dolls. She returned to find him staring out the window.

The view of the Manhattan skyline was usually thought of as a decorating element itself. It filled the length of the apartment, splendidly framed by her lavish curtains. Most people were drawn to the window and commented on how lucky she was to have such a spectacular view. But now she was seeing it as he must be.

She wanted to explain that this had nothing to do with Julie. These were the trappings of success in New York City. This was not what she really wanted, not what she had aspired to as a child. Nor did anything before them define her values and dreams. It all seemed so unfamiliar and alien.

And so very different from Camelot.

"Where shall I sleep?" His voice was strangely flat, as if he had just discovered something unpleasant about a person he cared for.

"Um, on the couch?"

Her fancy bedroom, complete with the unmade canopy bed and designer chintz wallpaper, was visible from where he stood. She had hoped he would just assume he was sleeping there, with her. But that was too much to ask, especially tonight, after all he had been through. In time, maybe, he would grow comfortable with his new surroundings. Perhaps in time.

He sat gingerly on the couch, staring straight ahead for a few moments. Then, with great effort, he pulled off his boots and stretched out. Julie scooted a pillow under his head, and he closed his eyes. She tucked a throw blanket around him, but he was too long, and his feet stuck out at the end.

She took the blanket from her own bed and returned to the couch, and that barely covered his entire length. After clicking off the lamp, she stared down at him in the dim light.

There was so much she wanted to say, so many things they had to talk about. Now was not the time.

"Good night," she said softly as she watched his chest rise and fall. She thought he was already asleep and had turned to go to bed when she heard him reply.

"Good night."

Julie Gaffney, lately known as the Crone of Camelot, did not anticipate a good night. Not at all.

At exactly three-fifteen, according to her brightly blinking digital clock, Julie realized she would not get any more sleep. It was her usual pattern—open-eyed panic about her job, guaranteed to ensure emotional instability fueled by caffeine the next day.

In the semidarkness of a city that never allowed complete blackness, she saw the number tumble to three-sixteen before switching on the bedside lamp.

The light, fitful sleep she had managed had been full of nightmarish images, of Malvern and the danger to Lancelot and the terrible expression on Arthur's face.

She sat up and punched her pillow. "And I'm *not* a crone," she whispered angrily. The Crone of Camelot, indeed. She slipped the brutally beaten pillow behind the small of her back and crossed her arms.

There was no sound from the living room. She hoped that Lancelot was in a deep, restful sleep. He certainly needed one.

Sure, he was in the wrong century, in a foreign land, with no way to rectify the wrongs that had destroyed an entire kingdom. But then, he did not have a major advertising campaign to present in the morning.

A familiar sense of panic began to overtake her, all the more awful because after the life-and-death struggle she had just witnessed in Camelot, intellectually she felt wrong to care about something as ultimately meaningless as an ad campaign for an all-purpose cleanser. Still, back in her own bed, surrounded by her own reality, it was difficult to focus on the lofty ideals of fifteen hundred years in the past.

What was she going to do? In a few short hours, she'd be in front of the clients with nothing to offer but a ripping yarn as an excuse.

As quietly as possible, careful not to disturb Lancelot, she slid open the drawer next to her bed and pulled out a legal pad and a red pen—her favorite writing combo to bring out creative ideas. She took off the pen cap and tapped the point against the paper, making patterns with the dots. The digital clock flipped and flipped as the minutes passed, and all she had was a yellow pad filled with dots and doodles.

Clearly, the creative ideas were not willing to be coaxed.

"Damn," she mumbled.

Maybe a glass of water would do the trick. Not bathroom water. Never bathroom water, so inferior to kitchen water.

And by going into the kitchen, of course, she could sneak a look at Lancelot. Not that checking on Lancelot was her main objective. It's just that it was impossible to get kitchen water without actually visiting the kitchen. Via the living room.

She stepped over to her closet, where her two bathrobes were hanging, the comfy terry one with frayed sleeves and a coffee stain down the front and the peachy pink one. Silk, with lovely beige lace insets.

The peach won out, simply because it was lighter. That was the only reason.

As softly as possible, she crept barefoot down the hallway and into the living room. It took a few moments for her eyes to adjust to the dark, and she coughed lightly, just lightly. Not that she wanted to wake him, of course. There was no movement from him.

Another soft cough, although ever so slightly louder, seemed to emerge of its own free will.

"Yes, Lady Julia. I am awake."

"Oh, sorry. Did I disturb you? Didn't mean to."

She heard him fumbling. "I can't light this lamp," he muttered.

"No problem." With a flick of the wall switch, the room was illuminated.

In triumph, she turned to him, and the smile left her face. He was sitting bare-chested on her couch, his expression one of such sadness that she was startled. She walked over and sat down beside him, careful not to touch his leg or arm, although she very much wanted to.

"Are you all right?" The question seemed ridiculous.

"I am unable to do anything here," he stated. "Unable even to light a lantern. Useless. Utterly useless."

"That's not true."

"You know very well it is." Although his words were emphatic, his manner was calm. "I am a man from another century. My life should be over. But here I am. Useless. Utterly useless." Then he turned to her. "Forgive me," he said softly.

"Forgive you?"

"Now I understand how you must have felt in Camelot. So out of place. So very different."

She placed her hand on his shoulder. "But that's just it. I really *didn't* feel that out of place in Camelot. I don't know why, but after the initial shock of being there, it was all beginning to make sense. It's just that . . ." Her voice broke off, and she shook her head.

"Continue. Please continue."

"Maybe it's because I had an idea of what to expect from Camelot, once I realized that's where I was. I've read books, seen movies, always heard about the legend of Camelot. But you, for you, it's much more difficult. You're in a place you have no way of knowing about, because it is in the future. How could you anticipate anything in the twentieth century? This is a completely different place from what you could ever, in a million years, imagine. You are truly lost. Not only that, but you've been wrongly accused of some horrible, vicious crimes, with no way to clear your name. You have Excalibur here and can't return it to Arthur. Not to mention . . ."

"Please." There was an undercurrent of anger in his tone. "Do you mind not comforting me at the moment?"

"Oh, sorry."

He took a deep breath and leaned his head back. Then he turned toward her. "Why are you unable to sleep? You're at home. You should be happy."

She shrugged. "I'm nervous about work, I guess. I have a big presentation to give tomorrow and have no idea what the heck I'm going to do."

"I see," he said in a clipped voice.

"What do you mean by that?"

He said nothing.

"Tell me."

"I thought perhaps the mayhem we left in Camelot would be the cause of your unease. The fact that you are viewed as a thousand-year-old hag."

"Crone," she corrected.

"Excuse me, crone. Or that I am an absolute villain. That Malvern is running about someplace, as evil in this time as he was in my own."

His voice was rising as he spoke.

"Or that we have the only hope for Camelot and the restoration of peace here, with us—Excalibur! I presumed those minor details would have plagued you."

"Well, of course, they're bothersome."

"Bothersome! Bothersome! Like a dog barking too early in the morning or a bit of soot in your eye!"

"Of course not! It's just that I have a presentation tomorrow, and, well . . ."

"Yes?"

"Well, let's face it, Camelot was a long time ago, and my presentation is tomorrow."

Immediately, she wanted to take back those words, but it was too late. She was exhausted; they had just slipped out.

"I didn't really mean that."

"Yes, you did. Of course you did. I'm irrelevant here, a living antiquity. An unwelcome reminder."

"Of course you're not! It's just that I need to straighten things out here. I'm back home, and that means I have responsibilities."

"Something, of course, I would know nothing about."

She hugged a pillow in exasperation. "You know

what? I'm not saying anything else for the rest of my life."

He said nothing. Finally, he said, "I believe that is a good decision."

The anger was gone. In its place was not defeat but simple fatigue.

"Everything is so different here, in your time," he began. "I'm ignorant of even the simplest things. Staircases seem to be beyond me. How to light a room. Me, Lancelot. I am useless, helpless."

"No, that's not true at all." She reached for him, hesitated, then touched his shoulder. "No. You're the best of men, the most noble. You've always been," she murmured against his arm, which she was now grasping.

"I've always been . . . continue," he urged.

As she spoke the words, she realized the truth. "You've always been my ideal, my dream."

He closed his eyes, then clasped her hand tightly. "You, Lady Julia, are the only person on the face of this earth who believes in me."

Their hands entwined, she stared at his fingers, hers, where one began and the other ended, and in spite of the vast difference in the size and the texture of their skin, it was almost impossible to tell.

"The funny thing is," she said, almost hypnotized by their hands, "I have always believed in you—even before I met you."

Time seemed to stop as they sat in long silence.

"You should go to sleep," he murmured.

"So should you."

Closing her eyes, she decided to say what she had been thinking, preparing herself for the probable answer. "Would you like to come into my room?"

"Yes."

"What was that?"

"I said yes. I would very much like to come into your room."

Rising, she turned and pulled him to his feet, and they walked slowly, her arm around his waist, his arm over her shoulder, pressing her close to his side.

In her bedroom, she slipped under the sheets first, and he followed, causing the bed to creak. Carefully, she reached for him, more to comfort than for anything else.

They lay very still together, falling into the rhythms of each other. She touched his face, her palm caressing the planes and angles, and gently, very gently, she pressed her lips against his cheek.

He moved, and his mouth covered hers, and suddenly the notion of simply comforting each other vanished. What began as a light kiss deepened, and he rolled on top of her, his weight heavy and reassuring. His mouth left hers and traveled down her neck, leaving a trail of warmth searing its path. She gasped, and her back arched. He slid his hand beneath her, pressing her closer to his mouth.

Her hands clutched at his bare back, and with a

single motion, he pulled her nightgown off and tossed it aside. Her breathing was shallow, and she felt a warm tightening in her lower body. Her hands were in his hair, alternating between combing it with her fingers and twisting it. Just the feel of his soft locks was sensual to her, sending tremors up her arms. And in an instant they were joined together. And at that moment, their world was every bit as glorious as it was in Camelot. Afterward, they lay exhausted, the sheets tangled around their legs and the cool night air drying the moisture on their skin. Her head lay on his chest, and his breathing began to even. As he held her close, she felt him smile in the darkness.

"What's so funny?" She returned the smile.

"It's good to know that some things have not changed. And perhaps, just maybe, I'm not so utterly useless after all."

12

❧

$\mathscr{M}$orning arrived.

Julie luxuriated in bed for a moment, Lancelot still asleep. With his eyes closed, his face so restful against the pillow, he looked so very young. But that was deceptive, for when she looked closer, she saw threads of gray in his hair and lines fanning from the corners of his eyes.

It had not been her imagination the day before when she had noticed something different in his features. Nor had the change been a result of the sudden trauma of finding himself in another place and time.

Lancelot was, indeed, growing older at a rapid pace.

She touched his hair, and he stirred but did not wake.

And then she glanced at the clock. It was just after seven. Next to the clock was the legal pad filled with little red dots, the extent of her work, all there was of the presentation she had to give in a matter of hours, minutes really.

"No," she groaned, hopping off the bed and grabbing clothes—any clothes. All she could think about in the shower was the presentation.

Of course, there had been times in her career when she had been unprepared. But never, absolutely never, had she arrived at a major client meeting with nothing except a legal pad filled with red dots.

She went through her morning routine with mounting panic.

And still, Lancelot slept. That was the one good thing about the morning, she thought. At least Lancelot was getting his much-needed rest.

Tearing off a piece of paper, she wrote him a note and placed it on the pillow.

Dear, dear Lancelot,

 I'm at work. Make yourself comfortable while I'm away, and help yourself to anything in the apartment. But please, please do not leave here until we can go over a few things . . .

 Love, the Crone

She smiled, rereading the note. And then, the unwelcome reality of her day hit her with full force as she grabbed her briefcase and her dotted legal pad and left a slumbering, naked Lancelot to face a battalion of humorless cleanser manufacturers and her advertising colleagues.

Sometimes life was just plain unfair.

* * *

"Gentlemen." Julie smiled as they filed into her office.

In the two hours between arriving at her office and this dreadful moment, Julie—the wunderkind of brilliant, last-minute ad pitches—had indeed been productive. There were now seven pages of red dots instead of only one.

No one else at Stickney & Brush knew how bad things were. Everyone, from the pathetically confident art director to the naively cheerful assistant account executive, assumed that Julie would manage to produce a viable idea. There was something sad about their happily expectant faces, she reflected. They were eagerly chatting with one another, digging into the boxes of doughnuts she had requested, and filling coffee cups. Well, at least they would get something from this meeting, if only a free breakfast.

They really had no idea, poor saps.

One by one, they grew silent and glanced up at their leader. Julie stood alone, hands braced against the front of her desk. She had a sudden urge to ask for a blindfold.

"Well," she began. "Please. There are more doughnuts for everyone. Lots more. And for those of you trying to cut down, here's a bag of doughnut holes."

There was a round of good-humored chuckles. "Anyone for a jelly-filled?"

There were a few more chuckles, a few head shakes. The president of Shine-All had an upper lip coated with powdered sugar.

"Welcome to my office," she began. "I hope you all had good weekends. Mr. Swenson? Oh, great! Yep. Well, I myself took a little side trip. Anyone else go away this weekend? Yes, David! Where did you go?"

The assistant in the art department shrugged uncomfortably. "Um, I went to my parents' place."

"How great! Where is that again, David? I know we've talked about it lots of times."

"Pennsylvania. Just outside Philadelphia."

"Oh, that's terrific. I'll bet you had a fabulous weekend, eh? Those great pretzels, cheese steaks. No wonder you look so rested. Must have been one boffo time!"

"Not really."

"Why not?"

"I was there for my aunt's funeral."

There was a thundering silence. "I'm sorry, David. I hope . . . oh, no. Please, here's a tissue."

She reached behind and handed him a fistful of tissues, and he sobbed quietly into them. Finally, after a loud sniff, he looked up at Julie and offered a watery smile.

"Are you all right?" she asked, mortified at causing him pain and embarrassment.

"I'm fine, Julie. Thanks."

"Okay," she said with false cheerfulness. "Well. Let's see. Shine-All is a fabulous product, as we all know. Its illustrious history harks all the way back to the turn of the century, and . . ."

Her intercom buzzed, and Julie paused and smiled

apologetically. She wanted very much to kiss the intercom but resisted the urge. It was the receptionist.

"Pardon me, Julie, but there is someone here to see you."

"Thank you, Audrey." Julie looked at her calendar, but there were no ten o'clocks scheduled for that morning, only this meeting. "Please tell the person there must have been some mistake. This meeting has been scheduled for weeks."

Then Julie went back to the front of her desk, this time with the legal pad.

"Let's see," she said as she flipped through the seven pages of pointillism. "Where was I?"

"Turn of the century," prompted a composed David. "Illustrious product."

"Oh, yes. Right. Of course. Okay, now. Picture the turn of the century, what it must have been like for those poor people back then, before Mr. Swenson's great-grandfather offered a grateful public Shine-All. Just imagine it! The dull brass, the dismal-looking metals, dingy sinks. That is, if they were lucky enough even to have sinks. Dreadful, simply dreadful." She shook her head at the tragedy. "How terrible everyday life must have been, and . . ."

The intercom buzzed again.

"Excuse me!" she chirped, reminding herself to give Audrey a nice potted plant. "Yes?"

"Julie, I'm sorry to bother you, but this man is most insistent."

"Tell him he'll have to wait."

"But Julie, I may have to call security."

"Security?" Mr. Swenson piped excitedly.

"Why security, Audrey?" Julie asked.

"This man here, well. He told me to tell you his name is Sir Lancelot!"

Julie literally felt the color drain from her face. "Oh?"

The art director beamed. "I just knew she had something up her sleeve."

With that, her office door was flung open, and Sir Lancelot, splendidly clad in his blue tunic, Excalibur drawn, entered the meeting.

"Lady Julia." He bowed, then turned to the round, glass-topped conference table littered with half-eaten doughnuts. Everyone smiled. "Ladies and gentlemen of the Round Table," he added gallantly.

"Lancelot," Julie began, pulling his arm. "How did you find me?"

From his belt, he pulled one of her business cards, complete with her job title and address. "This, Lady Julia. One square parchment containing your where-abouts. And there were others."

Of course, she thought. She had a box of them in her bedroom on top of the dresser.

Lancelot examined the card. "You must employ many fine scribes to do this work," he said sagely.

Betty from production clapped with delight, and

Lancelot bowed and rewarded her with a handsome smile.

"Okay, Lance." Julie began to push him out of her office. "Please, can you wait out front? I'll be done here in just a while."

The sword glinted under the fluorescent light, and she added, "And why on earth did you bring *that*?"

"And would I leave it in such a dangerous place as your apartment?" Lancelot countered.

"Fine. Just leave for a few moments, and . . ."

"And," he continued, "you put Excalibur under your bed! What kind of person can shove the mighty Excalibur under a bed with worthless boxes!"

"Hey, my shoes are there." She stopped before she mentioned the Barbie dolls.

"Very well. But now look at Excalibur, the dirt and smudges. I need something that will clean it. King Arthur will be most distressed."

At that, Mr. Swenson, like a congregant at a revival meeting, leaped to his feet. "Shine-All!" he shouted.

The office, except for Lancelot and Julia, erupted into spontaneous applause. She looked at Lancelot, torn between this magnificent bit of serendipity and wanting to prevent the further tarnishing of his name.

And then another thought crossed her frantic mind. Perhaps this could help elevate Lancelot. Maybe by using, of all things, an advertising campaign, she could fix some of the damage that had been done.

It was just slightly possible.

"Thank you, thank you." She nodded, grinning back at the Stickley & Brush crew, acknowledging the applause from the Shine-All executives.

"Yes, ladies and gentlemen," Julie began, warming up to the topic. "Just imagine how different history would have been had Sir Lancelot himself been able to take advantage of the stellar properties of Shine-All! Perhaps that was all that was needed to . . ."

"Shine-All?" Lancelot asked tersely. "What in the name of Merlin is Shine-All?"

"Aha, Sir Lancelot. How pleased I am that you asked. Shine-All is the magical combination of secret yet all-natural ingredients that will make your armor shine, your sword glow."

A sudden look of comprehension crossed Lancelot's features. She wasn't sure what he would do, whether he would simply storm out of the meeting—after all, she was using his very real name and predicament to sell cleanser—or follow her lead.

He blinked, and then, as if in anger and disbelief, he bellowed, "I cannot believe such a product exists."

He was playing along! She wanted to hug him, give him a huge kiss. Instead, she continued her pitch.

It was the usual ad routine, nothing new in the content. But in the delivery, that's where this was so very different. After hearing her praise the product, Lancelot held the sword.

"Then I must have Shine-All, to restore Excalibur for my king and Camelot!"

Julie applauded his performance along with everyone else, although she could see from his expression that he was more than a little dazed.

"Thank you," she whispered.

"In truth," he admitted, "I have no idea what transpired."

Mr. Swenson was very nearly performing cartwheels with delight.

"This is stupendous, absolutely stupendous! I think I can speak for the entire executive committee when I say that we wholeheartedly back this campaign." He turned to Lancelot. "And sir, I realize you are most likely a Shakespearian-trained actor of the highest rank, but I must shake your hand. What a twist! That all Sir Lancelot was doing was trying to clean Excalibur for Arthur—no stealing, no treachery. Just a decent knight trying to please his king. Excellent placement of Shine-All, naturally. Front and center. Brilliant, absolutely brilliant. I wouldn't be surprised to see this becoming a new trend: the great misunderstandings of history! I can just see Richard III selling breakfast cereal, because the little princes were not murdered but simply wandered off looking for a better breakfast. Or that Jack the Ripper would have been a great guy had he been able to get his hands on a package of safety razors. And . . ."

Julie nodded, trying to move Mr. Swenson along as gently and quickly as possible. "And what's your name?" he asked of Lancelot.

Without hesitation, he bowed. "I am Sir Lancelot du Lac."

Swenson grinned. "By golly, I'd almost believe you. Great job, excellent job."

The agency people were as excited as the clients, all wanting to speak to Julie, to shake Lancelot's hand. A few wanted to touch Excalibur, but after Lancelot's initial outcry, Julie said that the finish wasn't dry on the sword, and they didn't want it ruined before the first print ads were even shot.

"Lancelot," she said softly. "Could you please come with me?"

He nodded. "Yes, Lady Julia. We need to speak. It is most vital. I have been thinking about Malvern."

"Oh?" she responded, noting the nervous stares and double takes Lancelot and his sword were prompting. They rode down to the ground floor, and she walked Lancelot to the street, hailed a cab, gave the cabbie the address and fare, and turned to Lancelot.

"I'm so sorry, but I really can't talk right now. I have a ton of work to do. Here are my keys. Could you meet me at home? I'll try to get off early tonight and..."

"I see." His lips were tight.

"I feel awful about this, but really, I have to..."

He didn't wait to hear the rest. He grabbed the keys and got into the front seat.

The driver, a look of alarm on his face, shouted, "Hey! What's the big idea!"

"Sorry," Julie said. "He's from out of town. Lancelot, get into the backseat, not the front."

Again without speaking, he slammed into the backseat.

"Hey, lady," said the cabbie. "I ain't driving a guy with a sword. No way. So here's your money back, and get Prince Valiant here out of my car."

"No, wait." She bent to see into the backseat. "Lancelot, I'm sorry, but maybe I'd better take Excalibur."

"No."

"Please. You have to understand that in this time, in this city, a sword is not a very good thing to have."

"You said it was not safe in your home. Now you say I may not carry it with me to ensure its safety. Then what is to be done about it?"

"Well." She stood, looking over the roof of the car as she thought of a solution. "I have an idea. We have a safe at the agency. It's for when we have valuable items in the office, like rented jewelry for a shoot or something. I can put it in the safe for the day and bring it home tonight."

"No."

"What do you mean, no?"

"I refuse to be in this place unarmed."

The driver slid open the acrylic divider. "Listen, buddy, take it up with the NRA. Meantime, get out of my cab."

"Lancelot," Julie snapped. "Please. Just give me the sword, and I'll keep it safe. Promise."

He did not respond. He turned to her, just briefly, an expression on his face that was bleak and hollow. Then he looked away.

The worst part was that as right as she felt she was in sending him back to her apartment, as correct as her solution had been, she was the cause of his misery. She was the cause of his pain.

"I . . . listen. You've got to understand. Things are different here. And, well, maybe we can talk later," she said in a rush. He stared straight ahead.

"Okay? We'll clear this up later. It's just that they need me upstairs. I'll take care of this, I promise." She patted the sword. He continued to gaze ahead.

There was anger and humiliation on his face, and she longed to reach out, to apologize, to make up for what had happened, to thank him properly for saving the campaign and, in all probability, her job.

"Lady, I got to go," the driver said, and she nodded and closed the door.

The cab pulled away, and she clamped her hand over her mouth. "Oh, Lancelot," she said softly, watching the yellow car weave in and out of the Madison Avenue traffic. "I'm so sorry."

And for the rest of the afternoon, she was haunted by the expression that had been in his eyes.

*   *   *

"So, buddy." The cabbie glanced into the rearview mirror. "You from out of town, eh?"

Lancelot closed his eyes, wanting to be anywhere but in this moving contraption. Anywhere, anytime would be better.

"You hear me? I asked if you are from out of town."

"Yes," he said.

"What?"

"I said yes."

"Oh. Where you from?"

"Camelot."

"Yeah? I got a cousin lives there."

Lancelot looked at the driver for the first time. "You do?" he asked with interest.

"Yeah, yeah. Camelot City. It's in Indiana, right?"

Lancelot took a deep breath. "Yes. That's right." The driver continued talking, but Lancelot was no longer listening. Instead, he gazed out the window at the scenes of modern New York, watching the blocks roll past his view, the warehouses and the old factories from the last century.

He wondered, dully, what sort of place this was, what sort of place she was from. Now he understood why she wept back in Camelot, describing this place. Now he understood how she felt and why she did not want to tell him any more about a place where a man could not carry a sword.

The faces of the people. They were so different, so sad, as if they had long ago given up hope. When they stopped at a light, a woman wheeling a cart full of bags struggled to get across the street. Immediately, without thinking, he leaped from the car and tried to help her.

"Get away from me! Help!"

He stood, stunned, as others ran to her assistance, not to help her with the cart. To help her with *him*, with Lancelot.

"I'm sorry," he mumbled. "I was just trying . . ."

"Get outta here, you psycho," shouted a man with a patch over his eye. "Leave the lady alone!"

He did. Wordlessly, he climbed back into the cab.

"See what I mean, buddy? That's just what I was talking about. You can't do nothing nice for nobody."

The driver continued, and Lancelot, numb, stared at the passing scenes. It was a blur, a haze of buildings and faceless people.

Then he saw something.

It was a large sign, obscured by a tree with pink buds in its branches. That alone was an incongruous sight, a tree in bloom. But still he could read what it said clearly, in bold golden letters against a royal blue background. The sign read "Avalon."

It took him a few seconds to speak. "Please, stop!" he said, and then, tapping on the plastic divider, louder and more forcefully, "Stop!"

The cabbie, who had been entertaining himself with a running monologue, finally slowed down. "Yeah?"

"Please, could you stop?"

The car pulled over to the curb.

"You going to get sick or something?"

"No, no. What is that?" Lancelot asked, pointing back.

"Uh, the streetlight? The stop sign?"

"No. No, the place a few paces back. It says 'Avalon.'"

How odd it felt to say that word, a name that caused his heart to race. Avalon. It was an island he had heard of in Camelot, a place of magic and faith, of renewal and healing. Often, he had heard the tales of Avalon, of a wounded knight who was restored both body and soul by passing but a single night on the enchanted island.

It was a place of hope.

"Avalon? Oh, you mean the homeless shelter at the church."

"I'm sorry, I did not hear you correctly. Could you please repeat what you just said?"

"The homeless shelter. You know, the place where people with no homes go."

"No homes?"

"Yep. Men out of work, between jobs, some have emotional problems."

Lancelot craned his neck and saw a woman with three small children walk past the pink tree and into the door by the sign. "But there are women and children there." He pushed his hand through his hair in confusion. "There are children."

"Sure, buddy. Kids are homeless, too."

"I don't understand. There is so much money, so much wealth in this city. How could people not have homes?"

The driver said nothing.

"I'm getting out."

"The lady told me to drive you to . . ."

"I'm sorry. Um, do you have enough coin?"

"Coin? Yeah, sure." He hesitated, then, as if against his better judgment, he said, "Aw, hell. Here's the change—you've only used half the fare."

"Thank you," Lancelot smiled, accepting a handful of bills.

"Tipping is at your own discretion," the cabbie added.

"Tipping?"

"Man, you sure are from out of town. Tipping. You know, like at a restaurant. A little extra, eh, coin if you feel the service was good."

A dawning light crossed Lancelot's face, and he handed a few dollars back to the cabbie.

"Hey, thanks, buddy. And good luck."

"Thank you, sir."

The driver grinned. He could not remember the last time a fare had called him "sir."

Lancelot walked down the street, taking long, sure steps. He hadn't walked that way since being in New York, walking with purpose, with reason.

He was walking to Avalon.

Slowing his step as he neared the sign, he realized

there was a line of people waiting to enter or to be let in. A few of the people glanced toward him, then away.

It was as if he had been slammed in the midsection. He stopped, stunned by what he saw there. It wasn't their clothing, although some wore shabby coats, and one man's shoes were tied together with string. A child's hair was matted, although it had been tied with great care in a faded pink ribbon. It wasn't the outer trappings that caused him to halt.

It was their eyes. There was something in their gaze, something hopeless and so very dejected. The world had forgotten them. Life went on for others, while those clustered about the locked door waited for entry, waited for admittance to a place that would shelter them.

He recognized their eyes, for they reminded him of his own expression, the confusion, the loss, the uncertainty of what the future would bring.

There had been no such thing as a homeless shelter in Camelot. Everyone there had a home.

His memory stirred to a time before he found Camelot. Perhaps it had been more than a thousand years before, in a land vastly different. Yet the face of suffering remained the same.

The people in the line eyed him with suspicion, in his blue tunic and high boots.

"Hello," the little girl with a pink ribbon finally said.

He returned her smile. "Hello."

There was some commotion, and Lancelot was forgotten. The door swung open, and an exhausted-looking young man with glasses and a backward Yankees baseball cap held it wide, chatting with the people as they filed past him.

"Hey there, Phil, what's up? Melinda, you're looking sharp! Hi, Dave. How's the leg?"

One by one, he greeted them all, and one by one, they responded, sometimes with just grins, other times with shrugs, occasionally with snippets of conversation.

A strange thought crossed his mind. What if Julia were homeless? What if something happened, and she was forced to wait outside for someone to let her in?

Without thinking any further, he walked to the man with the cap.

The man's smile faded. He looked at Lancelot's clean attire, obviously well-buffed physique. "Yes?"

"What can I do?" Lancelot asked.

The man stared at him. "Nothing, man, nothing. This is an official shelter. We have a city permit, and this is our present location, buddy. Sorry if you're feeling the nimby angst of your property value going down, but . . ."

"Nimby?" Lancelot's eyes narrowed. "What does nimby mean?"

The man in the baseball cap crossed his arms. "You know very well, Mr. Workout. It means 'not in my backyard.' Listen, I've had enough with you rich guys. Have your lawyer send me a letter."

"No, no. You don't understand. I want to help."

"Say what?"

"I want to help you. I want to know if there's anything I can do. Absolutely anything."

"We could always use more money," he replied hesitantly, as if expecting Lancelot to pounce. "Why don't you just write me a check now, before you sober up?"

"I have no money. Oh, wait." Lancelot had forgotten the balled-up bills. "Here," he said, pleased. "Will this help?"

"Great. Eight dollars." He was about to hand it back, but there was something about this guy, something that made him stop and take another look. "Are you new to New York?"

The man nodded. "I guess it shows. But I do have a question."

"Yes?"

"Why does everyone here call me 'buddy'?"

The man took a moment to realize what the question meant. "Ah. It's an almost affectionate term if you don't know someone's name."

Lancelot nodded, then looked him directly in the eyes. "What are you doing right now?"

"At this moment? I'm about to serve lunch."

"Do you need some help?"

He stared at the guy dressed in a tunic. "You mean that?"

Again, Lancelot nodded.

"We're a little shorthanded now." For the first time, the man smiled at Lancelot. "Hell, we're always shorthanded. This is a volunteer job, but most people quit after a few hours."

His unspoken comment was that he expected Lancelot would not even last that long, but he only paused. "Well, here. Lunch is already made, but we have cleanup and then have to get ready for tonight. Grab a brush, and help us clean the bathrooms. Then the cots need making up, and we need some help with slapping together tonight's dinner."

Lancelot grinned. "Good. I'll be glad to."

The man in the baseball cap scratched his head and stepped aside for Lancelot to enter. "By the way, my name is Bill Kowalski. What's yours?"

"Lancelot," he said at last. "My name is Lancelot."

"Whew!" Bill laughed. "That must have gotten you into some heavy-duty trouble in school! Beaten up in junior high, girlfriends in college, right?"

"Bill, you have no idea," he answered solemnly.

They shook hands, and Lancelot entered the shelter, rolled up his sleeves, and scrubbed the toilets.

It was the most satisfying work he had done in a long time.

This was a first, Julie thought as the tuxedo-clad waiter took the next order. The client was treating the agency to lunch at the Four Seasons. Usually, always, it was the other way around, the agency groveling before the almighty clients.

She sighed, glancing around at the other tables. This

was the hour and place of the power lunch, and being taken there was a mighty statement to everyone. Just beyond the oversized flower display, she spotted a best-selling author and an A-list editor, huddled over bottles of sparkling water and platters of fruit. In the distance were a network anchor and a Broadway playwright. The place virtually smelled of power and wealth.

Before she had left her office, the president of the company had called from London to congratulate her. Word traveled fast in this industry, although usually bad news was the first to make it overseas. This was definitely a change.

She couldn't recall when a day at work had gone so well. It was as if she was unable to make a single misstep, as if every one of her spontaneous ideas had become pearls of wisdom, veritable treasures.

But there was a sick feeling in her stomach. All she could think about was Lancelot, how he had come into her office and literally saved the day, and in return she had stripped him of the sword and sent him home in a taxi like an unwanted houseguest.

"Would that work, Julie?" Mr. Swenson had been talking to her, but she hadn't heard a syllable.

"Pardon me?"

He laughed. "Ever the genius! Thinking up more slogans?"

"No. I'm sorry, Mr. Swenson. I'm just a little tired today."

"It's allowed, Julie. Especially after this morning.

What I was saying is that Shine-All is sponsoring the Shine-All City charity event at the Met."

"Yes, of course. I remember reading about it." It was, indeed, a terrific idea. The notion was to cluster a handful of charities under one umbrella and throw a single major bash. Instead of diffusing the wealth, competing with rival charities for the best guests and sponsors, this would be the one single event to see and be seen at for the entire season.

"What I was wondering was, may we use that sword of yours as a draw?"

"I'm sorry," she said, confused. "Why?"

"Don't know if you remember this from the press releases, but the theme is a medieval pageant. You know, the romance and elegance of days gone by. I hadn't really thought of it until this morning, but maybe we could add a Camelot twist to the event. After all, what's more romantic than Camelot?"

"Well, yes, of course."

"And not to mention, well, let's face it—it would be a terrific launch for the campaign. Two birds with one stone and all that. Now, this will be at the Met. So the sword would be protected. I mean, even with my jaded eyes, I could tell that was no bit of costume jewelry there. And didn't you lock it in the agency safe?"

"Yes," she admitted.

"Well, you don't do that for just any old prop, do you?"

"No, Mr. Swenson, you are absolutely right."

"Anyway"—he leaned back as his melon was placed in front of him—"Give it a thought. It would do a lot of good, Julie. For a lot of people who need it."

Her first course arrived, and she thought about what he was saying. He was right. Maybe if Excalibur could not help Arthur at the moment, perhaps something wonderful could come of it. That's what the enchantment was all about, wasn't it? Good triumphing over evil. That was the main thing.

"Mr. Swenson, that's a wonderful idea," she concluded.

"Great! Excellent! Now, may I add something else?"

"Of course."

"Again, I'm no expert, but that sword seemed rather, eh, special. I understand your office is secure, and I know you have great faith in your people. But frankly, I do wonder if Stickley & Brush is secure enough for something like that. I touched the thing, Julie. My God, what a feeling!"

Her eyes widened. He was right. Absolutely right.

"I just worry," he said, skewering a raspberry with a fork. "You see, if someone really wanted that sword, it would be hard for you guys at the agency to prevent someone who was determined, if you know what I mean."

One thought crossed her mind. Malvern. He was there, someplace around the city. What if he somehow found out where Excalibur was?

Swenson saw the panic in her eyes. "Not to worry.

I'm sure it's all right at the moment, but I just suggest that you send it over to the museum. No place in the world is as secure as the Metropolitan Museum of Art. They can keep it safe until the benefit, even do a little repair work on the thing."

"Sir," she said at last. "That is a great idea."

"So we can use it on the twenty-third?"

"Yes. I think . . ." She stopped.

"You think what?"

"I think the sword would like that." She smiled.

Swenson did not laugh. "You know, Julie, crazy as it sounds, I do believe you're right."

13

꧁

The very first thing Julie did after lunch was send Excalibur over to the Met, with instructions that they notify her the moment it arrived safely. And less than a half hour after the messenger left, she got word that the sword was there. It was an incredible sense of relief—the very thought of Malvern getting his hands on it was sickening.

After that, Julie leaned back in her chair and savored the success of the day. In spite of all the triumphs she had enjoyed so far in her career, this was by far the sweetest. And she knew a great deal of her feeling was thanks to Lancelot.

Maybe, just maybe, he could be happy in this time, in this place. With her.

The telephone ringing jolted her from her reveries.

"So, how's my favorite Camelot groupie doing today?"

"Peg! I'm so glad you called."

"Julie," she began. "Oh, Julie, I'll cut straight to the chase. Listen to me—I'm worried about you."

"Hey, don't beat around the bush or anything." She wasn't surprised by Peg's declaration, especially after what happened at Nathan's party. Julie herself would have been alarmed if the situation had been reversed, and Peg had suddenly appeared with a man who claimed to be a mythical figure more than a thousand years old.

"I'll bet you're concerned because I happen to be dating Sir Lancelot, is that it? If it's anything else, please do let me know."

"Julie, I'm serious."

"This is the one bad thing about having a best friend who's a shrink." Peg did not laugh. "Okay, I'll bite. Please clarify. What do you mean, you're worried about me?" She began to pull yellow Post-it notes from a pad and restacked them as she spoke.

"I think there is something very weird about this Lancelot guy. It's one thing to identify strongly with a mythic or historical figure. Remember that guy I dated a few years ago?"

"Sure. The one with the Robert E. Lee fixation?"

"Yep, the very one. As nutty as he was, he limited his activities to bidding farewell to his imaginary troops and an occasional stoic surrender to Grant. And he kept the depth of his fixation a secret from me until that unfortunate weekend."

"Oh, yeah," Julie recalled. "The bed and breakfast in Gettysburg?"

"It doesn't matter. We're not discussing me," Peg sniffed. "Anyway, Robert E. Lee is a benign figure compared to Sir Lancelot."

"How can you say that? Really, I think Lancelot's been given a bad rap."

"That's beside the point. What I'm trying to tell you is that for a mature adult male to identify with Lancelot is a very dangerous thing. Forget history, revisionist or not. How would you feel if he pretended to be Ted Bundy or Adolf Hitler?"

"Oh, come on!"

"Just because Lancelot is from a more remote past doesn't mean the identity he has selected is any less dangerous. To be honest, I think he might be a psycho."

"Peg, please."

"Really." Peg's voice lowered. "Have you ever seen the Majestic Comic version of *The Tales of King Arthur*?"

"No, I suppose I've missed that one. I'm way behind on my comic reading, but I've got an *Archie* on my bedside table."

"I think you should see it as soon as possible. I'll borrow it from Nathan and drop if off for you to study. Because, Julie, your friend has."

"My friend reads comic books?"

"He's clearly setting up some sort of bizarre scenario based on his own physical resemblance to the drawings in this book. Furthermore, there is a character who looks exactly like you."

"Peg, you've always told me that I have one of those faces that makes everyone think they went to high school with me. Maybe the character who looks like me is just someone else with a face like that."

"What do you know of this guy?"

"The guy who drew the comic book? Nothing. Haven't even seen the thing."

"You know what I mean." Julie had never heard Peg's voice so serious, so void of humor. "He came from nowhere. You've never mentioned him to me, and suddenly there is this incredible hunk with more than a few screws loose who goes on about being Lancelot and takes this whole game to a disturbing level. So what *do* you know of him?"

"A lot. I know a lot about him." She began to tear the yellow pad into small pieces. If only she could tell Peg the truth, explain everything. "I know a lot about him."

"You do not. You know nothing about this man. Everything you think you know is part of his twisted imagination. And let's just get to the practical basics. For one, Julie, he's huge. He's a big, strong man. Physically, he could really hurt you, especially if you decided to disagree with his little role-playing gig. This is no joke. I think he's dangerous."

"I really appreciate your concern. But I do know him, better than I can explain."

"You *think* you know him. He's merely a gifted actor who has convinced you his act is genuine. He's a fake. He has to be, because he sure ain't Sir Lancelot. Julie, please."

"Listen—I really have to go now."

Peg was not deterred. "The Lancelot in the comic book Nathan showed me looks exactly like your friend. I don't mean resembles him, I mean it *is* him, from the blue tunic to the boots to the way he speaks and his hair and everything. But that's not what worries me."

Julie sighed. "Go on."

"Right. Well, there is a Lady Julia in this version, and she is indeed a dead ringer for you. I think this guy saw you, and he's using you for his own twisted little stunt, to act out his own fantasy."

"Peg, you're way off base on this one." The urge to tell Peg the truth was overwhelming, to tell her everything, from Camelot to Lancelot and Arthur and Malvern. But Peg would be truly alarmed if she thought Julie had lost touch with reality. She'd never believe that while the boys were in the rest room, Julie had managed a side trip to Camelot. As it was, Peg made it clear she already feared Julie had lost a good deal of her marbles.

"Okay, I'll ask you this once. Why the hell was

he dressed up as Sir Lancelot? And why didn't he drop the whole thing once we left the restaurant?"

"It was a joke, I guess," Julie tried to explain. "I mean, he probably saw the comic book, and it was all a joke." She attempted to change the topic. "So, when was the comic book published?" Anything to get Peg off track.

"Well, it's pretty old," Peg admitted. "It first appeared in the late nineteen-thirties. It had something to do with the World's Fair. But it's been out of print since then, for almost sixty years. I got Nathan a copy at that bookstore you love so much."

"Cauldrons & Skulls? Such a charming name."

"Yep. Anyway, it's just too creepy."

"Well . . ." She tried to come up with a logical explanation, and her mind was blank. Over and over, she churned the possibilities to tell Peg, but they all returned to the one fact she could not possibly tell: that she had been to Camelot herself.

"Where is he staying? Not with you, I hope." Peg was employing her crisp, professional tone.

"Yes. As a matter of fact, he is. But listen, he really saved the day with the advertising campaign. I mean, he's a natural . . ." She stopped, realizing that being a natural in the advertising business was not the most ringing endorsement of a man's honesty.

"Good Lord, do you think that matters? Julie, just be careful. Be smart. I know, well . . ."

"Go on."

"I know you've been searching for a knight to rescue you. And then this crazy guy dressed like Sir Lancelot appears, and you seem to be projecting this whole myth onto him."

Julie smiled. If only she really knew. If only dear Peg had any idea how right she was, for all the wrong reasons.

"I know, Peg. Thanks. And I will be careful."

"Good. Now, call me later, or whenever you want to, okay?

"Sure. Thanks again."

She hung up the phone. It was past six in the evening. She imagined Lancelot in the apartment, but she didn't call simply because she hadn't yet explained to him how to use a telephone. He was already feeling inadequate. The last thing she wanted to do was add to the list of everyday items he was unable to use.

With a smile, she decided to go home. For once, she was not going to an empty apartment but to one with a wonderful man waiting for her.

This was, she decided, one of the best days ever.

The doorman greeted her with his usually friendly yet not quite effusive manner.

"Hello, Miss Gaffney."

"Hi." She smiled, adjusting her shopping bags as she checked her mail.

"Ah, been to the Gap?"

She looked down at the five blue bags filled with

clothes for Lancelot. "How could you tell?" It had been so wonderful to buy clothes for Lancelot, to pick out jeans and khakis and T-shirts and socks and shoes. All for Lancelot. She was in such a great mood that even a clinical attempt at conversation was welcome. "Oh, by the way, is my friend upstairs?"

"The one from last night?"

"Yes. Is he already upstairs?"

Of course, she already knew the answer to that. This was just a ploy to let the doorman know everything was all right, not to worry, and to let him pass without question.

"No. Afraid I haven't seen him, Miss Gaffney."

She stopped. "Excuse me?"

"I said I haven't seen your friend."

"Oh. Well, maybe he came in before you went on duty."

"Maybe. But I've been on since noon."

Noon? That was about the time she sent him back in the cab. He must have come back. "Have you taken any breaks or anything?"

"Nope. Things have been pretty slow here, and when I took a short break, I had Dave cover for me." Dave was the doorman next door.

"I see," she said, confused. "Charles, do you have an extra set of my keys I could borrow? I'll have more made tomorrow."

"No problem." He stepped behind the desk and gave her the keys.

Mechanically, she went to the elevator as Charles pushed her floor. She thought she thanked him but wasn't sure.

Maybe he was upstairs. He could have gotten by the desk somehow. Perhaps Charles had been engrossed in a newspaper, or Dave had stepped back to his own post for just an instant.

Maybe he'd be in the living room, just waiting for her.

But he wasn't. The moment she opened her door, she knew he had not been home. And her place seemed all the more empty because she had expected him to be there.

She put down the bags and began to worry in earnest. He was alone in a place he didn't comprehend, with enough potential disasters awaiting at every turn to alarm even the most tranquil of imaginations. And she knew if push came to shove and he found himself in a dangerous situation, he would loudly proclaim himself to be Lancelot, and a dangerous situation would become far worse.

How had she been so stupid? To have shoved him into a taxi, handed a suspicious driver a handful of bills, and turned her back on him was more than irresponsible. It was downright cruel.

In her mind, she saw him staggering about, lost and frightened but not knowing where to go. Perhaps the cabbie would know where he was, but she hadn't even bothered to get his medallion number or name. Lancelot could be lying someplace, hurt and bleeding.

She didn't even know whom to call. The police? Yep. Good idea. Tell them that a man with absolutely no identification, dressed as a medieval knight, and ignorant of the most basic realities of life in the twentieth century was last seen heading downtown in a cab. His age? Oh, about fifteen hundred years, give or take a century. Nationality? Why, he's from Camelot, so that must make him a Camelotian. Or maybe a Camelotite. Profession? Disgraced Knight of the Round Table.

Peg. She would call Peg. Surely, she'd know whom to call if someone who doesn't quite fit in happens to be missing. Someone who may be unequipped to be alone, perhaps confused or frightened. Certainly, Peg, with her practice, would have access to some service. Gentle people with white coats and pleasant manners.

On second thought, Peg was the worst possible person to call.

"Oh, Lancelot," Julie moaned, tears in her eyes. Had she lost him forever? Would she ever see him again? "Please forgive me."

Absorbed with her own misery, she did not hear the key in the door or the silent tumbling of the lock and knob.

"Are you ill?"

"Lancelot!" She stumbled over the bags to reach

him, her arms outstretched. "I'm so . . ." Pulling back, she looked up at him. He was smiling as if he had just had the most pleasant day imaginable. Then she noticed the distinctive fragrance.

"Pine cleanser?"

He sniffed. "I thought I got most of it off."

"Off what?"

"My sleeve. Bill forgot to mention . . ."

"Bill?"

"Yes, well, I'll get to that in a moment. Is Excalibur safe?"

Julie blinked, trying to follow his train of thought. "Yeah. It's in safekeeping at a museum."

"Oh. What's a museum?"

"It's a place with valuable stuff that no one can touch."

"I see. So, then, how does a museum differ from Bloomingdale's?"

"Well, Bloomingdale's is a department store, and . . . wait a moment. Where did you hear about Bloomingdale's?"

"From Bill. He asked me if that's where I got my outfit. I explained I was from out of town, and he explained Bloomingdale's. He said it's an expensive store that most people just go into to look at their wares."

"Who is Bill?"

"From the shelter."

"Oh, my God, you poor thing. Were you mugged?

Did you get hungry and get taken to a shelter? I knew I should have taken better care of you."

"No, no! Please, Julia, you're mistaken. I *worked* at the shelter. I volunteered. I saw it from the window of the cab and asked the driver to stop. I've been there for hours."

Julie was stunned. "What did you do there?"

"Mostly I got into people's way. But I also helped serve lunch, make up the cots for tonight, and open cans for dinner. Oh, and I scrubbed toilets."

"Scrubbed toilets?"

"That's why I smell like cleanser. Bill didn't warn me about how they flush, and, well . . . he assumed I knew already."

All she could do is look up at him, this noble man who had been torn from all he knew, from everything that he had worked a lifetime to achieve. And his immediate response, before the full impact of his own predicament could be fully absorbed, was to reach out and help others.

"What made you do that?"

He glanced over her head, formulating his thoughts. "The name drew me in at first. Avalon."

"Avalon?"

"The mystical island in Camelot, a place to heal, to be soothed and restored to health. I wasn't thinking clearly, just staring out the window. And then I saw something familiar, a word, a place. So I got out. There were people milling about, waiting to enter. I

looked at their faces and saw something else familiar—I saw fear, desperation, a hunger that went beyond the needs of the body. I saw a hunger of the
soul. In short, I recognized myself."

"Did you speak to anyone other than Bill?"

"I did. And for the first time since being here, I
understood. They are good people who are unable to
cope in this society. For some, it's temporary, a stroke
of bad luck or a house fire. A few were plagued by ill
health and lost employment. And some had lived their
entire existence just beyond the walls of this place, on
the fringe. One or two were angry and bitter, but the
rest were resigned to their fate. They have accepted it
not willingly but without a battle."

"That is the way you feel here," she stated.

"No. I was beginning to feel that way, but I refuse
to submit." Gazing directly into his eyes, she saw the
real Sir Lancelot, the man she had known in Camelot.
"We must find Malvern. No matter what the cost, we
must find him before he finds us, and before he finds
a way back to Camelot. If we do not prevent him
from going back, the destruction he will cause will be
absolute. And if we allow him to get accustomed to
this place, it is only a matter of time before he suc-
ceeds here."

"I understand what you're saying," she replied,
phrasing her words carefully. "But I have to confess,
as frightening as Malvern is, I really don't believe he

can do too much damage. Without Excalibur, he is powerless. And he will not get Excalibur."

He ran a hand through his hair. "I disagree."

"Lancelot, he is one man in a city of millions, in a world of billions. Believe me, there's only a limited amount of damage he's capable of here."

"Lady Julia, I spoke to people today who are desperate. There are many of them, I understand. And unlike the people who live in buildings such as this one, with jobs such as yours, they are searching for someone to lead them, to change their fate. Almost anyone will do. Malvern is a clever man, but what is more important is that he is vindictive. He will promise them anything to follow him, and he may even succeed in granting just enough to keep them following."

"Really, Lancelot, I don't think he could possibly . . ."

"Yes, he can. And mark my words, he will. I suspect that once he gets his bearings, he will indeed seek out followers. I believe he will go to shelters very much like Avalon and insinuate his way into their lives, inspire them with false hopes. And then he will be very dangerous indeed."

"He's only one man."

"He may be only one man. But tell me, has there never been a time or place where one man made a spectacular difference? For either good or evil?"

She paused, for he was absolutely right. History

was filled with individual names that changed the world, from Julius Caesar to Oliver Cromwell. There was Buddha, Jesus, and Joan of Arc. Napoleon, George Washington, and Lord Nelson. Marx. Lenin. Churchill and Gandhi. Of course, Stalin and Hitler.

Even on a smaller scale, one person could wield a tremendous capacity for good, touch millions without armies or governments, like Jonas Salk, Harriet Beecher Stowe, or Mother Teresa. Evil, too, could exist on a lesser scale, like Jim Jones.

When it came to Malvern, it wasn't a question of whether he would be good or bad. The only uncertainty was to what level his evil would rise, and that depended on how successfully he could sway others.

The fact that he had been able to persuade Arthur to distrust not only Lancelot but his own beloved wife was powerful proof of his skill.

Lancelot was right. Malvern was dangerous in this or any other time.

"Where do we even begin?" Julie said.

"I've been thinking about that. The first thing we need to do is get some help on our side, convince some key people that Malvern is real and that he is dangerous."

"Oh, Lancelot. Do you know how impossible that will be?"

"You believe. And you are from this time."

"Yes, but I actually went to Camelot. I don't think . . ." She stopped for a moment.

"Lady Julia?"

"I just had a thought. Peg's nephew has a comic book—um, a book with lots of illustrations—that apparently shows us."

"How do you mean?"

"Peg called me today, greatly concerned because she thinks you are pretending to be Lancelot."

"Pretending?"

"Well, yes. It seems this comic book doesn't only tell your story, but it contains drawings that look just like you and me."

"I see," he said thoughtfully. "Therefore, Peg assumes I am a pretender, and an insane one at that."

"I'm afraid she does. But the main thing is that whoever drew the pictures, well, maybe he was in Camelot when we were. How else could he have sketched us so well?"

"Interesting."

"And also, there is this weird bookstore downtown that specializes in the occult. You know, things that can't be explained by science."

"That covers just about everything."

"I'm beginning to think so. Maybe we could start there."

"Good. And I'll see if Bill just might be open to us. After all, he chose the name of the shelter. On some level, he must have sensed a truth in Avalon."

"Yeah, but as nice as Bill may be, what good could he do?"

"I'm not sure," he admitted. "But he knows other shelters and knows how the entire system works. Malvern is without resources, no coins or a place to stay. I would think that at some point, he will need help."

Suddenly, she was exhausted. Glancing down, she remembered the shopping bags. With a grin, she looked up at Lancelot, who was still mulling over his thoughts.

"Speaking of help," she began, "first, I want to thank you for helping me out this morning in the meeting."

He blinked, focusing his attention on her words, then he smiled. "Oh, yes. Shine-All, the all-purpose magical sword cleaner."

"Really, Lancelot. You saved my job."

He gave her a small bow. "My pleasure, m'lady."

"So I got you new clothes. I mean, just so that you won't feel as out of place as I did in Camelot wearing a paper crown and a bib."

"Is what I'm wearing now equivalent to what you wore in Camelot?"

"Close, but not nearly as humiliating. Anyway, here."

One by one, she opened the bags and pulled out the clothes, and one by one, he touched them with suspicion at first, then with growing interest.

"Yes. Bill wore something like this. And a man downstairs had on one of these blouses."

"Yeah, well. Men's tops are usually called shirts. You'll catch on."

He raised an eyebrow. "I have an idea."

"Yes?"

"Perhaps if I clothe myself in some of these garments, we can go to that shop you mentioned before?"

"Great idea! A place like Cauldrons & Skulls is bound to be open late."

"Cauldrons & Skulls? What a charming name."

Within fifteen minutes, they were on their way to the Village, in hopes of finding someone, anyone, who might believe in Camelot.

14

*I*t had been another slow day.

Sam sighed, wondering how much longer they could afford to stay in business. Luckily, Sam and his brother, Mel, owned the place free and clear. It had been in the family for more than a hundred years. Had they been renters, forget about it. In fact, they'd been offered incredible sums of money for the building. A very famous movie star wanted to open a restaurant, and all the Brillman brothers had to do was snap their fingers and they would be wealthy men.

They hadn't mentioned that offer to Mel's wife, Tina. She never did understand the store, claiming it gave her the creeps. Funny thing, the money it brought in—or used to bring in—sure didn't give old Tina the creeps. She was able to spend it just fine, thank you.

His sister-in-law, Tina, was the main reason Sam had never married. Mel seemed to get along with her, but that was because Mel did everything Tina told him to do. And he spent an unnatural amount of time looking at old books and attending estate sales and auctions to add to their stock. Poor schmuck Mel.

He looked around the place critically at the beaded curtains and the brick walls painted black and the stuffed owl positioned over the doorway. There were shelves of oversized books, rows of dog-eared paperbacks, an entire trunk filled with used tarot cards, and two glass cases to display the more exotic items. Even from across the store, he could see a layer of dust clinging to everything, including the owl.

"Mel, did you dust this morning?" he called out to his brother in the back room. Mel, as usual, was engrossed in another ancient manuscript. Always the egghead. Sam was the one with the artistic streak, the decorating flair.

He glanced with satisfaction at the gold unicorn painted on black velvet.

In the mid-seventies, when they founded the shop, it had seemed like such a good idea. The time had been ripe; everyone was exploring the mystical and unknown. Plus, they already had the space. The building had been their grandfather's old pickle store, and sometimes, when it was damp, he could still catch a whiff of garlic and vinegar and mustard seed.

But now Cauldrons & Skulls seemed as outdated as the pickle shop had been almost twenty-five years before. It seemed the more financially secure New

Yorkers became, the less inclined they were to worry about the good old things, like casting spells and reading about lost worlds.

What they needed was a good recession. Back in the fall of eighty-seven, the Wall Streeters were lined up six deep in the little store, avoiding one another's eyes as they bought their occult books and essence of spider in cobalt blue jars.

Who knows, maybe that's what turned the economy around. You get enough of those Morgan Stanley and Merrill Lynch guys casting spells on each other, and next thing you know . . . well, whatever.

The clock—made from a genuine human skull—read nine-fifteen. No sense staying open any longer. Wasn't as if a flood of customers would suddenly descend like locusts.

That reminded him. On his way over to the front door, round hoop keychain dangling, he double-checked on the dried locust supply.

And then he saw them. Customers. Clean-cut ones, too. Not like some of the oddballs who had been coming in lately. The man was large, dressed like one of those slick Gap ads but with longer hair. And the woman was a slender blonde. Actually, they were a darned good-looking couple, in a Hamptons-for-the-weekend, trust-fund sort of way.

He opened the door, the bells jingling overhead, and eyed them once more before stepping aside.

"Howdy, folks," he greeted somewhat incongruously.

"Hi," said the woman, edging toward the guy as if the store made her uncomfortable. "I'm not sure if you can help us . . ."

The guy cut in. "Excuse me, sir. But do you have any books on the lore and legend of Camelot?" He had a vague accent, British probably, although there was a slight lilt.

"Ah, Camelot. Sure, sure." Then he stopped midstride. "Funny, I had you guys pegged as love potion customers."

The girl smiled nervously, and the man just nodded, as if Sam had pointed the way to the shower curtains or drill bits. "Interesting," said the tall man. "And how is your potion done here? In Cam—" The girl jabbed the guy in the side. "Where I come from, we use herbs from the forest bed."

"Oh, yeah? I'll have to give that one a whirl sometime. We're purists here, none of that vegetarian stuff. Our recipe calls for a hummingbird wing stock, and we take it from there. Anyway, the stuff you're looking for is just above the crystal balls." Sam pointed to an eye-level shelf. "Camelot is very big these days, what with the Kennedy auctions and all."

The dark man seemed perplexed, and he heard the woman whisper, "I'll explain it to you later, Lancelot."

"Your name is Lancelot?" Sam asked, grinning. "Man, your parents must have had one heck of a sense of humor!" Then he peered more closely at Lancelot. "Hey, want to hear something wild?"

"Sure." The woman shrugged, glancing up at her companion.

"You're an absolute dead ringer for the Myrddin Lancelot. You ever see that classic? Damn, we just sold the one we had a week or so ago—it was in primo condition. It's a comic book from the late thirties. Hadn't seen one for about fifteen, twenty years—almost impossible to get hold of one. Wait a minute . . . mind if I get my brother, Mel, out here?"

Before either could answer, Sam called over his shoulder, "Yo, Mel! Come on out here—you won't believe this!"

The three of them waited for a few moments, and there was no response. Lancelot began to pull out a few volumes from the Camelot shelf, paging through with his back turned away from the other two.

"I know how to get him out here. Watch this." In a voice just above a conversational tone, he said, "Wow, Mel. Can't believe this. What did you say, it's from the tenth century?"

Within seconds, Mel appeared from the back room, a jeweler's glass stuck over one eye. "What did you say? Tenth century?" Then he blinked at Julie. "It's the Crone of Camelot! You're not tenth century—you're probably fourth, fifth max."

"What are you talking about?" Sam asked.

"I mean, she's lying about her age."

"Nah, Mel. What are you talking about? The Crone of Camelot was a hideous old hag. You telling me this lady here is the Crone of Camelot?"

"When she is Lady Julia, Sam." He rolled his eyes, the jeweler's glass making that one eye appear Cyclops-like. "Nice to meet you, Lady Julia." Mel smiled, extending his hand. "And my oaf of a brother probably failed to introduce himself, but he's Sam, the black sheep of the—"

At that moment, Lancelot looked up from the book.

"Sir Lancelot!" Mel stammered.

Lancelot smiled. "Have we met?"

"Myrddin's Lancelot! I don't believe this! Sam, where did you get these guys?"

"Um, we just walked in," Julie said. "We're really interested in Camelot—anything you have. Especially, well . . ." Again, she glanced uncertainly at Lancelot, and he nodded for her to continue. "Especially anything you may have on how to get there."

Sam and Mel said nothing, and then a sort of sad resignation passed over their faces. They exchanged shrugs, then Sam spoke. "Listen. You two seem like very nice people. And your physical resemblance to the illustrations in the Camelot book are fantastic, really fantastic. But let's face it, there isn't a way to Camelot. There probably never was a Camelot to begin with."

"I don't understand." Julie crossed her arms protectively. "I thought, of all places, here you would . . ."

Halting, she cleared her throat. "How can you have a shop like this and *not* believe in the magical?"

"Aw, come on," Mel said, finally removing the jeweler's glass. "We do this for fun, pure fun. Just because we have a painting of a unicorn on the wall doesn't mean we have a live one tied up in the backyard."

"Then you're running this place under false pretenses." Julie felt like crying. Somehow, the thought that at least two other people would believe them had become very important to her, almost vital. "Look at us. We're really Lancelot and Julia. We're not pretending."

"Lady, we were just playing along. It's all a gag," Mel explained. "We had a couple in here a few weeks back, claimed they were Rick and Elsa from *Casablanca*, both in trench coats. He looked a bit like Bogart, but she was a godawful Bergman. We played along with them, too. But we all knew this was tongue-in-cheek."

"This isn't fair. You were lying to us, then, making us believe you could help just by the nature of this store," Julie continued. Lancelot remained silent, just looking at the men.

"We aren't lying." Sam reached out to pat her shoulder, then stopped himself. "This is a business. Mel and myself, we're pragmatic guys. When I was a kid in college, I almost believed in some of this stuff. But that had more to do with the times, the 'sixties, Woodstock, and all that. I grew up, and once we opened this place, we saw what a crock most of it is."

Mel nodded. "Yeah. I was always interested in

the historical aspect of the items, of the antique books and all that. Fascinating, really. An insight into the psyche of man. But just because I study the stuff doesn't mean I believe it. It's like going to the movies—you watch Jackie Chan, you know he's not really being chased by the bad guys in the helicopter, but you stick with it because it's fun and it's entertaining and you never know what the heck's around the next corner. This shop is the same thing. It's entertainment, pure and simple."

"Why are you telling us this?" Lancelot asked.

"Because, like I said, you seem like nice people," Sam replied. "We've had other nice people in here who take this stuff too seriously. If we play along, enabling their superstitions to seem real, no good can really come of it."

Julie looked down at her feet, trying not to let her disappointment show. "But we belong there, in Camelot. We really do."

"A lot of us feel the same way," Sam said. His brother cocked his head at the gentle tone in Sam's voice. It was unfamiliar, certainly a tone he had never heard Sam employ with customers. "A lot of us wish this could all be real. God knows how many times I've prayed that the good things in tarot cards would come true, that a love potion would really work, that somewhere, if we believe enough, Camelot exists. But all that comes from that kind of thought is frustration and bitterness. You stop living in the real world so long that your chances, the genuine ones, are gone. The woman you could have loved, the opportunities you let slip through your fingers . . ."

He stopped, a flush rising in his face. Mel cleared his throat. "I'm in it for the antiquities, Sam's in it because it's more fun than the pickle business. End of story. But Sam's right, you're nice people. And I hope you find whatever it is you're looking for. Um, I'm going back." He pointed his thumb at the door to the back room. "Good luck. Sam will ring up anything you want to purchase. And Sam, let's give them a ten-percent discount, okay?" With a thin smile, he replaced the jeweler's glass and left.

Sam sighed. "There's almost an unspoken pact between the customers and us—we don't let on that it's fake. On the other hand, if you're sick and something we sell you makes you feel better, where's the harm? And if you love someone and want that person to love you back in the most desperate way, maybe our love potion will give you the confidence to win that person. When that happens, who's to say what works and what doesn't?"

Julie nodded. Lancelot wrapped his arm around her. He did not seem surprised at all, as if he had expected this reaction all along.

Sam looked at the two of them, then glanced over his shoulder at the back room where Mel was. "Listen," he said softly to the couple. "I don't know why I'm saying this, but, things have been slow here, so I have plenty of time to look stuff up. That's the only reason. Let's make that clear from the get-go, all right?"

Julie frowned, perplexed. "I'm sorry, you've lost me. What exactly are you saying?"

"I'm saying this." He crooked his finger, and they both leaned closer. "I'll look for you guys. I'll look through those books Mel has in the back. I'll go through his files. I'm the only one who knows how he organizes things, anyway. So give me your phone number, and I'll call you if I find something." He pursed his lips and shrugged.

Lancelot removed his arm from Julie's shoulder, as if that would help him to concentrate. "Why are you doing this? This seems to go against everything you just said in front of your brother. Why are you willing to help us?"

Sam stopped, an expression of bafflement on his own face. "I really don't know. It's just that, a part of me hopes this is all real, that maybe there is something genuine in this magical stuff after all. Also"——his eyes met Lancelot's, then Julie's, and he looked away, embarrassed——"I have a feeling you folks are genuine. If there is a Camelot—and I'm not saying there is, by the way, just *if* there is a Camelot—you two will make it there. And maybe"——he returned his gaze, unwavering, to them——"I'm hoping maybe you'll take me with you."

Then he took the books Lancelot had piled aside on the shelf. "You guys want these?"

They nodded yes.

"Terrific. Can't go wrong with the Tyson book, by the way." He carried the stack to the cash register and smiled at Julie as if the previous conversation had never taken place. "Cash or charge?"

Julie and Lancelot returned to her apartment just before midnight, after a leisurely late dinner in an out-of-the-way bistro. Lancelot enjoyed the meal and the wine, until he realized Julie had to pay for it.

"It's ridiculous," he continued as they entered her lobby, the large bag of books slung over his shoulders like game after a hunt. "Food is a necessity. Therefore, to force people to pay for a necessity is not right. Has it always been this way?"

Julie laughed, still glowing with the effects of the wine, the superb meal, and, most importantly, the nearness of Lancelot. Reaching into her purse for her keys, she smiled up at him in the bright lights of the lobby.

In modern-day clothing, he was staggeringly handsome. Yet by his gestures, by his every move, he demonstrated his complete naturalness, his utter ease with himself. And of course, that made him all the more attractive.

"Yes, food is a necessity, but not food and wine at a fancy pseudo-French . . ."

"Oh, Miss Gaffney!" Charles the doorman rose from his place behind the front desk. "Sir." He nodded to Lancelot, who returned the greeting. "I let your friend upstairs. I hope it's all right."

"Peg?" Julie asked. "That woman you've seen me with sometimes?"

"Why, no, Miss Gaffney," he said, an uneasy expression forming on his face. "No, it's a friend of your friend here. And he said that he needed a key because he was meeting you someplace and wanted to clean up."

"A friend of mine?" The smile fell from Lancelot's face.

"Well, yes. I mean, he was dressed just the way you were last night, only in black. He looked a bit untidy, and I hesitated, but he assured me that . . ."

"You stay here, Julia!" Lancelot shouted as he began to hand the bags to her.

"No! I'm going with you! Wait a moment." She turned to the doorman. "Do you remember anything else?"

"Oh, my Lord, Miss Gaffney! Did I make a mistake?"

"No, no. I did, Charles. You had no way of knowing." Julie tried to keep her voice calm. "Do you remember anything else about him?"

"Well, wait a minute. He wouldn't take the elevator. He insisted on taking the steps. Oh, my Lord!"

"It's all right, Charles."

"Should I call the police, Miss Gaffney?"

She was about to answer yes, when Lancelot

shook his head. "There are things we can't explain," he said softly.

He was right. They would need information about Lancelot, who Malvern was, where they had all met, what they thought Malvern had been after. Lancelot was right—they could not explain it to the police.

"No, Charles. Thanks, though."

The doorman seemed uncomfortable. "Really, Miss Gaffney. For security reasons, I should really notify the police."

Lancelot smiled warmly at Charles. "You're right, of course. But, well, he's an old friend of mine who has been having some bad luck lately. I'll deal with it."

Charles shifted his weight to his other leg. "Well," he began.

"He's right," Julie assured him. "But could you just answer a few questions?"

He nodded.

"What time did he come here? Did you happen to see him leave?"

"Yeah, I think I saw him leave after about ten minutes or so, but I was getting a cab for Mrs. Chestmire. She has a cane, you know, and needs a little help. And he must have come around ten o'clock, because Mr. Bealy on the seventh floor had just come back from walking Mr. Bigglesworth, that little dog of his. Mr. Bealy always comes back in time for the news at ten."

"Great. Thanks, Charles." She waved as they walked. "This is really more of a family thing."

That seemed to relieve him somewhat, and finally he took a deep breath. "Okay. But if I see this guy again, I *will* call the cops."

"You do that!" And Julie and Lancelot entered the elevator. "Maybe one of us should take the stairs," Julie began. "Just in case he managed to come back and Charles missed him."

This was like a strange dream. Malvern had been there. It was an absolute nightmare.

Lancelot shook his head. "I thought of that, but that might leave you alone. I believe we should stay together even at the risk of missing him."

Julie was not about to begin an argument for women's rights. Instead, she nodded as they reached her floor. "Lancelot, I'm terrified. Maybe we should call the police."

"Maybe. But I don't want to lose him if he's come back. And there is so much we can't possibly explain to the police. Julie, even the fellows at Cauldrons & Skulls did not believe us." Then he smiled and pulled her close. "It will be fine," he whispered.

The elevator stopped, and they looked at each other before stepping into the hallway. The moment they did, they saw her apartment door wide open.

He held a finger to his lips for her to remain silent, and she nodded.

The apartment had been ransacked; the entire place was a shambles. They quietly crept through each room, gingerly peeking into closets and looking under her bed.

"He's gone," Lancelot concluded. "I felt he was gone. But I wanted to make sure."

"Oh, no," she cried, flicking on the light switch. It was even worse when they could really see the destruction. The sofa cushions were scattered in the middle of the living room, clothing was strewn about, the lamps were knocked over.

"Anything missing?" Lancelot asked.

"Nothing seems to be missing. The television's here, the stereo, the VCR—all here."

"How about your jewels? Malvern could use them, sell them."

Julie went into her bedroom, noticing her shoe boxes had been pulled from underneath the bed, the tops scattered, her dolls tossed about. If Lancelot had not thought ahead, Malvern would have got hold of Excalibur.

That thought was the most horrible of all.

She opened her jewelry box and was surprised to see that it had indeed been cleared out. He had taken everything, the real pearls along with her flea market fakes. He had just scooped out the whole thing.

"My jewelry," she said as she walked back into the living room, stumbling over a tumbled lamp. "He took my jewelry. Everything."

Lancelot walked over and encircled her in his arms.

"I'm okay, really," she whispered, leaning her forehead against his chest. Then she stiffened. "At least no one was hurt. Wait a minute. The Gap stuff I got for you, all the clothes. They're gone."

"Of course." He reached up and rubbed his forehead. "Now he'll blend in better. He'll be more dangerous, Julia. You know that."

"Yeah, but thank God he didn't find Excalibur. That's because of you—you were the one who thought ahead."

He smiled thinly. "Perhaps."

The telephone rang, and it took her a moment to find it—under a throw rug. It was Peg, and Julie promised to call back.

Lancelot began putting the pillows back on the sofa, while Julie put the phone back on the table and reconnected the answering machine, which had become unplugged.

When she did, it hummed into action. "Hi, Julie. This is Orrin. I was wondering if . . ."

His voice faded out, and another voice came through, a woman's voice, in a tone of heartbreaking anguish.

"Dear Lord, help us!"

Then the machine went dead.

Lancelot stood slowly, a sofa cushion in his hand.

"Who was that?" Julia asked. "I don't recognize the voice."

His face tight, he closed his eyes before looking

at her. "I would know that voice anywhere," he said quietly. "That voice, Lady Julia, was Guinevere."

The disheveled man was strangely dapper in new-looking clothes.

Sam looked up from his morning coffee when he heard the bells jingling over the doorway. Immediately, he wished he hadn't opened up a few minutes earlier.

"Sorry, we're closed," he said from behind the counter.

"I do not care," the disheveled man replied. "I have need of your services."

The accent, Sam thought. This guy's accent is the same as Lancelot's. He looked closer at his features, for they were somehow familiar.

And there was something disturbing about the man's eyes that made him afraid to refuse. "What can I help you with?"

The man produced a piece of red cloth that turned out to be a woman's scarf. Sam's first thought was that it concealed a gun, but instead, it just held some jewelry, a jumble of real stuff and costume. Sam was relieved.

"Sorry," he said. "This isn't a pawnshop."

The man's eyes flashed, and in that instant, Sam recognized who it was. Malvern, from the same Myrddin book. Last night, Lancelot and Lady Julia. This morning, Sir Malvern.

What the hell was going on? Was there a full moon or something?

But this guy was different, dirty. More than the outward filth of his face and arms, there was a grime that seemed to reach to his soul, soiling his spirit, if that was possible.

It was all reversed. Lancelot the Evil had not seemed evil, not in the least. In fact, he had seemed like a nice guy.

Sam had been up all night, thinking about those people, unable to get them from his mind. He wouldn't dare tell Mel this, but he really thought there was something special, magical about them.

Couldn't Mel see it?

And now the gallant Malvern was here, corrupt and vile, making Sam wish to withdraw his hand immediately so it would not meet the other's on the counter.

"I understand you have information on Camelot."

"No," he replied, again relieved. "Sorry. We sold all of our Camelot books just recently."

"When? When did you sell them? And was it to a man and a woman?"

Sam swallowed. "I don't remember. We have so many people coming in here all the time, I really don't remember . . ."

The man was peering over Sam's shoulder.

"See that empty space on the shelf behind me?" Sam did not want to remove his eyes from the stranger. "Right above the crystal balls? That's where the Camelot books used to be."

Sam's mind was working. What should he do?

That number. He had the woman's phone number. He should call her, them, tell them Malvern had come into the shop, looking for information on Camelot.

"But we'll have more in stock in a few days," Sam heard himself say. What was he doing? He didn't want to see this man again. Not ever. But he continued, knowing somehow that Lancelot would need to see this guy. "Come on back in a day or so."

Malvern walked straight over to the shelf. "Here is one," he shouted. "I found one!"

Sam smiled as if vastly pleased for his customer, and he was, for the volume Malvern had was a next-to-useless picture book on the sites that might have been Camelot. It was a pleasant book, with lovely photographs of Scotland and Wales.

"You're right, sir. And that will be twelve ninety-nine."

Malvern's eyes shifted as he thought. "Take this," he said, handing Sam a pearl necklace that was probably worth a couple of thousand dollars.

He hesitated, then took it. The man grabbed the book, bundled up the rest of the jewelry in the scarf, and left.

Before the jingling of the bells over the front door ceased, Sam was on the phone dialing Julie's number.

15

❦

$\mathcal{J}$ulie did her best to hide the shock and genuine fear that coursed through her when she saw Lancelot in the morning light. The day before, his hair had been sprinkled with gray, difficult to detect under dim illumination. Now, his temples were almost white, and the rest was a slate gray.

His face, too, was altered. The once-vibrant skin was now a bit paler; the lines that had appeared earlier were deeper, more pronounced. But it was his eyes that truly revealed the change, for they lacked the spectacular luster she had first seen when he lifted his visor.

"Good morning." She forced a smile.

"Good morning." He ran a hand through his hair.

She wondered if he had any idea of the changes that were overtaking him. And then she wondered something worse: how much longer could he hold on here in this time? When would it simply become too late for him? For the two of them?

The telephone rang, and Julie reached for the receiver, glancing at the answering machine and aware that after hearing Guinevere's voice, anything was possible.

"Hello?"

"Hello, Miss Gaffney? This is Sam from Cauldrons & Skulls."

"Oh, hi. I can barely hear you."

"Yeah, well, I don't want my brother to overhear this. He's already worried that I may not have both oars in the water, if you know what I mean. But a guy came in here just a few minutes ago asking for information on Camelot."

"What did he look like?" She could barely breathe, and Lancelot was staring at her quizzically.

"He didn't look like anybody. He *was* Malvern."

"My God." She looked over at Lancelot. "Malvern was in the store this morning."

"Is he still there?" Lancelot asked.

Julie returned to the phone. "Sam, is he still there?"

"No. He took off toward Houston Street. He had no money but was dressed in khakis and a denim shirt and paid with a pearl necklace. I had a feeling I should tell you."

"My necklace. Yes. It was stolen, along with the

rest of my jewelry and some clothes I'd gotten for Lancelot.

"Did he threaten you in any way?"

"No. But there is something very wrong with that guy. I told him I would be getting more books in and that he should come back in a day or two."

"Sam." Julie smiled. "You're wonderful."

"Well." He cleared his throat. "I also looked up a few things in some of Mel's books. Listen, I can't be sure about this, but there was an old Italian manuscript from the sixteenth century—Mel translated it and stuck the English translation in the back. According to this book, those who leave Camelot are forever banished."

She closed her eyes, her shoulders slumped. "Please don't tell me this."

"But there is one exception."

"I'm listening," she prompted.

"If the individual has a physical link to Camelot, it just may be possible to return."

She glanced over at Lancelot, who was watching her intently. "What do you mean by a physical link?"

"Well, this is where it gets tricky, and it seems even brainy Mel had a tough time with the translation. The link must be something vital to Camelot itself. Can't just be, say, an old shoe or something. It has to be an important item. There's a word here, I can't be sure because Mel scratched it out about a dozen times, but I think the key word is *mystical*. There is some sort of incantation you can do when you have the item. I'm going to see if I can get anything else from Mel— I hope I can do it without letting him know what's going on. I think I can bribe him with a corned beef sandwich at Katz's. Because, to tell you the truth, what I have now doesn't make a hell of a lot of sense to me. Anyway, that was the only solid information I could come up with."

"A physical link," she repeated. "We need an important physical link to Camelot."

Glancing over at Lancelot, she saw a slow grin come over his still-handsome face. She raised her eyebrows in a silent question, and he answered.

"Ask Sam if the sword Excalibur would be suitable."

"Oh course! Sam, how would Excalibur work?"

"Holy Toledo, you guys have Excalibur?"

"Well, it's in safekeeping right now. We suspected Malvern would try something like this. But do you think Excalibur could do the trick?"

"Holy Toledo! Yes! I can't imagine a more powerful link. You guys really have Excalibur?"

She laughed. "Yep. I brought it back as a souvenir."

"Wow. Hey, listen, before you guys go back, before all this spell stuff happens, can I touch it? Just for a second?"

"Of course you can, Sam. Absolutely. Oh, just a minute."

Lancelot took the telephone. "Sam, hello. This is Lancelot."

"Uh, good morning, Sir Lancelot."

"Good morning to you, Sam. Thank you for all of your help. Just one question: did Malvern mention where he was staying? Any men's shelter, anything of that sort?"

"Nah. Frankly, he seemed anxious to get out of the store. He should be back sometime tomorrow, though."

"Sam, listen, I'll be there with you. You won't be alone the next time."

"Thank you." Sam sighed. "Thanks. And I'll let you guys know if anything else seems promising, okay?"

They ended the conversation, and she watched Lancelot as he replaced the receiver. As happy as she was about the information, part of her was filled with a kind of dread.

Why couldn't he just stay there, with her, in her own apartment? He could find a place for himself. He could fit into her life—he already had, and completed it in a way she had never imagined possible.

Before Lancelot, she hadn't known what was missing from her life. And now she knew.

How could she ever live without him? For he alone belonged in Camelot. She belonged where she was.

Again, she forced a smile. "This is wonderful, Lancelot. It really seems as if Sam is on to something."

There was an eagerness on his face, and he nodded. "We'll be going back soon, Lady Julia. Very soon."

She looked away, pretending to be busy with closing a drawer. "Well, I'd better call the locksmith to change the locks, then I have to get to the office."

"Yes. I'm going back to Avalon, to the shelter. Maybe Bill can help me locate other shelters, and I can ask about Malvern. Maybe we won't have to wait until tomorrow to find him."

"Yes" was all she could say.

He reached out and touched her arm before leaving. And she stood alone in her kitchen, wondering again how she was ever going to survive once he left forever.

How on earth could she learn to live without him?

"Julie," Peg said as the front door opened. The locksmith had just left, and Peg had a bag under her arm. "I called your office, and they said you were robbed last night. Are you okay?"

"Yeah, Peg. I'm just fine."

"Well, you look terrible."

"Thanks. You sure know how to make a gal's day."

"Did the cops catch the guy who robbed you?"

"Not exactly." Julie hesitated.

"What do you mean, not exactly? This is a straightforward question. Did the police manage to catch whoever broke into your apartment?"

"No. Not really."

Peg slapped her palm against her forehead. "You're trying to drive me nuts, right? Like the movie *Gaslight*. And here I went all the way to Long Island last night and endured a screaming Nathan to get this for you. I need it back this evening, by the way, or Nathan will have my hide." She tossed the bag onto Julie's couch.

"What is that?"

"It's the comic book. I want you to see how truly disturbed your pal is. So, let me get this straight—the cops gave you no information?"

"We didn't call the cops."

"What are you talking about?"

"Lancelot and I agreed that it wasn't a good idea to call the police on this matter."

"Lancelot and . . ." she sputtered. "Okay, I'm going to try to remain calm. And what I'm about to say will probably tick you off, but did you consider the very obvious possibility that Mr. Lancelot himself had something to do with your burglary? Thank God you weren't hurt. But Julie, get a grip here."

"Lancelot did not have anything to do with this," she began. "Peg, thanks for dropping this by. Really. But I have to get back to the office."

"No you don't, babycakes. You and I are going to complete this conversation."

"Peg, I . . ."

"Julie, I'm really worried about you."

"Ugh. I do wish you'd stop saying that. I promise you, I'm just fine. And . . ."

Peg, arms crossed, was scanning the living room when suddenly her mouth dropped open. "I don't believe this."

"Huh?"

She walked over to the chair where the Camelot books were stacked, the empty shopping bag on the carpet. "You went to Cauldrons & Skulls? I thought that place gave you the creeps."

Julie shrugged. "I guess I decided to trust your judgment and give the place another try."

Peg shuffled the books to read the titles. "Great. *Camelot—Reality behind the Myth*. Oh, and of course, the ever-popular *Lancelot: A Second Look*. Julie, are you serious about this?"

"You really don't understand the situation."

"You're right. I don't. And I also don't know how it feels to believe a very much alive guy can also be a medieval knight, or to convince myself that I broke every known rule of physics and science and traveled back in time. Why are you smiling?"

"It's just that, believe it or not, you sound exactly the way he did when I tried to tell him I was from the twentieth century. You two are really very much alike." Then she stopped, the smile fading. "Wait a minute. I never said anything about me going to Camelot."

"You didn't have to. It's obvious you somehow believe everything this guy tells you. You made a few comments that frankly spooked me. You're a smart woman, Julie. For you to be toying with a fantasy on this level is frightening. And another thing—I really think he may have slipped you something, some sort of hallucinogenic drug, for you to swallow without question all of these wild tales. I don't know how else to explain your behavior."

"You think he slipped me a mickey?"

"Julie, you need some serious help here."

"Actually, I think your friend Sam from the store is going to give us a hand."

"Sam? Don't get me wrong, Sam's a nice guy, but he's a little on the flaky side. Mel, now, he's the realist."

"How can you go to a store like that and not begin to believe in their books, all of their potions?"

"It's fun, Julie. I don't take it seriously, and it gives me—all of us, really—an idea of man's evolution. Before science, this stuff was a comfort, a way for people to deal with stuff that happens in life. I don't go to Caludrons & Skulls because I believe in love potions. I go there because I find the very notion of love potions fascinating, in a primitive way. It's a break from reality, a mini vacation. But you've gone way, way too far."

Julie stared at her friend for a few long moments. "I just figured something out about you, Peg Reilly. You really want to believe, don't you? For all of your pragmatic realism, there is nothing that you'd like better than to do something truly magical. Furthermore . . ."

"Boy, are you ever off base, Gaffney." Peg dropped the books back onto the chair and turned toward the door.

"No, I'm not! Oh, Peg, don't you see? It's all true! All of the magic and wonder *is* real. Let yourself believe, just for an hour or so, and you'll see."

"I have to go now, Julie. I'll check up on you later and see when I can come by for the book."

"Peg, come back! Really!"

She slammed the door on her way out, and Julie smiled. "She really does believe," she said to herself. "Poor Peg."

And then she got ready for work.

Mel could not touch his sandwich.

"All right, Sam. What's going on here? Why are you buying me lunch?"

"Can't a guy buy his brother a deli sandwich at Katz's without it becoming a federal case?" said Sam as he tilted his head sideways to get a better angle for the overstuffed corned beef.

"How can you eat that thing?"

Sam chewed a few moments before answering. "I can eat this thing because after I went home last night, I didn't eat dinner. I can eat this thing because I couldn't eat breakfast, either. That's how I can eat this thing. Do you want your pickle?"

Mel glared, then tossed his pickle over to his brother's plate. "The last time you took me out to lunch was when you heard Tina was running around with that guy from the bowling alley. So forgive me if I appear to be a little nervous here."

"It's nothing like that." Sam smiled with his mouth full. "Ain't life grand?" Then he stopped, watching Mel's obvious discomfort.

The deli was bustling, the steam rising from behind the counters, customers shouting their orders to the harried carvers, the constant tinkling and change-rattling slide of the cash registers, all in the neon-plastic interior with orange booths and chipped Formica tables.

Someone dropped a tray, and neither of them jumped.

"It's about those people last night, isn't it? The ones who looked like Lancelot and the Crone of Camelot. There's something going on with them, isn't there?"

Sam ate half the pickle. "They were nice people."

"Yeah, well, I thought they were a little strange. Too intense, if you ask me. Their faces, though.

Man——dead ringers, weren't they? I've never seen anything like it," Mel repeated.

A dapper old man in a Bavarian hat with a brush stuck in the side was passing when he heard Mel's lament.

"Take half home," he ordered. "That pastrami's big enough for two meals. No shame in that." And then he went on.

Mel did not even blink. "Sam, you're up to something, and it's not just my imagination, is it?"

Finally, Sam put the sandwich down, gingerly, as the middle began to slide out. "No. You didn't imagine that."

He looked at the sandwich, and suddenly he wasn't that hungry, either. Instead, he took a saltine from the bowl on the table and slowly, deliberately, pulled the red tag to open the cellophane. "Do you think there's a way to really get to Camelot, Mel?"

"Aw, come on, Sam. We both know there is no Camelot, probably never was. You don't really believe in all of that stuff."

"Yes, I do!" he shouted, and a few diners stared for a second, then went back to their meals. Sam looked down at the crackers, and instead of eating them, he carefully pressed the corners so they crumbled into the wrapper. "Okay. I just think it might be possible to go back there. And you, Mel, you know all of the secrets. You do all the translating, the studying." He lowered his voice. "So, you're the only one who really knows. We've never talked about this, but I do believe there is a Camelot. And I want to go there." He was finding it difficult to continue.

"And then?"

"And then maybe I'll be happy. Heck, it's worth a shot, Mel."

"Jesus. You've cracked up, you know that? You've seriously cracked up."

"Say what you want." Then Sam looked directly at Mel. "Listen to me, Mel. You have everything you want here. You've got Tina. You've got your work. You're about the most contented man I know."

Mel steepled his fingers, waiting for his brother to continue. "I suppose."

"Well, I have nothing. Half of a failing store, a few regular customers I think of as friends and who forget I even exist the moment they leave the store. That's it. No girl, no real happiness. And I wake up in the morning, and do you know what I think?"

Mel shook his head.

"Every morning, I wake up, and one thought, one thought only, runs through my head. *Is this all there is?* That's it. A simple enough sentiment, but when it's yours, it's terrible for all of its simplicity. Tell me, Mel. Please tell me that this isn't it for me, this is not all there is. For God's sake, tell me there's more."

For a long time, the two just stared at each other. Then Mel stood up. "I'm not hungry. We have a lot of work to do if I'm going to show you some of the special manuscripts."

Sam took a last look at the corned beef and nodded. "Thank you." His voice was barely audible.

They had begun to leave when the man in the Bavarian hat rushed to the table. "Boys! Boys! Come back! Take it home, there's no shame!"

Sam looked over his shoulder. "You can have them, Pops."

The man grinned. "Thank you, boys!" And he wrapped up the sandwiches, dinner for the next two nights.

16

The strange, unforgiving city was a little more familiar now to Lancelot. The constant sounds of car horns and sirens and drills blasting the pavement, the smell of asphalt when the streets were heated by the springtime sun at noon, and always the people—in every language imaginable and a few that weren't. All of these things were no longer so foreign to him, and he had learned to relish the welcome, relative silence of the basement of the church where the shelter named Avalon was housed.

Bill was surprised to see Lancelot, simply because most people only helped once, and then with their conscience clear, their token good deed completed, they would studiously forget the shelter. Occasionally, they would allay their guilt with a check or two, but then even the checks would stop, and Bill would have to train new people who would, in all likelihood, follow the same pattern.

"Lancelot." Bill grinned, his triangular face flushed with physical exertion. "Great! I can't tell you how much I need an extra pair of hands today. We have choir rehearsal before dinner, and these boxes have to be moved to make room for the chairs."

"Choir rehearsal?"

Bill nodded as Lancelot began to shift cardboard cartons filled with donated cans of food and assorted items of clothing.

"It gives the people a sense of permanency," Bill explained. "No matter where we are forced to move to, the choir offers stability, community. It's something they do together, and it also lends a feeling of giving something in return. That's important to everyone. They may not be quite professional, but there is a quality to their singing that's really quite special."

They were making room for chairs for that evening's rehearsal. "Besides," admitted Bill, "I have a degree from Juilliard. This is the closest I've come to doing anything I'm remotely trained for."

Lancelot wasn't quite sure what Bill meant but pretended that it all made perfect sense.

He'd been doing a lot of that kind of pretending lately.

"Bill," he began as he stacked one box on top of another. "Do you know of any other shelters?"

"Sure. Oh, could you put those more toward the window? Great." He pushed his wire-framed glasses back into place. "Other shelters. Yeah, there are lots of them."

Lancelot moved the boxes, then stopped, flexing and relaxing his right hand. It was bothering him today.

"You okay?" Bill asked, watching as Lancelot returned to work.

"Yes. Now, about those shelters . . ."

"My grandmother used to have that problem," Bill continued.

"Excuse me?"

"With her hands, I mean. Whenever it rained, or was about to rain, her hands would bother her. And it's supposed to rain this afternoon. Guess that happens when we get older."

That's why his joints were aching, he thought with mild interest. The dampness. It was going to rain. He recalled as a child an elderly neighbor used to be able to predict the weather in just the same way. If her joints gave her pain, it would rain, she would chant.

He was becoming just like her, the old woman with the gnarled hands.

Had Julia noticed the difference? She must have. The graying hair, the lines on his face. It wasn't simple vanity that bothered him. It was the knowledge that he was growing feeble, weaker. And if he became too weak and feeble, he could no longer be of help to anyone—to himself, to Julia. To anyone.

As if to prove himself, he hefted two cartons of

canned goods. But he put them down, his legs trembling, and just stared at the boxes.

"Here." Bill smiled. "Let me help you." With little effort, he lifted the boxes. Bill, a skinny, pale young man, was able to do what he, Lancelot, could not.

All Lancelot could do was nod his thanks and wonder what was happening to him.

Unlike the other knights, he had never suffered from the physical strain of training and battle. Instead, it seemed to rejuvenate him, to make him stronger, to give him a firm sense of purpose. There was a pure joy in besting a mighty opponent, someone who had trained hard and whose skill and daring would defeat a lesser man.

Now he was defeated by a box.

And soon Julia would feel pity for him. He could not tolerate that. Already, he had seen a glimpse of compassion in her eyes that morning, but it had vanished quickly.

It was humiliating to have those kind eyes of hers turned toward him with such concern.

For a moment, he did not care about returning to Camelot to clear his name or finding Malvern. All he cared about was having Julia see him as he really was. He wanted her to watch him in the context of her own life, to view him as a success the way he was back in Camelot.

"Would you like to rest a bit, old buddy?" Bill inquired.

He had said those words lightly, "old buddy," but they had hit their mark and stung.

"No. I'm fine," Lancelot snapped, returning to the job at hand and hoping he would be able to move the other boxes. Standing up, hands on his hips, he saw a full-length mirror. Reflected back at him was a man with gray hair and an ashen face, and it took him a moment to realize that older person was himself.

Just as quickly, he looked away, and he avoided the mirror for the rest of the afternoon.

Julie's return to work was nothing short of bizarre.

"Julie! Hello!"

"Are you all right? We heard about your robbery. Mr. Stickley just got back from London this morning and says you should take the entire day off."

"Hi there, Julie! Are you free for lunch? Bob and I were just . . ."

"Hey, stranger! The Shine-All people sent you a huge flower arrangement . . ."

She felt like a conquering hero returning from battle. There was also an element of guilt—she didn't really do anything to deserve such accolades. If anyone should receive praise, it should be Lancelot.

She smiled and waved as she made her way down the corridor to her own office, closing the door with relief.

Under her arm was Nathan's book. Instead of

sitting at her desk, which was now crowded with flowers, she sank into the couch and kicked off her shoes. All she needed was a minute to collect her thoughts, to calm herself down.

It wasn't easy. A vision kept flashing through her mind like a flickering movie, an image of Lancelot growing old so quickly, of the pain he would endure, of the sorrows and triumphs that life would deny him. There was so very much he had yet to accomplish. And she felt absolutely helpless, powerless against the forces of nature that seemed to be working against his very existence.

Maybe there would be some clue in the book, something to help him. It was as good a place as any to look for answers. If not an answer, at least she could find the question. While Sam was searching through his brother's texts, she could at least page through this one.

The book itself was an oversized, oblong volume, lavishly illustrated with vibrant colors. The inset was a depiction of King Arthur pulling the sword Excalibur from the stone. What struck Julie immediately was the amazing likeness of Arthur—it really looked like the man she had seen. A youthful version, of course—the boy Arthur, his features screwed in effort, pulling the sword from the stone, propelling himself into legend. Not only did it look like him, but he was even wearing the same sort of tunic she had seen in Camelot.

Just before she opened the book, she glanced at the hilt of Excalibur as it was depicted on the cover, in the unblemished hands of the youth Arthur. It was a precise rendering of the sword, accurate in every detail, from the placement of the gemstones to the curious etched swirls on the hilt.

Then she turned the pages to the first chapter, with a meticulously rendered drawing of Merlin, looking almost as he had when she met him at his home, although his nose was a little less bulbous and his eyes were less puffy. It was Merlin after a cosmetic makeover, the same man with slightly more dashing features. Even his robe, although the same one she remembered, was free of stains.

Then came more illustrations of Arthur, older than on the cover, a mature adult. And he was just the man she had seen in the banquet hall. His expression was every bit as calm and serene, wise and compassionate as it had been in Camelot. With a jolt, she realized something she had not comprehended before. King Arthur bore a striking resemblance, of all people, to a young Abraham Lincoln. It was as unmistakable as it was improbable. Peering closer, she even saw the same irregularities that had made Lincoln's face so distinguishable, the deep lines, the uniquely clipped beard. It was mesmerizing.

"Enough," she mumbled, paging on. In spite of her mission, she swiftly became involved with the story itself.

And then, with another jolt, she saw him. Lancelot, in one of his blue tunics, looking every bit as impossibly handsome as he was when she had seen him, visor up, in her first moments in Camelot.

Now she could really evaluate the changes in his appearance since arriving in Manhattan, and those changes were startling, brutal. He looked at least a dozen years older, perhaps more.

Gently, she touched the page, as if that would allow her to reach back to the brief time in Camelot, tracing his features, the dark, straight eyebrows, the vibrant skin glowing with health, the strong white teeth.

Nothing was overdrawn in this comic book. Although it had originally been published in the late nineteen-thirties, there was nothing stylized about the words or the illustrations. There were no telltale reminders of the era in which it had been written. In fact, it was as timeless a rendering of Camelot and its people as she had ever encountered.

The author must have visited the place. It seemed unlikely, but she couldn't imagine how else he could have known. And after all, she had somehow traveled there. She wasn't arrogant enough to presume that she alone had been gifted with the trip. Others had gone to Camelot, just as others would follow.

An uncomfortable chill ran up her arms as she realized something else. The author must have been there at the same time she was. Was he still there?

She looked at the cover. The author and illustrator had been a man named Ralph Myrddin. Odd name, certainly.

Was he still alive?

Continuing along in the story, she read of Lancelot's daring exploits, of his gallantry and dash. There were even flashes of his humor, the humor she had grown to know so very well.

And then she turned the page, and there she was—the young squire in a bib and paper crown. But Lancelot was already beginning to change. His eyebrows now arched with a slight menace. There was something different in his eyes as well, a glint of something behind the pure blue.

Whatever it was, the change was more than disturbing, especially since Julie could not recall the changes taking place while she was there. She was a witness, yet the Lancelot she knew most certainly did not transform into the frightening vision Ralph Myrddin had portrayed.

Then she saw a rendering of Malvern, looking almost kindly. The artist had gotten it all wrong. She realized he must have confused the two. The dark eyes and the corrupt glint had been rendered on Lancelot, but in reality they had belonged on Malvern.

She read further about Lancelot's growing treachery and Malvern's attempts to keep Lancelot noble.

"All wrong," she muttered. "It's all reversed."

And then she saw a plot line that literally made her gasp.

According to this version of the legend of Camelot, Lancelot went mad. This part was accompanied by the most terrible drawings she had ever seen, of Lancelot ripping out his own hair, stalking through the realm, and finally . . . finally . . .

Finally, there was a detailed illustration of Lancelot killing Malvern. She was unable even to look at the illustrations, much less read the words. It was just a blur of violence, of hands and hair and an open mouth. She quickly turned the pages, taking in as little as she possibly could. Still, it was too much.

Then, according to Myrddin's account, Lancelot killed a woman known as Lady Julia, who was also the Crone of Camelot. There were two renderings of her, one in the blue gown, the other as a horrible, bent creature reminiscent of a female Cryptkeeper.

"This is all mixed up," she breathed. "This is all impossible."

She understood about the confusion of Lady Julia and Malvern, for they had disappeared with Lancelot. But Lancelot's transformation. That was completely peculiar.

Her phone began to ring, and she slipped the book under the couch. She could look at it later. And perhaps it would all begin to make sense.

Mel was uncomfortable in the front of the store. He always had a firm belief that it was Sam who belonged out front, with all of the customers. It was Sam who had a bantering way with people, could chat easily about all of the weird, mystical stuff that came with the territory. His brother could make tarot cards, magic potions, and little black bags filled with charms seem as normal as the parts of an automobile engine. And that sense of normalcy was needed, especially with new customers who might be uncomfortable with this sort of stuff. Sam had a way of putting them all at their ease.

His own specialty was the dusty old texts, weird in their own way, but no one seemed all that interested in ancient books in foreign languages.

But Sam was at the bank, depositing the week's earnings. He was supposed to have done it the day before but had never gotten around to it, and Mel had already written checks to the utility companies. The last thing they needed was a bunch of bounced checks.

Poor Sam. He'd really gone around the bend. Mel suspected it was just a phase, like that time in high school when Sam had wanted to be a rock star. The chances of Sam making it as an opening act for the Rolling Stones was only slightly less likely than Sam appearing in Camelot.

The mere thought made Mel grin.

Still, Sam seemed genuinely excited, and he couldn't help but wonder if he knew something, a secret perhaps. He could always tell when Sam was keeping something from him, and this was no exception.

What could it possibly be?

Then the front door opened, and the overhead bells jingled.

"Hello," Mel began, then stopped.

It was the gallant Malvern! At least, this guy looked exactly like the Malvern in Ralph Myrddin's book. He was nicely dressed. Maybe he'd buy a bunch of stuff. Mel tried to keep himself calm.

"How can I help you?"

"I am looking for books on Camelot." The man did not look him directly in the eye, and Mel assumed the poor fellow was embarrassed about being in a store like this. Wasn't everyone's cup of tea, exactly.

"Camelot? What a coincidence. We had a couple in here the other night looking for stuff on Camelot."

The stranger's gaze snapped to Mel. "Who were they?" He smiled and softened his tone. "I have friends, you see. I thought perhaps you might have seen my good friends."

"Well." Mel chuckled. "You're going to think I'm nuts, but they looked exactly like Lancelot and Lady Julia from an old comic book. He was a big guy, dark hair. She was blond and pretty." He decided not to mention this guy's own resemblance to Malvern.

"How very interesting." The man smiled.

"Yep. They were Lancelot and Lady Julia, all right."

The stranger smiled again. "I was told you would have more information on Camelot. I was told it would be here tomorrow, but I need the information now."

"You must have spoken to Sam. Well, jeez." Mel looked behind him at the empty shelf where the Camelot books had been. "I'm afraid you're out of luck."

The stranger stood, still smiling. "I certainly hope not. It's time my luck turned around."

"Ah, one of those days, eh? I've had a few myself." Mel thought for a moment. Sam probably hadn't ordered new books yet, especially since he was only just depositing the cash. So he wouldn't have been able to refill the stock.

"Listen. I feel terrible about this, but we probably won't get the new books for almost a week or so. I don't know why Sam told you that. He must have been preoccupied or something."

The man simply stared at Mel, his dark eyes glinting.

Damn, Mel thought. He hated to lose a new customer. "I'll tell you what," Mel began. "I don't normally do this, but I have some rare books in the back. Come on with me, and we'll go through them. I think you may find them interesting, even if they're out of your price range."

Mel began to walk around the counter.

"I want to find a way to go to Camelot," the man said.

Mel stopped. "You don't say? Jeez, there must be something in the water. Sam's asked me for the same stuff. We were looking at it just a while ago. Hey, is there some sort of contest or something? Like find an ending to the Camelot legend and you win some terrific gifts?"

"Yes," he began slowly, then his grin spread wider. "In a way, there is a contest, a tournament coming up. And whoever wins will get the greatest prize of all."

"Well, come on back. I may have just the thing you're looking for—just translated it a few weeks ago." Then he stopped, wondering if what he was doing was disloyal to Sam. What if Sam didn't win some prize because Mel showed the same stuff to a customer?

"Nah," he muttered to himself. "Business is business. Even Sam says that all the time."

Together they went past the beaded curtains and into Mel's back room.

Julie's day had passed in a whirl of activity. Although she thought she'd be exhausted, especially after the emotional trauma of reading the book, she had more energy than she could remember.

And everything she did seemed to be just right. In a meeting for a foot powder ad, she suddenly thought of the perfect slogan and blurted it out. Perfect! Then she added a single line to the graphics for a copy-packed advertorial, and the layout artist shook her head and declared that, too, was perfect.

Late in the afternoon, Mr. Stickley, the president of the entire agency, asked her if she would like to have drinks at the 21 Club. In the past, she wasn't sure if Mr. Stickley had even been aware of her existence. Now she was being invited into the inner circle.

Out of the blue, a major sporting goods company dumped the agency they'd been virtually married to for a decade and asked S&B to handle their six-million-dollar account, specifically mentioning Julie's name. And just as she was freshening up for the 21 Club, the biggest fast-food chain in the country—in the world—left word that they were going with the idea Julie had pitched a month before. Since she hadn't heard from them, she'd assumed S&B was out of the running.

As exciting as the day had been, she knew, deep down, that the sudden success was entirely due to Lancelot. He was the one who changed everything, who caused every known equation to be tossed away. His mere presence had transformed every facet, every corner of her life. Nothing remained the same, including Julie herself. For now, she was thinking of herself as Julia. Now she was someone of importance.

It was all Lancelot.

*   *   *

Peg looked at her watch impatiently, shifting on the sofa in Julie's apartment lobby.

This wasn't like her to be late. If anything, reliable Julie was always early. It was that damn guy, that Lancelot jerk. He changed everything.

He'd even changed things at Julie's office. Peg, whose own schedule was not exactly lax, had not been able even to speak to her when she called to double-check on the time they would meet. Instead, she'd had to go through a ditzy receptionist. That had never happened before.

She flipped her wrist and checked her watch. Only a minute since the last time she'd checked.

Luckily, Peg's six forty-five had canceled, and there were no evening appointments tonight. Even therapists needed a night off.

And hers was being ruined by that Lancelot jerk.

"Calm yourself, Peggy," she whispered. The doorman gave her a curious glance, and she smiled.

The doorman was a jerk, too.

She began to tap the heel of her black pump on the marble floor. All she needed was the damn book. It was probably right upstairs. Nathan would kill her if she didn't get it right back to him.

Two minutes had now passed since the last watch check.

Then she saw him. The jerk. He was wearing new clothes. Obviously, Julie had taken her Lancelot on quite a spending spree.

He wasn't only a jerk. He was a gigolo. Double whammy.

And then she smiled, because in the light of the lobby, she realized he wasn't as young as he'd seemed before. His hair was not just touched with gray, it *was* gray, and white at the sides.

"Forgot to use the old Grecian Formula this morning, Lance?" For some reason, the fact that he looked so much older than she remembered did not give her the pleasure she thought it would. Her smile faded as she watched him help a woman with luggage into a taxi. When he straightened, she saw his lips tighten, as if the movement had been painful.

Actually, it was sort of sad. Pathetic, perhaps.

He walked into the lobby, reaching into the pocket of his khakis when he saw her. And he smiled, a genuine smile of surprise and pleasure.

"Lady Peg." He gave the same strange bow at the waist she had seen him do before. "What a pleasure it is to see you. Is Julia home?"

"No." Peg stood up. No doubt about it, the guy was indeed charming. All the more reason to mistrust him. "Do you know when she's coming back?"

He shook his head, pulling a set of keys from his pocket. "No. I thought she would be home by now."

He seemed worried. More worried than the daylight savings evening would warrant. Maybe he thought she was out on a date.

Peg hoped that was the case. Then she was grazed

by a pang of guilt. "I called her at the office, and I think she had to go someplace with a coworker. Her boss or something."

Immediately, his face relaxed. "Good. Thank you for telling me. I . . . well, I'm not used to this city yet, and I am concerned for her safety."

"Yeah. Well. Whatever."

"Would you like to come upstairs? She should be back soon."

Peg eyed him warily. Would he dare to hit on her? To use his poor-lost-out-of-towner routine to snare his next Sugar Mama?

Nah. This guy was too slick. But he couldn't fool Peg. After all, she was a trained psychologist. She could spot even the most accomplished liar a mile away.

But this guy was good. Very good. She owed it to Julie to find out whatever she could about Sir Lancelot. She hoped he wouldn't become violent, but that possibility was all the more reason for her to find out all she could about this guy.

It might be dangerous. She knew how to deal with agitated patients. Besides, she had a can of mace in her purse.

"Why, yes, of course. I'd love to come up, Lancelot," she purred. "I could certainly use a drink."

If he tried to slip her anything, she would catch him red-handed. That would sure be worth the risk.

He smiled, and Peg tried to see if there was something else in his smile. Anything. But all she saw was a tired, very handsome man with a warm smile.

She changed her tactic, opting for the peppy friend routine.

"So, Lancelot, what did you do today? Catch a movie? Buy yourself some new clothes?"

They stepped onto the elevator, and he punched the button. "No. I worked at a homeless shelter."

"You what?"

Rubbing his eyes, he continued. "Over at the Avalon shelter in St. Anne's church basement. I helped out with lunch, choir rehearsal, and setting up dinner. I hope there will be enough cots for everyone."

"You're kidding!" They were on Julie's floor, and Peg followed him to the door. "You actually worked? Then what's the name of the shelter's director?"

"Bill Kowalski. Do you know him?" An eagerness came over him, making Peg feel uncomfortable. She shook her head. "He's a fine man. And the choir he's put together is quite good, especially some of the children."

"I've never heard of a homeless shelter with a choir," she admitted.

"It seems Avalon is the only one. But it makes sense, especially to hear Bill explain it."

The locks clicked, and they entered Julie's apartment. Lancelot stared out the large picture window for a moment, dusk over the city. "I wonder if I'll ever get used to being so high."

Peg followed his gaze, aware that she, too, had often had the exact same thought looking out that window.

"So." He put the keys on the kitchen counter. "The choir is to give the people a sense of belonging, of being part of a community. For the most part, they don't feel connected to anything in this city, they're disenfranchised, isolated. But when they sing, it's unique. Would you like a drink?"

For a long moment, she simply stared at him. "Excuse me?"

"You mentioned that you would like a drink. And so I offered you one."

"Oh, yeah. Sure. Maybe a vodka tonic with a twist?"

"Right," he said uncertainly. He opened the refrigerator door and began looking at bottles. "Coke. Orange soda. Spring water . . . tonic?" He read the label. "I'm afraid this isn't vodka tonic."

"You have to add the vodka."

A dawning expression passed over his face. "Oh? Interesting." He ducked back into the refrigerator. "Milk. Dairy-free cream. What is dairy-free cream? Let's see . . ."

"Um. I hate to bother you, but the vodka is usually in the liquor cabinet."

"Vodka is liquor?"

Was this guy for real? "Yes, Lancelot. Most people consider vodka a liquor. Here, I'll get it." She reached past him and pulled out the bottle.

He was still looking at labels. "Lady Peg, I believe Julia has run out of twist. There's not a single bottle of it in here."

"Run out of . . . oh, for God's sake. Okay, let's stop this little act right here. It's wasted on me anyway. I can see right through you."

Lancelot stared at her, then looked down at himself. "What manner of sorcery do you employ?" His arms were stretched out, as if he would float to the ceiling.

"What the hell are you talking about?"

"You can see through me. How is that possible without sorcery?"

"Without sorcery? Why, you big lug. You really think I'm stupid enough to fall for your tricks?" She tried to keep her voice calm, the fury in check. "I know exactly what you're up to. You see Julie as an easy target. Yes, she's lonely. But she's better off alone than with someone like you."

"Julia? Lonely?" It was as if he hadn't heard anything else she said. "How can someone as beautiful as Julia ever be lonely?"

"Come on. You saw a sad young woman and made the best of it, didn't you? Well, you chose well. Because you have her convinced that you're really Lancelot. And . . ." She crossed her arms. "Are you listening to me?"

"Yes, yes. Please continue." But his manner was distracted.

"I would like you to pay attention," she snapped, irritated by his behavior.

"Would you be offended if I sat down?" he asked, his voice hollow.

"Well, no, I don't think so."

She watched as he walked slowly across the room and sank into the sofa. Elbows on his knees, he rested his forehead against his clasped hands before looking up at her. "I never imagined her as lonely."

"Julie?"

He nodded.

"Of course, she was lonely. Most of us are."

"You, too?" There was genuine concern on his face, a flickering in his eyes that was pure compassion.

"Well, yes. I suppose so."

There was something wrong. This wasn't going the way she had expected it to go. "Are you all right?" Peg heard herself asking.

He looked at her, his gaze clear and direct. "Why must there be so much sadness? You, Julia, the people at Avalon. How can such misery be allowed?"

"Well, I never really thought about it." She settled on the couch next to him. "It's just the way things are, the way they have always been. It's the natural human condition." She smiled wryly. "Good thing, too. Or I'd be out of a job."

Lancelot closed his eyes. "That's not true. It's not

the natural human condition. Not at all. And it hasn't always been like this."

"You mean, it wasn't like this in Camelot."

He took a deep breath and opened those clear cornflower blue eyes, and Peg felt a strange fluttering inside her.

"No. It wasn't like this in Camelot."

"Tell me about it there. Tell me about Camelot."

Then he smiled. "I used to think it was the place that was so magical, Camelot. The flowers and the fragrances, the sparkle of the castle and the walls, the sky and the birds. And it is indeed a beautiful place. But I've only now realized, since coming here, that the real magic in Camelot lay within her people."

"I'm not sure I understand."

"There is no genuine heartbreak in Camelot."

"That's impossible. Everyone suffers. Everyone survives the suffering."

"But that's just it. Camelot is the one place where suffering is not necessary. It's obsolete. Rather, it's been rendered obsolete. But someone tried to introduce it to Arthur and Guinevere, and that's when the kingdom fell apart."

Peg stared at him in wonder. "You really believe in Camelot, don't you?"

"Yes. Now more than ever. I believe I needed to leave to restore my faith. In a strange way, I've never felt Camelot more keenly than I do at this moment."

The front door opened, and Julia, her face radiant

as she saw Lancelot, entered. She dropped the half dozen shopping bags.

"Hi, Peg," she said, her eyes on Lancelot.

Peg just watched, fascinated.

Slowly, he stood and walked toward Julie, his arms gently opening to take her. And she, too, moved to meet him. They did not seem to be creatures of this earth as they came closer, closer, and finally they met.

He embraced her with such tender ferocity that Peg heard herself gasp, and then she saw Julie's face, an expression of such sublime love and joy that Peg clenched her hands.

And then there was a strange hum, as if the world had become a single note, a tune. As Peg stared in astonishment, a mist seemed to encircle the two of them, twirling and flowing around their bodies, brilliant in its pure whiteness. It was as if a heavenly cloud had arrived to dance with two divine creatures.

Finally, their lips met, and Peg realized that what she was witnessing had nothing to do with her world. What she was watching was a little bit of Camelot.

17

Sam returned to the store with deposit slips poking from the pocket of his plaid shirt.

"Whew. Killer lines at the bank." Then he noticed the expression on his brother's face, the same expression of barely contained excitement that blew Aunt Bertha's surprise party on Staten Island last year. "What's up?"

"We are." Mel grinned. "We're up."

"You're making me nervous here."

"Let's just say that maybe I'm the one with the real customer pizzazz. Maybe I'm the one who should be up front."

"Oh, yeah?"

"Yeah. Guess who just got us five hundred bucks without selling a damn thing?"

"What are you talking about, Mel?"

With great flourish, he produced a handful of crumpled bills. "Viola," he announced.

Sam resisted the urge to mention that a viola is a large violin, and looked down at the money. "This stuff looks like it's seen better days. So, where did it come from?"

"This is the greatest idea of all time. Get this. The five hundred bucks is for a copy of a few pages of a manuscript. It was funny, the guy kept on slapping more bills on the counter. He thought I wanted more money, but I was just confused about why someone would pay so much for a plain paper copy. Straight from the fax machine, in fact."

"You're kidding!" Sam paused. "What manuscript?"

"This is the real coincidence. It's the same book we were looking at. You know, the sixteenth-century Italian text with the incantations. The Camelot book."

"Who took it? Was it the couple from the other night?"

"Nah. This is the other odd thing. The guy who was in here looked exactly like the gallant Malvern. Weird, eh? He said he was in here before and that you said you'd have more stock tomorrow. Why on earth did you tell him that? Aren't you the one who says never to disappoint a customer? That it's better to call up and tell him his order is early than to tell him it's late?"

Sam stared at the money. "He must have pawned the rest of her jewelry. What did you tell him? Did you mention the part about the physical link?"

"Calm down, Sammy. Yeah, of course, I mentioned it. Listen, I know there is some sort of contest thing going on. I hope I haven't messed up your chances."

"Contest?" He wiped the perspiration from his upper lip. "What contest?"

"The guy said there was a contest or tournament. Hey, what's going on here? Is this some sort of reenactment group?"

Sam shook his head. "It's complicated. I should have . . . Listen, Mel. If that guy comes back in here, do not give him anything. Absolutely nothing else. Copy or not, no matter how much he offers you, do not give him a shred of paper."

"Sammy, no contest is that important. You need to get a grip, Sammy boy."

"This isn't just a contest. It's crazy. You'd never believe me."

"Try."

Sam hesitated. His brother was the pragmatic one, the one who spent his summers in accelerated language courses while everyone else played. He'd have Sam locked up. But there was no way to keep this from him, not now.

"Okay, here goes," Sam began. "There was something I left out at Katz's. There *is* a Camelot. And those people have come from there, and they need to get back. This isn't just something to amuse me or a stage I'm going through. Somehow, Lancelot, Lady

Julia, and Malvern have slipped through time, something like that. They're all trying to get back there."

"You gotta be kidding."

"No. I'm serious."

"Then there is no contest?"

"Well, there's not a contest in the sense of sending in box tops or writing an essay. It's as if there's a competition, but that's not it, either. It's bigger, more important. Almost like a good-and-evil thing, and I've got a gut feeling that Malvern is not as gallant as we've always thought he is. I'm not sure exactly. Something's going on. I just can't figure it out."

Mel stared at his younger brother, uncomfortably aware of the improbability of the whole story and also aware that Sam was right. Something sure was going on. He could feel it, too.

"I got another text a few months ago," Mel blurted out.

Sam blinked. "Good. I'm happy for you. But back to the issue at hand."

"This is the issue at hand. I haven't translated it yet—it's Latin, and you know how Latin can drive me crazy. It was in all that junk I got at the estate sale in Buffalo."

"Oh, yeah. From that old vaudevillian guy."

"That's the one. Had an act in the thirties that went nowhere. He was heavily into the occult. Thought it might help his act."

"Wasn't he a tap-dancing ventriloquist?"

"Yep. The dummy was the tap dancer, that was his whole shtick. Anyway, this guy bought everything he could get his hands on."

"He should have bought tap-dancing lessons."

"Lucky for us he didn't, because one of his books was the earlier Latin version of the Italian Camelot text, the vulgate, if you will."

It took Sam a moment to follow the line of thought. "So? It's the same book in a different language. What's the big deal?"

"The big deal is that the Italian was just a translation of the genuine Latin. Let me put it this way. Any translation is only as good as the translator. It's an art form by itself. Remember that game we used to play as kids, Telephone? You go around a circle and see how the same little piece of information gets mangled with every retelling? Old manuscripts were like that. This wasn't printed material, it was done by hand. And without an original manuscript for comparison, you're at the mercy of the guy who translated."

"So?"

"So, I'm saying that I don't think the Italian was such a hot translator. I looked at the Latin, and even on a first once-over, it was clear there are nuances the Italian missed. Maybe he left them out on purpose, who knows? But there are significant differences."

"Such as?"

"Okay—just off the top of my head, the Italian

copy states that a physical link is needed to return to Camelot."

"Right. And it has to be something mystical."

"See? That's exactly what I mean. The Latin version is a little different. It states that not one but two links are needed."

"Two?"

"Yep. One physical, the other mystical. This is what I've been trying to tell you all along, Sammy. I don't think you appreciate my work. Sure, you're out front schmoozing with the customers. But what I do is also schmoozing, only I'm usually schmoozing with dead guys."

"Yeah, yeah. I know what you do is important. But what's this about two links? I thought there was only one."

"See, that's just it. The Italian either didn't catch this or deliberately omitted it, which would mean he did not want this information passed on to just anyone. You've got to remember that anyone who could read Latin back then was something of a scholar. Hell, anyone who could read anything back then was a scholar. But this guy may have been an elitist. Didn't want the wrong people to get hold of this, because he seems to have thought this was mighty powerful stuff. No matter. The upshot is that the incantations and the material items needed are different. Nothing radical, just in the subtleties."

"What else is different?"

"This is why Latin drives me crazy. Little things change the meanings. It's going to take a while to compare the texts side-by-side, line-by-line. This is a fine-tooth-comb thing we're talking. You've gotta give me some time."

"How much time?"

"I don't know." He scratched his neck as he thought. "About a week or two. That is, if I do nothing else."

"No good. We've got to get this done much sooner."

"What? Camelot can't wait two more weeks? Okay, okay. I'll get right on it and see how far I can get. But I've got to warn you, Latin drives me crazy. I might get real cranky."

"So what else is new?"

Finally, Mel smiled. "Okay. I'm not sure why I'm doing this, but okay. Oh, and Sam?"

"Yeah?"

"While I'm working on this, the take-out food's on you."

Peg grabbed the bottle of vodka and poured the entire remaining contents into her glass.

"Are you okay?" Julie asked as the glass rattled in Peg's grasp. Finally, she just put it on the coffee table, tilted against the edge of a book on Shaker furniture, where it spilled happily, soaking the book, the coffee table, and the carpet beneath.

"Sorry. So sorry," Peg muttered, blotting the mess with an already damp napkin.

"No problem."

Lancelot was in the bedroom resting, spent from a day of physical labor, spent from yet another day in this time and place.

"I can't believe this," Peg said with confusion. "I saw the room glow white with my own eyes. Did you see that?"

Julie lowered her gaze for a moment. "I didn't exactly see it."

"You didn't?"

"No. It's more as if I *feel* it. To tell you the truth, I didn't realize there was anything to see. It's just, well, it's just sort of there."

Hands trembling, Peg grabbed her oversized leather satchel and pulled out a pack of cigarettes. She stared at them, tapped the unopened end, then shoved them back into the dark depths. "I keep forgetting I quit."

Julie mopped up the rest of the spill with exaggerated care. "So, how are things with work?"

"Swell. Couldn't be better. Thank goodness for my sake there are a lot of psychologically ill people out there."

"Yeah. Thank goodness." She blotted the last drop in the corner.

"Julie, what's happening?"

Finally, she dropped the soaked napkin. "I don't know."

"Whatever you know is a hell of a lot more than what I know. So I'd really appreciate it if you'd fill me in."

"I've tried, Peg. Really, I have."

"And I've been unresponsive. Sorry. But can you blame me? I mean, I've been trained to help people get over their delusions. And then my old pal comes up with Sir Lancelot, and I'm expected to accept him as something other than a psychiatric case?"

"Of course, I understand. It took me a while to believe, and I was there."

Peg just stared at her for a long while, her expression blank. Julie half expected her to launch into another diatribe about the insanity of the whole notion.

Instead, she fumbled again with her backpack, located the cigarettes and a book of matches. With great deliberation, she lit the filter end before righting the cigarette, relighting it, and taking a long pull.

"Tell me."

"Tell you? About what?"

"About everything. Do you have an ashtray?"

Julie rose and returned with an old ashtray. "To tell you the truth, I don't feel quite comfortable telling you all of this."

"Why on earth not? Just because I've told you how mentally disturbed you've been, that Lancelot is a total psycho with sociopathic tendencies, and that you're clearly in the middle of a massive breakdown? Talk about thin-skinned."

"Well." She shrugged. "This is so deeply personal. I'm not sure if I can articulate it."

"Try."

Julie glanced up, and Peg snuffed out the length of her cigarette. "Please try to tell me. Because, Julie, you may be my last chance."

"Last chance?"

"Yes. My last chance to believe in anything. I mean, really believe, without clinical trials and placebos. I . . . it's something I've missed. Desperately. And for years, I've been looking for a way to get it back, the pure faith, the belief. Please. For my sake, please try to tell me."

Julie closed her eyes and tucked her feet beneath her. "It happened so swiftly. There was no transition. Not really. One moment, I was in the corridor of the restaurant. The next, there was this overwhelming fragrance."

"A fragrance?" Peg was surprised, and Julie looked at her.

She nodded, a smile curving her lips as she recalled the sensation. "It was a perfume, really, of fresh flowers and clean air. The only way I can really describe it, I think, is to say it was green. It was a fragrance of the light, pale green of springtime before everything blooms, when the buds are soft and delicate on the branch, almost white. That's what I smelled at first."

"And then?"

"I touched metal, the metal of his armor, and it was hot and vibrating. And then the scent of leather that had been seasoned with wear and the salt of perspiration. I opened my eyes and saw his helmet, and then his face. He spoke first, and he lifted his helmet, and there he was. His eyes this incredible shade of blue, his features, well, so strong, so full of life. And that was only the beginning."

Peg leaned forward and rested her chin on her palms. "Go on."

"Then there was Camelot."

"What was . . . what is it like?"

"It's a fairy-tale world. I don't know if I can explain it." She bit her lip for a moment, searching for the words. "It was a little like looking into a kaleidoscope. Bright colors twirling at every moment, never knowing what to expect next, shapes and colors and things you could never imagine in a million years."

"Do you think that was the place itself or the magic of being with Lancelot?"

Julie paused. Peg had just acknowledged Lancelot by his name. It was a relief and unsettling at the same time.

"Both, I think," Julie admitted. "I was overwhelmed by everything. I never knew what would be around the next corner or who would approach next."

"But what was your overall view of the experience? I mean, was it a good place or a bad place?"

"It was wonderful," she breathed. "Beautiful. It was the way I always hoped the world could be when I was a child. There was this incredibly strong sense of right—everything was right. And then there was King Arthur."

"You met King Arthur?"

"Yes. And Peg, you've never met anyone like him. It's as if a sense of justice shines from him like a beacon. And there was Guinevere and, of course, Malvern."

"Malvern! Oh, he was always my favorite! I used to have such a massive crush on him when I was a kid. Was he wonderful?"

"Wonderful? No. Not at all. He was absolutely horrible." She was about to tell her that he, too, was there, and that it had been Malvern who robbed her apartment, but she didn't.

"How can you say that? He was Arthur's most trusted knight. Just because, well, never mind."

"Just because what?"

"I was about to bring up the fact that Malvern discovered Lancelot had betrayed Arthur. So it makes sense that you would defend Lancelot. I see it all the time, women who fall in love with bad boys."

Julie shook her head and realized that Peg didn't understand, not in the least, in spite of her longing to do so. Perhaps she was asking too much of Peg, of anyone, to comprehend the whole story without actually experiencing Camelot.

"Well," Julie said at last, "I'm really beat."

"Oh, sure. Sorry." Peg looked at her watch. "Wow. It's past eight. I'd better head out." She stood up. "Do you have Nathan's book? I have to get it back to him as soon as possible."

"I don't believe this. Peg, I left it under my sofa at work."

"No problem. Nathan will literally kill me, but other than that . . ."

"Wait. How about if I send it by messenger first thing in the morning?"

"First thing? You promise?"

"Absolutely."

"Okay. Thanks. And Julie, thanks for telling me everything. It really helps."

Julie hugged her. "Oh, Peg, I know this is hard for you to understand, but maybe one day it will all make sense."

Peg returned the hug and was about to leave when she stopped. "One thing I don't quite get." She swung her backpack over her shoulder. "Why you? Why did you get to go there, to experience everything? I mean, there are so many people who would have given anything, *anything*, for that chance. I've loved the legend all my life, studied it. My thesis was on how Camelot has altered psychological perspectives through the centuries. But you, of all people. You . . ." She shook her head in confusion.

"I don't know, Peg. I honestly have no idea."

After Peg had left, Julie crossed her legs, hugged a pillow, and asked herself the same question.

By the next morning, Lancelot was running a fever.

It wasn't terribly high, and after Julie gave him aspirin, he seemed to feel much better. Still, it was just another indication that all was not well. He was not made for the late twentieth century.

"There is one comforting thought." He smiled. "Perhaps Malvern is faring as poorly as I am in this climate."

She returned the smile, aware that today he was looking even more worn, exhausted, and just plain ill. Yet he insisted on helping Bill at the shelter even as he continued his search for Malvern.

As she slipped on her jacket, thinking about Avalon and Lancelot working there, an idea came to her. "Lancelot, where does your friend Bill get the money to run the shelter?"

"Donations, mostly. And the city itself gives some amount of funding. But according to Bill, it's a week-by-week thing. This is the third church they've been in this year, simply because other needs arise. Why?"

"Well, this charity thing we're doing at work with the Shine-All people. One of the groups scheduled to perform has been forced to drop out. And didn't you mention there's a shelter choir?"

"Yes. And they are quite good."

"Maybe, just maybe, we can get the shelter in on this thing. All of the charities are going to split the proceeds evenly. It's sort of last-minute, but should I talk to Mr. Swenson about it?"

"Bill would appreciate it," he said, reaching for her hand. "And so would I."

Their fingers touched for just a moment, and then they pulled away from each other. Only later did Julie realize that he was every bit as apprehensive as she was, and every bit as uncertain about what the day would bring.

He watched as they left the tall building.

It had been surprisingly simple to follow their movements. And they had been foolish from the beginning, underestimating his resourcefulness.

Of course, he had been confused at first. Everything was so very different here, so loud and fast and hard-edged. But perhaps being alone honed his adapting skills, for in the matter of one short day, he had begun to understand the truth that had made the rest of the journey almost laughably simple.

Malvern had discovered that, unlike Camelot, this place was propelled by greed and desire. Compared to the people he saw on the streets or watched on the television box in the shelters he had slept in, he was a rank amateur. His modest aspiration, to return to Camelot and rule the kingdom, was admired here. They had names for what he wanted to do. Sometimes he thought it was called a takeover, but then he heard the word *politics*. Although he was not sure precisely how his own particular quest would best be labeled, he was certain he would be applauded for his success.

In a way, he wished he could stay here, in this time with these people. But the competition was too great. There were too many other Malverns, more accomplished than he could ever hope to be.

Besides, he was not feeling well. It had come on gradually, and he attributed the aches and the chills to the strange foods and climate. Luckily, he found the home of Julia almost immediately. A kind lady at the place where he had landed—a sort of banquet hall—had offered him a ride into the city and had generously told him about something called a telephone book. It had been such a simple matter of finding her home in the tall building and taking her jewelry.

What he had really wanted was Excalibur. For then, he would be celebrated upon his return, praised as the new king. And without Lancelot, Camelot would be ripe for his grasp. It could all be his. Everything. Even the queen.

That thought alone had made him smile, even while sleeping in strange places among strange people.

The two, Lancelot and his Lady Julia, were talking on the street. Now he did have a dilemma. Which one should he follow? Who would be more likely to lead him to Excalibur?

He looked over at Lancelot. He was not looking well, his old friend. Indeed, he was looking rather, how should he phrase it? Fragile. Yes. The mighty Lancelot appeared to be frail.

Not Lady Julia, however. She was looking quite enticing in her short dress. That was an improvement over Camelot. Legs. Everywhere he turned, there were women's legs. Especially her legs. For some reason, they were particularly nice. And if truth be known, it was far more enjoyable to follow her to her place of work than to trail Lancelot to his Avalon.

A sharp pang touched Malvern at the thought of Avalon. All that was good, all that was noble. Avalon and Camelot and Arthur.

But they would not have him! They didn't understand that all he had wanted was to be one of them, to be a part, to belong. That was all he had asked. And they denied it, all of them. They had robbed him of his right to be noble and good, so now he would have to go in another direction.

And with just a little luck, he could take all of Camelot with him . . . forever.

18

❦

It was as if Julie's office had become the Grand Central Station of the advertising world.

From the moment she arrived, the telephones had all but melted down from use, fax machines were spewing out page after page, messengers were coming and going with packages, and frantic assistants were waving the latest urgent note from whatever client or campaign needed the most attention at that precise moment.

Everyone, everything, seemed to need Julie. Right then. At that exact second. Or entire campaigns would collapse, and Stickley & Brush as they knew it, perhaps the universe itself, would cease to exist.

She had not even had a chance to sit down, literally. And even if there had been that spare instant, her chair and sofa were all piled high with unread faxes and promotional folders and boxes of the newest athletic equipment.

On top of everything else, the Shine-All people had

involved Julie in their big charity event so she could help them properly coordinate the new campaign with the event itself. It was now just days away. Along with her usual job run amok, she was suddenly fielding calls from newspapers and television reporters about the celebrities attending, names that were being added by the dozen, each jostling for extra attention and publicity.

As crazy as the day was, she managed to handle it all. The details she could not attend to herself she delegated to the assistants, young women dashing about the office, still in their sneakers from the walk to the office, and young men with pencils stuck behind their ears and wild-eyed stares.

When there was a brief lull, she added the Avalon shelter to the list of charities and had them included on the official list. That gesture alone gave her great satisfaction, as if both she and Lancelot were sharing one goal.

And then the phones began their buzzing, and more messengers and assistants waited for their orders, and she was once again consumed with the hectic pace of success.

Peg tried once again to reach Julie, and once again she was put on hold listening to bad "lite" rock, only to be informed eventually by yet another breathless person that Julie was engaged in another vital meeting.

She slammed down the telephone, frustrated and annoyed. She had managed to sleep only a few hours the night before, haunted by what had happened, the strange light she had seen Lancelot and Julie evoke.

Now she couldn't even reach Julie, while her whole life had been turned upside-down by all of the inexplicable events. Her friend Julie had not only visited Camelot but had brought back Lancelot as a souvenir.

Then, in the middle of the night, she remembered the sword. Lancelot had called it Excalibur. Had it *really* been Excalibur? That was all Peg wanted to know, but she couldn't reach Julie to ask that one simple question. Or to see if Nathan's comic book had been sent as promised.

Meanwhile, Peg herself was such a wreck that she canceled all of the day's appointments. There was no way she could listen to Mrs. Gibbons complain about her daughter-in-law's housekeeping, or hear about Mr. Murdoch's dilemma with his imaginary companion, Binky. Not only would she be unable to focus, but she knew if any of her patients had the slightest notion of what their therapist was going through, they would undoubtedly urge her to seek help.

And there was something else, something of which she was not proud. Deep down, she was jealous of Julie. Jealous because her friend had experienced something so incredible that it defied all reason and logic. Jealous because she could not figure out why Julie had been offered this opportunity and Peg had not. In short, Peg was envious because her closest friend had been handed a chance that she could only dream about.

Plus, she had come out of the whole wondrous trip with Sir Lancelot. Granted, Lancelot was not exactly the most romantic of choices. Still, she had to admit he was charming, far more so than any of the stories had ever indicated. In fact, he did not seem the least bit dastardly. Above all, Julie seemed blissfully happy with him, although there was clearly something bothering them both.

Still, Julie had made the most of an amazing twist of fate. So that left a simple question. What was Peg's destiny? Was she to spend the rest of her life listening to other people's problems and glories, never to have anything of her own? Was she destined to experience life second-hand, adventures retold?

Peg had to get out of her apartment, to take a walk. She needed to seek the anwers to the one question she had always asked herself.

Is this all there is?

The homeless trickled into Avalon in a steady stream, not so very impressive until it hadn't stopped and Bill realized there was no more room. It was time to start turning people away—the one thing he dreaded most. And this was only lunch.

At least, Lancelot had been there to help. And that idea of the Shine-All City charity event was nothing short of spectacular, if they could really pull it off.

He'd been reading about it in the papers but had no idea there was any way to get involved. That guy had already been more help than all of the other volunteers combined. He had left just moments ago but would return later.

More people arrived, and he realized he would have to use some of the food stored for tomorrow. Well, that was another day. He'd deal with it then.

"Over there, Frank. There's an extra dozen cans in the box by the corner. Yeah, you've got it. And you know where the can opener is."

It was getting so that he could give the orders in his sleep. And while that was helpful and made life easier, he was beginning to wonder if he was on the verge of accepting the idea of homelessness. He no longer felt the urge to fight the condition. Instead, he just dealt with it.

"Hello, Wilma. Nice to see you."

There had to be something else, someplace where he would make a difference and be able to see it. At times, he even wondered if it was really a help to these people to have a warm, dry place to sleep. It was a short-term cure, not a genuine solution. What if the very existence of this shelter prevented them from seeking a better life? What if it kept them from having permanent homes?

And when his thoughts turned in that direction, he always scolded himself. Most of these people had multiple problems and were in this situation through no fault of their own. It was like blaming a patient for contracting a disease.

"We'll have a short practice tonight, guys," he announced. "And I may have some exciting news."

Who was he kidding? They didn't care about the choir, about singing the stupid arrangements he had created with his Juilliard-trained ego.

It must be torture for the people, literally to have to sing for their supper. It did nothing to raise their self-esteem or create a sense of community. He was simply putting them through a trial before they were allowed to eat.

He glanced around the room, his gaze resting on that new guy, Vern, who had just arrived. There was something unsettling about the man. It wasn't his clothing, since he was better dressed than most of the others, including Bill himself. There was something else about him that was disturbing.

It was probably a case of running the shelter for too long. Probably just a case of reality. He no longer saw people as individuals but as open hands begging for help.

When did he start having these thoughts?

He glanced away from Vern. And when he did, a strange thought came to him; he only felt true despair when he was there. At all other times, no matter how tired he was, no matter how short-handed, he felt a sense of joy when he knew he was helping people. His personal life was nonexistent, he lived in a single room in the Bowery across from a man who collected live chickens, and yet he had considered himself happy. That is, until recently.

In fact, the one place he felt sure of himself was there, at Avalon. Only recently, with the arrival of Vern, the guy with the beard and the unpleasant eyes, did he begin to doubt himself and the way he had lived his life for the past decade.

He wanted Lancelot to meet Vern, to see if he had any vibes. But they never seemed to be there at the same time. Vern arrived just as Lancelot left, or vanished as Lancelot arrived. Bill watched as others reacted to him, scooting over so they would not be close, averting their eyes when he looked in their direction.

It was as if the new guy had the magical ability to suck every ounce of positive energy from the room.

And as Bill was mulling those thoughts, Vern was watching him, an odd smile twisted on his lips.

"Okay, everyone," Bill announced. "There's enough for all of you, no need to push."

Still, Vern just sat and watched.

And waited.

Lancelot entered the chaos of Julie's office with mild amusement.

"I'm so sorry," she said, hand cupping the end of the phone. "I don't think I'm going to be able to . . ." Then she held up her finger and spoke into the receiver. "Hello? Yes. Of course, we can look into it right away. We'll need added security if they are coming. They do? Great! Just a minute."

She turned back to Lancelot. "I'm so sorry, but there's absolutely no way I can get away right now. I thought I might, but . . ."

He nodded, just as a harried-looking young man with oversized sketches pushed past.

"Sorry. Um, Julie? Here are the preliminaries for the Shine-All print ads. When you get a chance, can you . . ."

She gestured for him to come closer. She flipped through the sketches, then scribbled her signature before returning to the phone call.

Lancelot turned to walk away.

"Wait! Just a moment." Again, she cupped her hand over the phone. "Sam called this morning and says he has some new information down at the store. I thought we could go together, but I don't know when I'll get away from here."

"I'll go, then."

"Do you mind? I'm so sorry about . . . hello?"

With an apologetic shrug, she got back to work and her calls.

Lancelot made his way through the office, sidestepping the Rollerblading messenger and picking up the stack of papers a young woman with a cup of hot coffee had just dropped.

As he rode down the elevator, he was very much

aware of two things. One, he was not feeling well. Indeed, he was so exhausted he needed to sit down. And two, he did not belong there. Not in her office, certainly not in her time, and perhaps not even in her life.

For her sake, he had to decide what to do next.

Peg had been walking for hours without being aware of where she was going.

It was a cleansing walk, something she needed to do in order to clear her mind. And as she strolled, the sights and sounds of the city presented themselves as only mild distractions, interesting only in their fleeting presence. Then she could go back to herself, a topic she had managed to avoid for far too long.

Pausing at a streetlight, waiting for it to change, she took a deep breath and looked around. Somehow she was in the Village.

She had just walked more than ninety blocks!

That knowledge pleased her for some reason. Ninety refreshing blocks. Now she was in familiar territory, in the East Village, where all of her favorite funky stores were. She couldn't have planned it any better. What a perfect place on a warm spring day.

She turned left instead of crossing the street. Cauldrons & Skulls was less than half a block away. In the mood to poke around among old books and bottles, she thought someone there might have more information on Camelot. She hestiated just a moment.

Had she remembered to bring the wallet with her credit cards?

Looking down, she began to rifle through her purse and saw the right wallet, and then . . . she looked up and saw him.

More important, he saw her.

"Hello." She smiled. She knew this man. In the jumble of her thoughts, she couldn't recall how she knew him, she just did.

He seemed busy, with a couple of oversized books under his arms.

He nodded once and tried to pass right by her.

"Wait a moment!"

But instead of waiting, he kept walking.

Perplexed, she saw him turn a corner at such a brisk pace that he was all but jogging.

Where had she seen him before?

Then it hit her, the proverbial ton of bricks. It was the gallant Malvern! The very same man she had spent her adolescence dreaming about—that is, until she discovered Mel Gibson.

Well, she wasn't going to let him get away. He must have come from Camelot, along with Julie and Lancelot. And then another thought crossed her mind.

What if he was there for her, the way Lancelot was there for Julie!

It made so much sense that she didn't want to think about it any further, for fear that it would no longer make so much sense. Too often, she had allowed her sensible side to choose the path. Too often, she had missed out on adventure and excitement. For once, she was not going to play it safe.

It took only an instant for her to decide. And for the first time in her life, Peg did something impetuous and romantic.

With a thrill of pure delight, she followed the gallant Malvern. She followed him, hoping against all reason that he would lead her to her own destiny.

Lancelot sensed something was wrong the moment he saw the shop door swinging on its hinges, the bells tinkling softly overhead.

He stepped softly, not wanting to startle anyone who may have been inside. There was no one behind the counter, no sound other than the bells. Carefully, he separated the beaded curtains and crept into the back room.

It took a moment for his eyes to adjust to the darkness, and then he saw the crumpled form of one of the brothers.

In one large bound, he was at his side, gently touching his shoulder.

The man began to stir.

"Be easy," Lancelot whispered. "I'm going to see if I can catch who did this."

He patted the shoulder and began to stand, when the man moaned, "Oh, my head."

"Please remain silent."

Then he moaned in a louder voice. "My head!"

"I know, someone must have hit you . . ."

"Someone? I know exactly who did this. Wait until I get ahold of that cartoon guy."

Mel sat up, holding his head, gingerly testing to see if there was any blood. With only very slight disappointment, he shrugged and began to rise to his feet.

Lancelot had checked the back room, and, as he suspected, there was no one there. "Here, let me help you."

When Mel was settled back in the chair by the desk, he patted the empty surface.

"He took them. He took them both."

Lancelot was about to ask what was taken when the bells jingled in the front.

"Mel? You back there?"

"Yeah, Sam."

Then Sam appeared with a large white bag with grease stains just forming on the sides. "I got you the extra sauce for the—" Then he saw Lancelot and the way Mel was cupping the side of his head. "What's going on?"

Lancelot began, "I just arrived, and the door was open. Your brother seems to have been injured by a thief."

"What?"

Mel nodded. "Yeah. He's right. It was that Malvern guy, and he came in here all nice and pleasant, asked how I was and if the books had arrived yet. Then next thing I knew, I was on the ground, and Lancelot here was saying it was all right."

"You okay?"

Mel shrugged. "I'm not bleeding. I'm just beginning to feel the way I did on New Year's Day in seventy-nine."

Sam winced. "Ouch. Wait a second. I've got some ice in here for the celery tonic." He began to gather ice in a napkin and handed it to his brother.

Then he paused, hands on his hips, and surveyed the room, the large, empty desk with the magnifying glass pushed to the side, the jeweler's glass on the floor. He shook his head. "He got them, then." He bent over and put the jeweler's glass back on the desk.

"Sure did."

"What did he get?" Lancelot asked.

"The Latin and Italian texts." Sam closed his eyes for a moment. "Damn." He shook his head once more, then looked right at Lancelot. "Mel was translating some old texts. They were the ones on Camelot. The ones with the incantations and spells about how to return."

Lancelot looked at both brothers, then turned to Mel. "Do you recall any of the details?"

Mel shrugged. "I was just beginning to make sense of the Latin. It was all a jumble, a real mess, and then I was on the verge of a real breakthrough. Between the two texts, there was a common thread that was just beginning to emerge."

"Remember what it was?" Sam asked eagerly.

"Nah. I would have had it in another twenty minutes. I swear I would have. But no. I saw the pattern, but I didn't have time to figure it out."

Sam rubbed his eyes, then looked at Lancelot with hope. "Hey, does Malvern know Latin?"

Lancelot nodded. "I'm afraid it was part of our early training. We all know Latin."

"How about Italian?" Mel offered.

"I don't know. It was certainly not required, although some of the other knights had language skills. Of Malvern, I am not certain."

Mel smiled. "This may not be so bad. As I was going over these texts, I realized the Italian was not meant as a simple translation of the Latin. It was not just a matter of nuances. I'm pretty sure that they were meant to be used together. One would not work by itself—the other version was needed to complete it. If he doesn't know Italian, then he has only half of the stuff he needs."

"What about the English translations?" Sam asked.

"Never got around to writing them all down. He may have some of them, but not all, and certainly he would not know where the translations came from, what part of the book. So this may not be so bad."

A vague sense of cautious optimism was beginning to surface. And suddenly, Sam snapped his fingers. "Mel! I've just thought of something. Remember a few years ago we went to that New Age conference in California?"

"Don't remind me. What a bunch of fruitcakes."

"Yeah, but remember that professor from Columbia? He gave you his card. Said he was teaching a course on magic and mythology or something. It's a long shot, but maybe we could give him a call. He might know something."

"Oh! Nice old guy. Sure, where did I put that damn card? I usually shove them all in this little side drawer here. Can you shine the light this way, Sammy? Okay, here we go." He began to thumb through a stack of torn, yellowed business cards, some with cross-outs, handwritten numbers scribbled on the sides. "Here we go. I . . ." He blinked and held the card closer. "This is impossible."

"What? Did you find it?"

"Yeah, yeah. But this is impossible. I would have remembered. Hell, *you* probably would have remembered." Then he looked at both men, a strange, puzzled smile on his face. "The man's name is Professor Ralph Myrddin."

Lancelot slowly uncrossed his large arms, and Sam took a moment to understand. "As in the book?"

"As in the book," Mel confirmed. Then he pointed to the white bag. "Did you say you got extra sauce?"

19

The day before the Shine-All City Charity Gala, there was so much breathless press coverage that some people were convinced it had already happened.

There were columns on who was wearing what, designed by whom, accessorized with what jewels on loan from Harry Winston or Cartier or some recently deceased fabulous person's estate. There were gossip tidbits on what couples were going together, who would be sitting at what table of fellow celebrities, and who would be trying to avoid whom under the glare of overhead lights and the flash of the paparazzi.

Actors, actresses, rock stars, models, producers, writers, directors, titans of business, and celebrities of the moment were all descending upon Manhattan, all touting their pet causes or at the very least their upcoming projects. In short, the glittering world of fame and fortune was consumed with elaborate preparation for this single event.

One columnist likened the gathering to Mrs. Astor beckoning the fortunate four hundred who could fit into her legendary ballroom in the last century. But that notion was contradicted by a rival columnist who stated flatly that, as a whole, this group was far better-looking than Mrs. Astor's fleshy ton, and furthermore, this was a charity event. So these far-better-looking folks were actually doing some good with their money, besides supporting the piggyback industries that kept them so darned good-looking, such as plastic surgeons, personal trainers, nutritionists, the fashion industry, and the various clinics and detox centers.

It made the city as a whole feel good to think of itself as one big handsome do-gooder, and the mayor of New York jumped on that idea, stating with characteristic smug flair that New York at that moment was, indeed, the center of the universe.

Very few people disputed that point when it was learned that Madonna herself would be dressed as Guinevere, and Donald Trump, without consulting Madonna, was being fitted for a splendid King Arthur costume.

And then there was the rumor that a Kennedy—no one was quite sure which one—was going to auction a rare piece of JFK memorabilia. It was all in keeping with the Camelot theme, and everyone was supremely confident that whatever the mystery item to be auctioned was, it would be in the best possible taste.

No one could wait until the evening itself arrived. No one.

*   *   *

Julie had been trying to reach Peg but with no luck. She assumed Peg was simply embarrassed. After all, she had confessed a lot the other day about her dreams. It must not have been easy.

It was incredibly early to be going into the office, although if she had never gone to sleep, she still would have been hard-pressed to get everything done. They'd all worked late, and she'd be the first one in this morning. It was only fair, really.

The security guard waved her on, and she held up her employee card after he had already returned to his tabloid paper and doughnut. Some security. She smiled as she entered the elevator.

Although it was early, not speaking to Peg was really bothering her. She'd give her a call the moment she got into her office. There was so much to tell her, about that professor at Columbia. Although they had not been able to reach him by telephone, and even the switchboard at Columbia couldn't get through, she was going over later that afternoon with Lancelot to see what they could discover. He might really be the same guy who did the comic book.

And Peg didn't know anything about the texts being stolen or the importance of the Italian and Latin. She even wanted to let Peg know about how well Lancelot was doing with the people at the shelter.

He'd been helping the choir, coordinating their little five-minute stint at the gala.

There was just so much to tell. Hang it if it was barely five-thirty in the morning. The moment she got to her desk, she was going to call . . .

There was something very wrong.

She felt it the instant she stepped off the elevator. The doors closed behind her before she could step back, and she began pushing the down button, hoping another elevator would arrive soon. Because even from where she stood, she could see that someone had been in there.

The couches in the reception area had been torn open, the glass behind the floor plants shattered. Even the plants themselves had been pulled up from the roots and tossed across the lobby.

A *ping* announced the arrival of the elevator, and Julie pounded the close button, not unclenching her hands until the doors had shut and she was on her way back to the lobby.

All thoughts of calling Peg had vanished for the time being.

Lancelot and Julie took one more look at the card with the address of Professor Myrddin.

"This must be it," she said, glancing at the building on the campus of Columbia University. "I don't know why, but I'm nervous. I mean, if he's the same guy who wrote and illustrated the book, he'll recognize us right away. And he probably won't be too thrilled, either."

They entered the strange building with "Arts, Humanity, and Mystery" etched over the doorway. "Weird," she mumbled.

Lancelot smiled. She was keenly aware that he was not feeling well. In fact, he would have been much better back at the apartment, but he had insisted on coming with her. Sam and Mel had also wanted to join them, but they had to fill out insurance forms and complete the police interview from the robbery. Mel's injury was considered an assault, so the police were treating the crime seriously.

And even as Lancelot and Julie had gone uptown, the police were examining the crime scene at Stickley & Brush.

"This is it. Number seven," he said as they stopped in front of a small door. In gold lettering, it read, "Professor Ralph Myrddin." But the door was so tiny, unlike the other offices or classrooms, that it seemed impossible that anything other than a broom closet could possibly exist in that space.

Lancelot glanced at her, then knocked once. There was no answer. He was about to knock again when the door flew open.

"I've been expecting you," he said, an unlit pipe clenched between his teeth.

"Merlin!" Julie shouted. It was him, the same bulbous nose, the pinkish skull dotted with tufts of cottony white hair. Now he was wearing a battered tweed jacket and a moth-eaten sweater underneath, but there was no mistaking the identity of the man before her.

It was Merlin.

Lancelot just stared at him. "I do not understand."

A couple of students came down the corridor, and Merlin opened his door wide. "Both of you, come in here."

Amazingly, his office was precisely the same as she remembered his home in Camelot, complete with a long, heavy table topped with various boiling beakers, another table filled with ancient-looking books of crumbling parchment. And in the corner, chattering between seeds, was a parrot.

"Charo," Julie mumbled.

"Sir Lancelot, please sit down," he offered, and with only a slight hesitation, Lancelot sank into a deep chair.

Julie turned from the parrot, recovered enough to ask questions. "Merlin, what's happening? There is so much to tell you, I don't even know where to begin."

"I know, my dear, I know. You did the best you could. Would you like a biscuit?"

The bird let out a single screech, and Merlin whirled around. "Not you, silly thing. I meant our guests." Then he looked at Lancelot with a brief expression of pity in his eyes and turned again to Julie. "But how are you, my dear? I'm afraid I've put you through a terrible ordeal."

"Well, I've—" Then she stopped. "*You* did this? This was all your idea?"

"Please sit down. You make me nervous standing there. Thank you." He sat down in his own chair, the same battered furniture she recalled from Camelot.

"What do you mean, you've put us through an ordeal?"

His mouth rotated around the bite of the pipe before he answered in his gloriously British, BBC Shakespeare voice. "It was I, as a young sorcerer, who created the whole notion of Camelot."

"You created Camelot?" Lancelot all but shouted.

"Yes, I did. You see, the world was in a dreadful mess at that time. And—"

"What time?" she interrupted. "When did you create Camelot?"

"Oh, let me see, I was very young. Very young indeed. I suppose it was about"—he counted back on his fingers—"yes, that was it. About two thousand years ago."

"Two thousand years!" She dropped her purse on the floor.

Lancelot shook his head. "But that's impossible. Arthur himself told me that Camelot had only been in existence since he became the true king."

"Ah, he would say that, wouldn't he? He wouldn't be much of a king if he felt otherwise. But Arthur is wrong, although Camelot, as we all know it, as the world knows it, did indeed begin with Arthur. But before that, it was in an earlier form. So, yes, I began it about two thousand years ago, but you see, it's still very much a work in progress."

Lancelot said nothing, but Julie could see his obvious anger. Merlin, however, seemed oblivious. "I take whatever I like from whatever time strikes my fancy. I should have thought you would have noticed my cell phone back in Camelot. I tried to hide it, but it began to ring just as I asked you to leave."

"A cell phone . . ." She mulled over the idea. "A telephone. Is that how Lancelot and Guinevere's voices were on my answering machine?"

"Of course. I have to use whatever tools are available. In earlier times, if I wanted to get someone's attention, I would use Morse code, the Pony Express. Once I tried smoke signals, but that was an utter disaster."

Merlin winked and went on with his story. "But you see, as I was such a very young wizard at the time I came up with Camelot, there were glaring imperfections in my creation. For example, the whole notion of Arthur and Guinevere was never supposed to have become a romance."

"Really?"

The anger left Lancelot's face for a moment as he leaned forward to hear the explanation.

Merlin went on. "No, indeed. She was to be the one for me, you see. I wanted a companion, so I cast a few spells and came up with Guinevere."

"What went wrong?" Lancelot asked in spite of himself.

"Well, you must understand that for every spell I cast, there is a fifteen-percent chance that something unpredictable will occur and throw off the whole works. In this case, I made Guinevere a woman with spine, a woman of passion and intelligence."

"And?"

"Unfortunately, with the intelligence came a free will. She saw Arthur. I really thought that beard would put her off. It didn't. I tried to toy with the formula, just as Lancelot came to me."

"I came to you?" He stood, towering over Merlin, who remained in the chair. "You made me up? I am nothing but the invention of a meddling old wizard?"

Julie rose and placed her hand on his forearm, but he did not even glance at her.

Merlin merely took a pull from his pipe. "Perhaps I should phrase it differently. I recruited Lancelot. When I say he came to me, I mean he literally happened upon me. Don't you remember, lad? The darkness, the mist. The hunger. Goodness, you were the most hungry child I had ever seen."

"Recruited?" Lancelot sat back down, stunned. "From where? Where did I come from?"

"It doesn't really matter, dear boy. It can make no difference to you anymore. But you see, I couldn't possibly create an entire Camelot using only my own imagination. It would be so very dull. Imagine making up hundreds of people. After a while, say three or four, you're reduced to repeating yourself. Do you see what I mean?"

"So Lancelot came from someplace else," Julie said softly. "Just like the rest of us."

Lancelot shook his head. "There was nothing special about me after all. Nothing at all. There is no reason to fight for my honor, to clear my name, because it makes no difference."

"Of course it does!" Merlin sputtered. "You are Lancelot, the best of the best. I could never have created you. Not that you're perfect—that would be dull as well. But your qualities never cease to amaze me. I believe you're my very favorite of the whole batch."

"Then why are you making him suffer so?"

"That uncertain fifteen percent, my dear. It happened when Guinevere fell in love with him." He removed the pipe, thinking to himself. "In all honesty, I just don't work with women as well as I do with men. They tend to be shallow, one-dimensional things when I get through with them. They always look absolutely smashing in a gown, and they always have superb legs—that's my trademark. I'm a leg man. But there's always something missing. In Guinevere, she was intelligent but too passionate. So when she met Lancelot, well. In the original version that you know so well, my dear, you know what happened. That pesky fifteen percent kicked me right in my teeth. And there wasn't a blasted thing I could do about it . . . until you."

"Me?"

"Yes, my dear. Before I recruited Lancelot, he was in love with you. That was the perfect love I had envisioned for him. I couldn't create it myself. You two worked the magic, and I just sat back and watched."

Julie felt as if the world were spinning. "Lancelot and I were reincarnated?"

Merlin barked with laughter. "Do you believe in that rubbish?"

Julie shook her head at the absurdity of the moment. "Me? Of course not."

"Good. You began to worry me for a moment, my dear. No, you two are not reincarnated. But you have always been together, reaching for each other. The problem was, every time things would be just right between you, something would happen. Always the same thing, or a variation. You know only one of the versions. Well, two now, thanks to my work in the late thirties. I believe it holds up rather well, don't you?"

"So you *are* the author of that comic book." She ran her hand through her hair, trying to absorb everything that was being said.

"Of course I am. There aren't too many Ralph Myrddins running about. Oh, sorry about that crone thing. And I believe you two are aware of two more of my lesser-known publishing efforts."

Julie and Lancelot exchanged perplexed shrugs.

"The Italian and Latin texts that Malvern stole. Don't tell me you've forgotten them already."

"You wrote them!" Julie laughed. "Then you can tell us what they say, and Lancelot can take Excalibur back and clear his name!"

"Well, I'm not so sure about that," Merlin admitted.

"What do you mean?" Lancelot asked, his voice rising.

"There's more to it than just words. Surely, you both must know that by now. If not, well, I'm afraid there will soon be another version of Camelot, one with an equally unhappy ending."

"You have to give us more than this," Julie pleaded. "It's not fair! How many other ways can this story end?"

"I believe you know, my dear. You were always skipping off, leaving Lancelot heartbroken. Let me tell you, Lancelot is close to worthless when you go away. If I had a coin for every monastery I've had to rescue him from . . ."

"Monastery!" Lancelot shouted.

Julie continued. "Please, Merlin. Please give us more so we can save Camelot."

He stopped, then leaned forward. "By jig, you really don't know, do you?"

"No. So could you please tell me?"

Merlin put down his pipe and leaned forward,

looking Julie directly in the eye. "In order to return to Camelot, you both will need one thing you have held but given away, and another that you have held but never known."

"Excuse me?" she asked.

"I will not repeat it. That is all I can say. That fifteen percent, you see. And we're so close this time, my dear. It would be such a shame."

"Please, I'm not sure if I remember what you said." Julie was beginning to get frantic. "And Lancelot. Can't you see? He's not feeling well. He's, well . . ."

"I'm aging." Lancelot completed her thought. "Every day seems to be years, decades. It's happening faster and faster. How much time do I have?"

Merlin counted on his fingers again, muttered to himself, then counted some more and looked to the ceiling. Then he faced her. "When is that charity ball?"

"Tomorrow. Why?"

"And it's not outdoors, is it?"

"Why, no, it isn't."

"Good thing. We don't have time for a rain date, my dear."

"You mean he won't be able to live here much longer than tomorrow?"

For the first time since they had entered his office, Merlin's face, the kind folds and lines, became genuinely sad, a mask of sorrow. "I am so sorry. When I created Camelot, when I was so very young, I thought I'd be very clever and add some rules. Unfortunately, I was a good

enough sorcerer even then to make them unbreakable—
even by my own hand and deepest wishes."

"Then tell me what I need to do. Tell me now,
Merlin. There isn't much time. Please tell me."

"I can't. I've set things in motion, I've set up the
playing field, and there is no reason to believe that it
will go mucky once again."

"Can you give me anything else? Something to
hold onto?"

"Other than what I said, there is nothing that can
help you but yourselves."

Julie just stared at Merlin. "I . . . please." Lancelot
took her hand, but she did not want to leave. Not
without more. "Please tell me what to do!"

"You'll know. You always do. Figure out what I
told you."

"But I always seem to screw things up! Why else
would we be here right now?"

"I must admit, my dear, there is a very strong
element of truth in what you say."

Lancelot took a deep breath and nodded to Merlin, a vague smile on his lips. But Julie began looking
around the office, imprinting it in her mind in case
there was something, anything, that might help her . . .
help Lancelot. On a deep chair, she saw books. As
Merlin reached for her purse and handed it to her,
Julie peered at the names on top of them.

"Jane Austen?" She faltered. "Mark Twain?"

Again, Merlin chuckled. "Of course, my dear.

With Camelot almost done, I have to think up other ways to amuse myself. Besides"——he leaned close to her ear——"you don't really think two mortals could ever come up with all those ideas, do you? Now, be gone, the two of you. And Julia?"

She turned to him, still stunned by the encounter. "Good luck, my dear. I hope to see you at home soon, very soon."

They left the office, and suddenly Julie had another thought. "Wait a moment . . ." But the door was closed. No, it was more than closed.

It was gone.

Where the office door with its sign and room number had once been, now there was an undistinguished little door with "Broom Closet" stenciled across the top. Julie grasped the knob and turned, and the door opened, to reveal . . . a broom closet. There were buckets and mops and the scent of cleanser.

And they knew they were truly on their own now. No one else could help them.

There were two messages on Julie's machine when they returned. The first was from Sam. Interesting news from the police: the same fingerprints that were all over Cauldrons & Skulls also appeared at a crime scene in midtown. An advertising agency had been broken into and ransacked, although it was uncertain if anything had been taken. The prints, however, were not on record.

Julie shook her head, still trying to remember Merlin's words even as she listened to the machine. "So it was Malvern. Why would he break into my office?"

Lancelot sat down. "I do not know. Unless . . ."

"Unless?"

"I do not know," he repeated.

The next message was muffled at first, and then Julie recognized the voice and turned to Lancelot. "Peg." She identified the speaker, but it was hard to understand her words, for she was crying.

"Julie, Lancelot, please forgive me. I'm so sorry . . . I didn't realize what I was doing, who he was. I followed him. He acted as if he was interested in me in a romantic way. You know how long I've . . ." She sniffed, then began again. "Julie, please be careful. He's not right. I thought he would be so different, and once I realized how malicious he was, it was too late. He didn't hurt me, but he got a lot of information from me before I realized what he was doing and what he was really like. And then I read about the break-in at the agency, and I remembered how he thought the sword was in your office. He must know where it is now—it's all over the press. Please, please, forgive me. And please, for God's sake, be careful . . ."

Then her voice drifted off. Julie tried to call her back immediately, but there was no response.

And Lancelot said only one word. "Malvern."

20

❧

*T*he day had finally arrived.

Most of the city was anticipating a glorious stream of celebrity arrivals on the red-carpeted steps of the Metropolitan Museum of Art, with live television coverage beginning at four in the afternoon. The blue police barricades were put in place early that morning, and a large royal-blue silk banner was unfurled over the main entranceway. Fifth Avenue itself was swept clean of stray newspapers, rolling cans, and unsightly debris of any kind, human as well as the more inanimate forms.

In her apartment downtown, Julie prepared for a far more significant event. For others, this would be a spectacular gala, a chance to see and be seen, the social affair of the year and the glittering East Coast rival of the Oscars.

For Julia and Lancelot, it would be a chance to

save Camelot, perhaps the only hope they had for a life together.

After seeing Merlin the day before, she realized what she had known instinctively, that Lancelot had been fading in this time, ebbing away into oblivion, and that whether or not she followed him, Lancelot had to go back to Camelot. There was no choice for him, absolutely none. Just as that one simple fact was drawn with such clarity, her own role was still unclear.

Would she know what to do when the time came? Would she let them down—Lancelot, Merlin, everyone?

One thing was certain. If nothing else, Dr. Peg Reilly was changed forever. She had said little after the encounter with Malvern, and Julie suspected she would never say more. But later she had called asking if there were any possible way she could come to the gala. It hadn't been easy, she had to call in a few favors, but Peg was now an officially invited guest.

Julie sighed as she got dressed. She would need all the moral support she could get.

"Do you need any help?" she asked Lancelot.

He just shook his head no.

There was a strained understanding between them. It was so obvious that he was unwell, so impossible to deny, that they did not discuss it anymore. There was no point, not really. It was a fact, just as indisputable as the color of the sky or the day of the week.

She did everything possible to keep their moments together from taking on the dynamics of caretaker and invalid. But it became increasingly difficult, and she had to stop herself from supporting him as he took halting steps, from watching with concern as he dressed.

With a brisk smile, she returned to her own preparations.

There was no doubt what she would wear. There was only one option, and that was the blue gown from Camelot, the one she had worn both there and when she returned.

As she slipped it over her head, she felt like a high school senior before the prom. And then, as she watched before her mirror, a strange thing happened. The gown itself changed. In the moments from the hanger to her body, it went from the beautiful dress she had worn in Camelot to something truly extraordinary.

She stepped back from the full-length mirror to get a better view. The basic lines of the dress were unaltered. It was still a stunningly cut, rather simple, yet wonderfully executed gown of deep powder blue. What was so different?

Running her hands down her sides, she watched a shimmering effect as her hands passed over her hips, like a finger trailing in a cool green pool of water. Then she saw it, the difference.

It wasn't the gown. It was Julie. She seemed to have an inner radiance, a luster that made even her skin reflect light. She turned on another light, an unforgiving overhead globe that she always flicked on when she had a perverse desire to see her physical flaws at their most glaring.

Still, she remained a vaguely luminous creature. Had she put those pearls in her hair? She couldn't recall. Had her hair been that long, halfway down her back? Surely, she would have remembered, even with all of the recent distractions, if her hair had suddenly grown almost twenty-four inches and her skin had started to glow. Those weren't the sort of changes one usually missed.

"Julia."

He stood behind her, Lancelot, again in the blue tunic he had worn when first she saw him. And he, too, was changed, as if the mere act of wearing the clothes in which he belonged had the power to revitalize him. Perhaps he wasn't quite the Lancelot of Camelot, but he was closer to that perfect knight than he had been in days. It wasn't just a physical change. There was an aura about him, a transformation that went far beyond the outer trappings.

Neither spoke. He placed his hands on her shoulders, solid hands of great strength and gentleness, and she closed her eyes and leaned back against him. His arms slipped about her, encircling her, holding her close, his cheek resting against her temple.

It was a moment she wanted to last forever.

Then, all too soon, he spoke, as she knew he must.

"After tonight, perhaps it *will* be forever."

She could only open her eyes and look at the image reflected back at her, the two figures so perfectly matched, illuminated as if by an otherworldly flame.

And together they left to meet their future.

Bill wasn't quite sure what to expect.

His name was, indeed, on the guest list, and he smiled to see the way Lancelot—or someone—had rendered it: William of Avalon. It did seem more appropriate than Bill Kowalski.

The great, vaulted hall of the Met was as intimidating as always, a seemingly endless dome arching toward the sky. The marble floors echoed like musical notes as the guests arrived, the excitement humming, the expansive staircase of tiny stone steps reaching endlessly to the next level, each step dotted with a celebrity or an anonymously gorgeous person striving for celebrity.

Bill took it all in, straightening in his rented tux. Somehow, this was more than just the survival of his shelter. Something bigger was swirling. He could feel it, and the men and women who entered in either lavish gowns or elegant white tie could sense it, too. It was on their faces, an expectancy, a knowledge that they were about to be part of something important.

"Are you Bill?"

A young man in a hopelessly trendy suit—not

a tux, like every other male not dressed in costume—rapped him on the shoulder. Bill nodded.

"Yes. Can I help you?" Bill laughed, wondering why he offered help when he was so obviously the one who needed help.

"Actually, Julie Gaffney told me to look out for you. I'm Max. I'm an assistant account executive at S&B, and she wanted to make sure that you got a good look at where the risers are set up for your choir."

"Oh, great!"

"Come with me, over to the Hall of Armor. That's where all the big stuff is happening tonight, you know. Camelot and all that."

"Of course. I mean, that makes sense."

Max led him to the hall, past clusters of lights mounted high on metal stands, their reflections flashing off the shiny surfaces. Brilliantly colored banners were hanging from the walls as if in preparation for a medieval tournament, and pages in garishly colored tights stood against the pillars, smiling and pointing out directions to socialites and their escorts, the stars and the fortunate ones with invitations.

The Hall of Armor was dazzling, nothing like the way it had seemed the last time he was there, when friends from Illinois had come to visit. Then it had been impressive, with the massive horses in their armor, the mounted knights looking down from their hollow suits.

Now, the metal itself seemed to gleam as if it had a life of its own. The banners were all new, flocked with gold brocade, the still horses seemed almost alive, a hoof poised in midair ready to continue its pace, to move forward, to do battle. And the knights, which had always seemed stiffly lifeless—the silent guards of a faded past—now seemed on the verge of stirring to life once again. It was as if they were awaiting a signal, and then they would burst forth and shame the mere mortals with their glory.

There was even a fountain at the center of the room, flowing and swirling, a constant source of gentle noise and motion in a room that had been still for too long. Bordering the fountain was an exquisite collection of flowers, all at the peak of their bloom, the height of a temporary beauty.

"Is this okay?" Max asked. "I'm supposed to do anything you ask. What did Julie call me? Oh, yeah. I'm your squire tonight."

Bill grinned. "Great. That's just great . . ." His voice trailed off as he looked around. "Hey, is that a new suit of armor over there?"

"The one on the podium?"

Bill nodded, and Max explained. "It sure is new. Julie had it shipped in from a restaurant in New Jersey. It was sort of weird, but hey, the boss is the boss. And another new thing is that sword over in the middle in the Lucite case. It's really incredible. I don't know where it came from, Julie also managed to get it from someplace, but when the crowds go away from it, you should really get a look. It's more impressive than the Crown Jewels."

"Well," Max said. "I'll be around if you need anything."

More people were arriving, a tide of the well-heeled clustering, nodding and smiling as the newer ones entered.

"Isn't that Elton John?"

"My goodness, did you see what Madonna is wearing?"

"Here we go again. The Donald is with a new model, and Ivana is with a new European count."

"Henry Kissinger is in the corner with Colin Powell . . ."

Then a hush descended over the assembly in a slow wave. And two people entered.

"Who is that guy? He's gorgeous . . ."

"Who is the woman? I've never seen anyone . . . anything like her."

Lancelot, his arm crooked, with Julie's hand resting lightly on his forearm, walked straight, not looking at the crowds, not stopping as the cameras flashed and the news crews stepped toward them.

He was still not well. Julie could feel the will-power it took just for him to get this far. Although he looked nothing short of glorious, she alone knew the toll the effort had taken.

"Do you know where we're going?" she said.

He smiled. "Yes, I do."

"Have you come up with an answer from what Merlin said yesterday? I can't get it out of my mind.

'One thing you've held and given away, the other you've always held but never known.' "

"No, Julia. Even Sam and Mel were stumped. Just smile. We'll both find out soon enough."

As they walked to the Hall of Armor, the other guests returned to their conversations or watched as newcomers arrived. In a gathering as sensational as this one, attention spans were short.

Lancelot spotted Bill almost immediately and introduced Julie. And then Peg arrived, splendid in a peach gown.

"Lancelot," she said when she turned to him. "Please, please, forgive me."

He took her hand and kissed it, and the no-nonsense Dr. Reilly blushed furiously.

"It looks as if things are about to get started." Bill nodded toward a makeshift stage. And he was right. There was a blaze of talent on display, a veritable Who's Who of the entertainment world punctuated by speeches and testimonials by the world's most successful men and women of business.

It was numbing, and Julie glanced around, noting that even this stunning show was beginning to wear on the audience milling about. It was almost too much, overwhelming.

Bill left to gather the choir from the Avalon shelter, who had just arrived by bus. It was almost their turn to perform.

But so far, nothing had happened, nothing extraordinary. Part of Julie was relieved, the other part panic-stricken. If not tonight, when? And would that mean that because of Merlin's fifteen-percent window of error, they were not to be given a chance this time?

Lancelot was charming, mingling with his usual aplomb. Yet she could see how exhausted he was, the tight smile and the stiff greetings.

This, she knew, was the last of his strength. After tonight, there would be nothing in reserve.

She went to stand by his side just as the Avalon choir was announced.

Bill stepped out as the others filed onto the risers, all looking their best, all with eager expressions on their faces.

One member had separated himself from the others as they lined up to sing. He had arrived with the choir, his face shaved, his eyes gleaming, wearing a yellow and black tunic under his shirt. And then, with stunning ease, he blended into the crowd. So many others were dressed in similar clothing, so very many others in similar colors.

"Ladies and gentlemen." Bill smiled, then nodded to the suits of armor. "And tin. We are the Voices of Avalon choir, and it is our privilege to offer ourselves for your enjoyment."

The evening had begun in earnest.

Malvern ducked slightly as he wove among the people, all standing still and listening to the choir, their chords sour to his ears.

And then he saw it. Excalibur. It was glittering

under lights, the stones and precious metals shining like beacons calling his name. That was it, the reason he was there. The Latin incantations were fresh in his mind, everything he had gleaned from the texts. He was prepared. Now, with Excalibur within reach, under a clear dome that was little more than a dust cover, he was about to claim his destiny.

It was almost too easy.

Lancelot was there. He could feel his presence, although he had yet to see him. Lady Julia was there as well.

Lady Julia. He grinned. Maybe he would take her with him, back to Camelot, where he would rule. Guinevere was not as enticing to him as was Lady Julia. Now, that would make his triumph complete and absolute—to conquer Lancelot so sublimely. How he would laugh at Lancelot. How he would gloat.

He saw her then, Lady Julia. Yes, he would have her. Soon she would be his, to do with as he pleased.

Another thought came into his mind. Perhaps he would take both Lady Julia and Guinevere. And then later, at his leisure, decide which one to keep. Maybe both. Maybe neither. It would be a pleasant task at any rate, one suitable for the king.

King Malvern.

He straightened at the thought. Mighty King Malvern. Powerful Malvern. He could hear the accolades now. They were in his head, singing his praise, overlapping in their lush glory, drowning out the sounds of the miserable choir.

It was only a matter of time now, and then the world would sing the praises of Malvern, the greatest king of all.

Lancelot had been scanning the crowd, looking back at the sword, watching Julia. She was with Mr. Swenson, who was obviously pleased with the event. Good. As long as she was occupied, she would not be aware of the turmoil around her.

For he was there, within striking distance. Malvern. Lancelot could almost taste his presence.

He heard her laugh, and again his eyes fell upon her, the incandescence of her being. She leaned toward one of the men, and he saw her features change from intent listening to delight as he spoke and she responded. It was a marvel, a joy, simply to observe her movements, her every gesture and expression. As he watched her, he realized something both strange and ordinary, terrible and wonderful.

Lancelot loved her.

It was a truth he had known from the beginning. Perhaps even before the beginning. He had never told her. And as he stood in the distance, he wondered if he would ever have the chance.

The sword was still safe. She was still safe. For the time being. And he vowed that no matter what the consequence, he would keep it that way. Or die trying.

Julie could not believe the joke Mr. Stickley had just told her, slightly off-color but very funny. When she laughed, it was a relief, she felt so wonderfully normal.

The choir from Avalon had just left the stage, and they had done a wonderful job. It had been a refreshing change from the ultra-slick performers who had gone before and those who would follow. Mr. Swenson had mentioned something about sponsoring the shelter on a regular basis, funding that would be permanent, and she felt a marvelous rush of pleasure at the thought of being just a small part of that success.

As Mr. Stickley continued with yet another joke—how could he remember them all?—she looked for Lancelot. He was easy to spot, taller than the rest, certainly more handsome than anyone else there, anyone else she had ever seen.

Max from the agency whispered in her ear that someone from the *Daily News* wanted a quote from her, and with reluctance she pulled her gaze away from him.

As she walked past all the people, she took a deep breath and wondered if perhaps everything would just fall into place for them. He would adjust to this time and could exist there happily with her. Together, they could forge a new life.

She smiled. It would be wonderful, wouldn't it?

*   *   *

Everyone grinned at the man in the yellow and black tunic.

"Who's he supposed to be? Basil Rathbone?"

"No, no. He looks like the Black Prince."

"I thought the Black Prince wore a crown, not yellow and black."

"Maybe he's the Bumblebee Prince."

They began to giggle, and the man glared at them. Immediately, the laughter stopped.

He continued his progress, slowly, so as not to attract too much attention.

The crowd parted just slightly, and he saw her, Lady Julia. For some reason, he had changed his mind once again. The best revenge against Lancelot was so obvious! Not to take Lady Julia, to coddle and comfort her in Camelot, but to leave them both here. The twist would be to leave Lancelot alive and to leave Lady Julia dead.

Now, *that* would be a triumph! He would be stripped of everything then, no consolation of knowing that Lady Julia survived. Lancelot would have nothing!

And it would be so easy. His faithful Excalibur could assist in both deeds, ending Julia's life, beginning Malvern's new one.

Then it struck him: that is what the Latin text had meant! Two items, two special items. Of course! One was Excalibur, the other was the destruction of

Lancelot through Julia. How utterly perfect and symmetrical, like a delicately balanced work of art.

He searched again for Julia. He needed her to be closer to both himself and the sword. And he needed to start the incantations.

So he began. He spoke the magical words softly, almost to himself, but loudly enough to be heard by the powers that be. A few people stared as he walked, this dark man so obviously alone, speaking to himself.

"That's the problem with an open bar," someone commented.

But he didn't hear, nor did he care.

Across the room, Lancelot sensed the beginning. Slowly, he searched the faces of the hundreds of guests, watching their movements, looking for just one. As if by some unseen force, he turned, and there he saw Malvern.

He was inching closer to Excalibur. But what caused every nerve in his body to hum was Malvern's gaze. For he was glaring at Julia with the look of a starving beast.

She remained oblivious.

"Julia, be alert!" he said aloud, and others nearby stared at him. But she didn't see, nor did she feel his warning. Instead, she was in an animated conversation with a young woman who was writing down the words.

Slowly, Lancelot moved toward the sword, his focus still on Julia. "Give me strength," he murmured.

Malvern, his body angled just slightly, raised his elbow and with one single blow crashed through the Lucite and grabbed the hilt of Excalibur.

A stunned silence descended wavelike through the crowd, and Lancelot was at Malvern's side, cautious, waiting for his chance.

Malvern raised his voice slightly, in his Latin chant, and rays began to emanate from the sword.

Julie heard the commotion.

"What's happening?" she asked Mr. Swenson, who was tall enough to see over the throng.

"How marvelous." He winked at her. "There seems to be a little stage play going on. It's the Lancelot actor and someone else. Fabulous launch to the campaign, Miss Gaffney."

But she was already rushing to Lancelot, pushing through the assembly, going over the words in her mind: "one thing you've held and given away, the other you've always held but never known."

Oh, Lord, she thought frantically. *Please make it clear to me . . .*

And then she saw them both, Lancelot and Malvern. She froze, not wanting to make a sudden movement for fear of distracting Lancelot.

Malvern had Excalibur.

The sword seemed to be alive, whirring softly like the wings of a bird.

She moved closer, stepping gently. If only she could reach the sword.

Malvern grinned at Lancelot. "You know I will win this time. I have everything. And soon, I will have her as well, to do with as I please. But I find her dull. The only sport will be to kill her like a . . ."

At that, Lancelot, who had kept himself under control, pounced on a stunned Malvern. There was a smattering of applause from the audience, and Excalibur bounced a few yards from the men.

The two were locked in a mortal struggle, and only Julie knew what was at stake. *What do I do?* she cried to herself as she watched the battle, skirting closer.

No one touched the sword, and she clenched her fists, terrified to do nothing but panicked at the thought of doing the wrong thing, of harming Lancelot in any way.

The crowd was beaming. They assumed this was part of the act, the three people dressed in similar clothing, the men in tunics, the woman in the blue gown. No one questioned what was happening.

Julie was close enough to hear Malvern's words now, the incantations. What if they worked? He almost reached the sword, and she came close enough to kick it away.

Lancelot's features were contorted in fury.

Between his Latin, Malvern was hissing directly at him.

"You never said farewell to her, did you? Pity!"

They flipped over, the sword scooting further,

and Lancelot realized that with the incantations, Malvern could very well journey to Camelot and take Lancelot with him if they were in physical contact.

As he battled, Lancelot saw Julie from the corner of his eye. If he left her now, he would never get the chance to tell her how he felt, to tell her of his love. If they left, she would be forever safe from Malvern, and he could clear his name, reclaim his honor.

The sound of the sword was louder now, over-powering the noise of their scuffling on the marble.

He could save her, protect her . . . and never again see her face or hear her laughter. He would never touch her hair or inhale the fragrance of her perfume.

He saw the hem of her gown, the slipper poking from beneath the velvet.

And in a startling instant, Malvern pushed with his legs and scooped Julie up by the waist.

"Ha!" he shouted in triumph, and a few people clapped, then stopped. Even they were beginning to realize something was very wrong.

Panting, Lancelot slowly rose to his feet, his eyes on both Julie and the sword.

Malvern began chanting his Latin louder now, ever louder. But Julie, after her initial surprise, began to elbow and kick Malvern, jabbing him with every ounce of her strength.

"You jerk! Let me go!" she shouted over his chanting, and then she turned and bit him on the shoulder.

His voice hopped an octave as she did, and people began to laugh uncomfortably, enraging him further.

"You are all doomed!" he wailed.

Julie looked around and saw Lancelot, the expression on his face heartbreaking. She struggled, her legs pumping, and then she saw another face.

For an instant, she stopped, wondering if it could be her imagination. In the middle of the crowd was Merlin, in his wizard robes. A slow smile spread over his face, and her mind tumbled.

One thing you've held and given away, the other you've always held but never known.

And then he winked at her.

She gasped. That was it! All the time! The answer to his riddle . . . Excalibur.

And their love!

Before she could act, Lancelot rushed to Malvern, and in the shock, Malvern let go of her for just an instant, just long enough for her to grab Excalibur.

The crowd fanned out further now. Excalibur's sounds were becoming human, the voices of layers of song.

With both hands, she steadied the sword. And the song of the sword became louder, ever louder. She was going to try to speak, but she could not be heard over Excalibur.

Lancelot finally had Malvern in a headlock, his teeth clenched in the effort, and he looked up at Julie.

Malvern deserved punishment. Not only for what he had done here but for everything else, for a lifetime of treachery.

And gently, Julie let one of her hands leave Excalibur, and it floated to the song of the sword, upward, reaching to Lancelot.

Now he had a choice. To punish Malvern or to take the hand that Julie now offered . . .

Malvern crumpled to the floor when Lancelot dropped him.

And slowly, Lancelot walked toward the light, the radiant halo of love, and their hands touched.

In an instant, there was a brilliant, blinding flash . . .

And then they were gone.

For long moments, the room remained silent, and then they applauded and cheered, the most joyous sound imaginable, a sense of awe filling every being present.

Malvern tried to run, but a security guard stopped him and led him roughly away.

Everyone exchanged glances, uncertain what had happened. They all knew they had just seen the biggest show of all, and no matter what the papers would write, no matter what they themselves would say the next day to explain what had happened . . . for the moment, it was pure magic.

And they had all been a part of it.

21

"Help me," he murmured.

Julie smiled. "Haven't I done enough?"

Lancelot took her hand and kissed it gently. "As a matter of fact, you have not." He gave her a pointed look with his cornflower-blue eyes.

She just stared at him for a moment, wondering if she would ever lose the thrill of simply being this close, of having him speak to her, of his touch on her hand. And she knew it would never pass, this wondrous feeling. Never.

"So," she said. "Just what is it you wish of your former squire?"

"Another kiss," he demanded. "As the groom, I claim my rights."

"Can we wait? We are, after all, in the middle of the wedding banquet."

The Great Hall had never been so spectacularly bedecked, with floral garlands arching gracefully over every door and window and tables filled with cakes of every shape, form, and size.

Lancelot shrugged and looked at the hundreds of people gathered before them in the hall, every man, woman, and child of Camelot. To their left sat King Arthur and Queen Guinevere, who were in deep discussion with Merlin. Occasionally, Arthur would scan his subjects, his gaze finally resting on Lancelot and Julia, and his eyes would soften. Then he would return to the conversation with Merlin.

"What do you suppose they're talking about?" Julia asked, leaning close to her Lancelot, brushing the glossy black hair away from his forehead.

"Perhaps they're talking about old times." Lancelot smiled. "And that unpredictable fifteen percent."

They laughed, savoring the simple, extraordinary chance to be with each other. Their laughter faded, and he clasped her hand.

Julie sighed, not wanting to look away from his face. "I can't believe we're really back home."

He glanced down, his dark eyebrows slightly drawn. "I need to ask you something."

"Yes?" Leaning closer, she snaked her hand up his arm. Then his eyes met hers.

"You left everything you knew. Everything. Your career was splendid, you had a good life there, Julia. I need to know . . ."

"Go on," she whispered.

"Do you regret anything? Is there something you will miss in your life?"

"Lancelot," she breathed. "Don't you know? You *are* my life. You always have been. I just haven't always known it. This is my home, where I belong."

He pulled her closer, his strength overpowering, his need for her overwhelming.

"Julia," he rasped, and she closed her eyes, hoping the moment would never end.

Then he slid her onto his lap, his massive arms slipping about her in a tender caress. "It won't, my love. I promise. This time, it will last forever."

It did.

Epilogue

❧

$\mathcal{D}$r. Peg Reilly had been dying to enter the quirky little store with the strange name, Cauldrons & Skulls. The only thing that prevented her thus far had been her professional reputation and an intense aversion to quirky little stores in general.

But this time, she had a mission. In less than two weeks, her nephew would be ten years old. In addition, treating Nathan and his friends to an afternoon at Knight Times, that medieval-themed restaurant, she needed the perfect gift for a knight-obsessed fifth-grader. So she entered the store with a purpose, the jingling bells over the threshold announcing her arrival.

A pleasant-looking man was behind the counter. "Hello." He smiled. "May I help you?"

He was a surprisingly pleasant-looking man, she revised.

"Hello. I'm looking for something for my

nephew. He'll be ten, and . . ." She sniffed once. "Do I smell vinegar?"

The man put one hand on a hip. "I don't believe this! Yes, in fact, you do. This used to be my grandfather's pickle store. You have some nose on you, lady."

For some reason, the comment pleased her, and she felt an unfamiliar blush creep up her face. "Well, um . . . my nephew."

"Let's see. Is he at all interested in the Camelot legend?"

"I'm not sure," she admitted. "He's just now emerging from a Power Rangers phase."

"That's encouraging," he said, and they both smiled. "Over here, I have a rare comic book, hardcover. It's about sixty years old, a classic."

The book was beautifully bound. "Myrddin? What an unusual name."

"Yeah, it is. Actually, it's Merlin in Welsh."

"Really?"

He nodded. "See, it's all here. Camelot, Merlin, Arthur. Then here comes Guinevere, and on this next page . . ."

"Lady Julia! Oh, she was always my favorite."

"Oh, yeah? I was always a Lancelot man myself."

"They're the best! When she disguises herself as his squire . . ."

They both said the name at the same time. "George!"

"And then with the evil Malvern," she continued, unable to repress a shudder.

"That's great. And wait until you see the job Myrddin did on Malvern. Pure evil."

"Oh, and Lancelot! He's wonderful," she sighed. "Wow. They are so realistic. Look at Lancelot's eyes. And Julia's hair. They just look so honest and real."

"Hey. Um, you should have some time to look this book over. It's not cheap." He cleared his throat. "How about if I take you for a cup of coffee? My treat. And you can really look it over. Decide if . . ." His face reddened. "You can decide if it's what you want."

Peg was still smiling at the illustrations when she looked up. "I . . . well, yes, I believe this is exactly what I want. But coffee . . . sure. Yes."

He grinned. "Great! Just a second." He went to a beaded curtain. "Hey, Mel? I'm going out for coffee. Be right back."

Then he offered his arm. "My name is Sam."

And she accepted it. "I'm Peg."

The bells on the door tinkled as they left.

Author's Note

The legend of King Arthur has spawned so many versions, over the course of so many centuries, and in so many languages, it's impossible to pin down one as correct or definitive. In fact, there is no actual proof of Camelot's existence. Even tales of finding the remains of Arthur and Guinevere sound suspiciously like myths themselves.

So, in creating a Camelot, there is always the danger of offending purists who have rigid notions of what the kingdom would have been like. The double whammy of Camelot is that if you create a historically accurate environment, you're stuck with the misery and hardship of fifth-century Britain. Not much fun, no matter how diverting the romance. And if you stay with one source, especially an earlier one from the tenth century, or even the more modern John Dryden (*King Arthur*, 1691), you're likely to leave out elements that are more recent and much-loved additions.

In other words, no matter what path you chose, you've messed up. Royally.

All of this is simply by way of explaining that, yes, I do know there were no full-length mirrors, specific locks and keys, cellular phones, and toilet-trained horses fifteen hundred years ago. People spoke differently, not in the modern speech patterns used here. There were probably a hundred ways to say *vermin* and no word at all for *chocolate*.

This was an attempt not to re-create an era but rather to flesh out my own vision of a sparkling Camelot and a shower-fresh hero. A magical place not of this time, nor of any other.

Besides, is there anything more wonderful than pure love? No one, no matter how gifted, could ever be audacious enough to invent *love*. Now, that's the real magic in this story, and the only thing that happens to be absolutely true.

Go figure.